𝒮

A thinness in Shap[...]
expect. "It's a bit [...]
that bush over there [...]

In fact she did not find devastation on this scale as
horrific as lesser injuries to living flesh. There was
no question of Kerry Page having survived, even
momentarily, the blast that took her face away.
There was no need to wonder how much she had
known, how bad the pain had been and how long it
had lasted. One moment she was alive and well, the
next dead meat. She was beyond reach of their help,
beyond need of their sympathy. All she asked of
them now was to find her killer.

─────────────── ★ ───────────────

Forthcoming from Worldwide Mystery by
JO BANNISTER

CHARISMA
A TASTE FOR BURNING
NO BIRDS SING

Jo Bannister

A Bleeding of Innocents

W🌐RLDWIDE®

TORONTO • NEW YORK • LONDON
AMSTERDAM • PARIS • SYDNEY • HAMBURG
STOCKHOLM • ATHENS • TOKYO • MILAN
MADRID • WARSAW • BUDAPEST • AUCKLAND

A BLEEDING OF INNOCENTS

A Worldwide Mystery/June 1997

First published by St. Martin's Press, Incorporated.

ISBN 0-373-26241-8

A
Bleeding of
Innocents

I

ONE

FUNERALS WERE ALMOST the only thing left that still made Frank Shapiro feel Jewish. He was not a religious man, had not had a religious upbringing; he did not eat pork but told himself this was because he did not like it; he did not attend synagogue and even the main holidays always took him by surprise. Apart from his name there was nothing in his personal or professional life that singled him out from the bulk of the British people who were at least nominally Christian, except this. He could never get used to the idea of signifying respect by uncovering his head. So at funerals he tended to look as if his mind was elsewhere. Occasionally somebody jogged his elbow and nodded, and then he smiled gently and explained. But for the most part the funerals he went to were those of colleagues or friends where his sturdy figure in its dark coat was easily recognized and his undoffed hat passed without comment.

Alan Clarke had been both a colleague and a friend, and his wife would think nothing of Shapiro's hat. Watching her with deep compassion from under the brim, he doubted she would have noticed if he had taken the hat off and withdrawn from it a rabbit or a string of silk hankies. Her face was grey and drawn in deep lines, her eyes vast and remote. She had a strong son at each elbow: without them Shapiro thought she would have swayed. She was not crying, was still too shocked to cry. She looked at the coffin as if she did not know what it was doing there. Twice Shapiro saw her glance distractedly round the mourners and felt sure she was looking for Alan.

His death, coming out of the blue as it did, had stunned her like a physical blow. Shapiro had gone to the house to tell her about the accident, had driven her to the hospital and sat with her for four hours while they waited for news. He was still with her when her husband died. She had not cried then either. At first she seemed to think there was some kind of mistake, looking up quickly when anyone passed in case they had better news for her. Later, when she accepted that Alan was gone, she began looking for someone to blame.

In part she blamed the job, which was why Detective Inspector Alan Clarke did not receive the full panoply of a police funeral that his service entitled him to.

Shapiro didn't blame her for her anger. She was entitled to it. It remained to be seen whether the job was the cause of Alan's death, but the police force was big enough to carry the can until the individual responsible, the man driving the car, could be found. What Shapiro did regret, though he understood this too, was the way her anger had focused on Donovan. After four days it still was not clear exactly what had happened or why but Marion Clarke knew who she blamed. But for Donovan Alan would have had his feet up in front of his own fire that night. The driver of the car that broke him in a hundred pieces would have roamed the streets in vain.

That was why Donovan wasn't here, was probably hunched over the bar of a local hostelry instead, drinking fiercely and showing few signs of intoxication. Marion had told Shapiro that she would make a scene if he came, and Shapiro had had to tell Donovan. He had hoped it wouldn't be necessary, that the hospital would hold on to him till after the funeral. But he went there yesterday and found Donovan had discharged himself. Then he had to go to the man's home and tell him he wouldn't be welcome at his DI's funeral.

The pity of it was, Marion was cutting herself off from someone with whom she could have shared her grieving. Donovan had been Clarke's sergeant for two years. It was an unlikely partnership—Clarke a comfortable middle-aged golf-playing family man, Donovan a saturnine Celtic loner—but it worked well. The two men thought in complementary ways that did wonders for the clear-up rate, despite some blazing arguments. Over those two years professional respect had grown to personal friendship so that the Clarkes were the closest thing Cal Donovan had to family.

And now when they should have been grieving together Marion had chosen to end the friendship. It was the shock, of course, and in time she would see how unfair she was being. Meanwhile Donovan was hurting perhaps as much as she, and without the benefit of someone else to blame.

Except that Donovan too had his scapegoat. Donovan didn't believe it was an accident. He couldn't afford to believe that. If it was only random misfortune, if in prowling the back streets in the middle of the night they had by merest chance encountered someone who, because he was drunk or because he panicked, drove on after hurling them into a brick wall, then that—because being there was his idea—was at least arguably Donovan's fault. The alternative, that it was a deliberate attempt to murder them both, lifted that burden. If as Donovan believed they were marked men, sooner or later, in one dark street or another, that car or another or a man with a gun would have been waiting for them.

Shapiro did not as yet either support or dismiss the theory. If they could find the car he would have a better idea whether DI Clarke died because of the case he was working on or because he failed to look both ways before crossing a road. He wanted evidence and there was none.

The service was coming to an end as a symbolic few handfuls of earth, soft with the rain of the last few days, pattered on the coffin-lid. The vicar read a last passage and closed his book. When other people stepped forward to offer Marion their condolences Shapiro did the same. Soon he would want to talk to her, to find out what she needed, how he could help, but this was neither the time nor the place. She was barely hanging together. The boys were watching anxiously and as soon as they could steered her to the car and took her home.

Shapiro had been asked back to the house. He wondered if it would be better not to go. Then he thought of Alan's sons waiting to receive his friends and no one coming, and decided that the best thing was to spend a little time here, give the family a chance to get their breath, then drop in but not stay. When he glanced round he saw that everyone else had come to the same conclusion.

He exchanged a few words with people he knew, then with a man who was putting flowers on a new grave a few plots along from Clarke's. From the pushchair parked beside him Shapiro surmised the grave was his wife's and wondered who he would blame for being left alone while he had a child to raise. At least Marion's sons were grown. But the man looked up and smiled over the flowers in his hand, and his eyes were composed.

Then something on the periphery of Shapiro's vision

struck him as at once familiar and out of place, and peering at the little knot of saplings in the corner of the cemetery he picked out a figure almost as slender and tall as the young trees. He sighed and, excusing himself to the man with the pushchair, walked over.

'I thought you weren't coming.'

Donovan did not look at him. His eyes brooded on the middle distance. 'I said I wouldn't be at the funeral. I wasn't. Sir.' He always, but never more than now, tacked that courtesy on to the end of his sentences as if he'd found it stuck to his shoe.

'No,' agreed Shapiro softly. 'Well, it's a big cemetery. And a public one, of course. And Marion—well, she's away home now. She's not herself, lad. You can understand that.'

Donovan's eyes flicked at him like a whip, inky in the pallor of his thin face. He looked as if he should still be in bed. The car that hit Clarke hit him too: youth, faster reactions, perhaps mostly luck had let him off with concussion and bruising the length of his body. There was a row of stitches in a purpling gash on his temple, one eye was blackened, and when he moved it was cautiously, like an old arthritic horse, easing his body under his clothes. But he had escaped essentially uninjured from the incident that killed his DI, and it was there in his eyes that that hurt more than his head.

As to whether he understood Marion Clarke's reaction, Shapiro could not know. Donovan was not an easy man to read. He had been variously accused of letting his heart rule his head and of having no heart at all. Shapiro suspected he was a young man who could be disturbed by the power of his own emotions; but the only one who could have said with any confidence was Alan Clarke. Clarke had picked Donovan out when he was a raw new detective constable with the hungry eyes of a young wolf. He had taught him, moulded him, used Donovan's restless energy and street-wise intellect to counterpoint his own different talents so that the combination was greater than the sum of its parts. But even Clarke might have hesitated to claim knowledge of how Donovan felt, and the rest of the division regarded him warily. That was before the accident. Shapiro had no idea what he would do with Donovan when he wanted to work again.

'The family's gone now, everyone else is drifting away.' He ventured cautiously, 'If you wanted to go and drop a clod on him—'

Donovan barked a silent laugh, his face in profile drawn down to the bones. 'I think they may have a more dignified name for that part of the ceremony.'

Shapiro smiled down at his polished shoes. 'Probably. Well, whatever they call it...'

Donovan shook his head. 'I'm not bothered about the formalities. I just needed to be here at the end.' He glanced at Shapiro. 'I wanted to see him in the hospital but they wouldn't let me. He was already dead when I came to.'

Shapiro knew. When Alan's sons had arrived at the hospital to sit with their mother he had slipped away for a spell to see Donovan. He wanted very much to know what had happened, what they'd been doing round the back of the gasworks, what Donovan had seen before the car sent him reeling. But Donovan was unconscious. The doctor said he was in no danger, he'd wake up in the next few hours. But while Shapiro was there all he did was mumble and make loose, uncoordinated pawing gestures at his bandaged head.

Then a nurse came to say he was wanted in the intensive care unit and a woman still in theatre greens broke the news that they'd lost DI Clarke. They'd done all they could but realistically his injuries were too great for him to recover. Shapiro took Marion and the boys home, and stayed as long as he was needed, and when he returned to the hospital Donovan was awake and already knew about Clarke.

Shapiro rather regretted that. He had not been looking forward to the job but Clarke had been a copper and Donovan was a copper and he should have heard it from another copper not a doctor who, however well-meaning, could not understand the kind of relationships forged on the streets where men routinely saved one another's skin. In two years at the sharp end Clarke must have owed his life to Donovan, and Donovan his to Clarke, perhaps several times over.

Shapiro said, 'I don't suppose....' and stopped.

Donovan looked at him, the dark eyes haunted. 'What?' The Irish accent was always more pronounced when he was tired. Today he sounded as if he had just got off a potato boat.

'That anything more's come back.'

Bitter and somehow ashamed, Donovan's gaze licked his face before returning once more to the middle distance. 'There is nothing more. I told you. Do you think I'm lying?'

'Of course not,' said Shapiro. 'But a bad concussion can leave your memory disjointed for a while. If you keep going over it, sooner or later you may find something else. You're a detective, for God's sake, you know that.'

Donovan nodded. He went through it again. There was nothing new. It was told in a few sentences. He spoke the words as if they tasted bad. 'We went on foot from the railway depot. I watched our backs: nobody followed us. We went under the viaduct and suddenly there was a car behind us, headlights full on, coming fast. I don't know what make: light coloured, but you know that from the paint chips.' He meant the ones picked out of Clarke's flesh. 'Anyway, it's no help: it'd be stolen specially for the occasion.' Shapiro said nothing.

'We were in close to the wall, there was plenty of room for him to pass. But he hit us. Then he stopped the car and walked back. I didn't see his face, just the movement against the tail-lights. He walked to where DI Clarke was lying. Then he stood over me for a couple of seconds, then he went back to the car. The reversing lights came on. Then another vehicle came into the tunnel behind us and he drove off. Then I passed out.'

Shapiro nodded. The first time he'd heard this Donovan had been shaking, whether from shock or fear or fury he couldn't tell. 'I know you couldn't move. But when the man was standing over you, what could you see?'

'Striped trousers, leather shoes, knee-length coat. Smart.'

Still nothing new. 'What did he say?'

Donovan frowned. 'He said something? I don't remember.'

Shapiro shrugged. 'It's likely he said something. If it was an accident he'd be shocked, that can make people babble. And if you're right and it wasn't an accident he maybe wanted to crow a little. For his own satisfaction, you know? He couldn't know you were still conscious. He probably thought you were both as good as dead.'

The edge on Donovan's voice sharpened. 'He didn't

think I was dead. He thought he had to run over me again to be sure.'

'Well, maybe,' allowed Shapiro. 'Or maybe he hit reverse when he wanted second gear. Have you never done that?' Perhaps Donovan never had. 'Well, I have. Without being in shock.'

Donovan was still frowning, his brows drawn together under the rather long black hair that the wind was whipping in his face. The autumn day was swinging between Indian summer and bleak midwinter depending on whether the sun was breaking the clouds. 'He could have said something,' he said slowly. 'I don't know. He stood over me and—' Then his face cleared, surprise smoothing the skin. He had thought there was nothing more to remember but there was. 'He rolled me over with his foot. And he said... And he said...' But it wouldn't come.

Shapiro caught his breath. 'He kicked you?'

'No, not really. I was on my face, and he stuck his toe under my shoulder to turn me over.'

'And he said something?'

Donovan's profile was hatchet-sharp against the scurrying clouds. There would be no more sun that day. He shook his head as if to clear it. 'Yes, I think so. I don't know what he said. But I can—you know—hear his voice almost. I just can't get a grip on it.'

'Don't worry about it,' said Shapiro. 'Just give it some thought. If it's in there it can be got out. It may not help, but you never know. Whoever he was, whether it was an accident or not, I want this man. I don't like burying my officers, and I particularly don't like doing it while those responsible are still at large.'

Donovan said, 'Has anyone been to see—?' and Shapiro cut him off in mid-sentence. That was not a matter he wanted Donovan taking an interest in.

'Yes,' he said shortly, 'I have. He has an alibi.'

Donovan's eyes kindled. 'Of course he's got an alibi. He'd have that fixed up first! You can't believe a word he says. He knew we were on to him, there's nobody in this town had a better reason for turning Alan Clarke into hamburger!'

'That's enough,' snapped Shapiro. More gently he added, 'I do know the background, Sergeant. I know the kind of man he is: he's a liar and a thug, and I'm not going to rule him out of the enquiry just because he throws up his hands in well-feigned horror. But I'm not going to try and fit him up either. Before I charge him I want some evidence, because if you're wrong and this was just a happy accident for him I could end up losing both of them: the one through trying to frame him for the wrong crime, the other—the driver— through not looking for him at all. Trust me, Donovan: I've been in this business a long time, I know how to do it.'

He looked at his watch then and it was time to make his appearance at the Clarke house. 'Look, I have to go now. And you should be at home. Can I drop you?'

Donovan had been leaning, string-thin, against one of the young trees with his hands fisted deep in his pockets. Now he pushed himself upright and shook his head. 'I've got the bike outside.'

Shapiro shuddered. 'Do as I say. See if you can coax up any kind of memory—what he said, something about how he looked—from that half-minute before you passed out. Call me if you think of anything. Otherwise, try and get some rest.'

He watched Donovan walk away, stiff and slow, his

thin shoulders hunched in the black leather jacket, his head down, no sign of the restless energy that had irritated Shapiro so often in the past. Two thoughts competed for his attention. One was that Donovan didn't look well enough to ride a bus, never mind a 750cc motorcycle.

And the other was that while anyone might have an accident, and almost anyone might panic and hurry away, there was a degree of deliberation about turning an injured man over with your foot that gave a sort of credence to Donovan's conspiracy theory, after all.

TWO

MR WILKS CLAIMED there was a thief in the nursing home who had stolen his left slipper. Mr Prescott and Mr Fields agreed: Mr Prescott's right slipper had disappeared, as had the twelve-foot rock python which Mr Fields had left watching *Neighbours* on the dayroom television. Sister Page faced the challenge of solving the crimes before she left for the weekend.

The python problem was readily disposed of. There was no snake; or rather, though it was perfectly real to Mr Fields it remained obstinately invisible to everyone else. Kerry Page asked gently if Mr Fields had thought to look in the bathroom; and when she saw him a minute later there was a seraphic smile on his well-scrubbed face and she supposed the python was back where he wanted it. Mr Fields spent his boyhood in India and had kept snakes there. Now he was over eighty and living in a geriatric home. His wife was dead and his children lived at the far end of the country; when they did manage to visit half the time he did not recognize them. So it was to those sunny far-off days he turned for respite from the dreariness of old age. The imagined python was his security blanket.

The Great Slipper Theft did not detain her much longer. She looked in Mr Wilks' locker, then in Mr Prescott's. She gave Mr Prescott the slippers she found there and he, rather shame-facedly, gave the slipper off his left foot to Mr Wilks. She wished them a pleasant weekend and said she'd see them on Monday.

In the office she completed her paperwork before handing over to Sister Kim. But there was still no sign of the blue and silver 4×4 in the car park so she settled on the edge of the desk for a bit of a gossip while she waited.

'Where are you going this weekend?' asked Sister Kim. Kerry Page had arranged to leave early; she assumed there was some reason.

'Oh, only down to the cottage,' said Kerry. 'But David said he'd be finished by three o'clock so we thought we'd make an early start and miss the traffic.'

'Traffic?' exclaimed the Chinese nurse. 'I didn't think they had *roads* down there.'

'I meant, getting out of town,' smiled Kerry. Actually there was a perfectly good road to the cottage. The 4×4 was an affectation.

'One day, when I'm old and rich and married to a jet-setter,' sighed Kim, 'I shall have a cottage in the country. In the mean time I'm trying to persuade my landlord that hot running water is not a passing fad.'

Kerry grinned. She had visited her colleague's flat often enough to know it was perfectly comfortable. 'I keep telling you, David is not a jet-setter. He flies a plane for a living. It's a very small plane. It'll take three passengers if they're good friends. Cabin service consists of one packet of crisps each and a supply of paper bags.'

Kim sniffed. 'If my husband was a professional pilot I'd weekend in Monte Carlo.'

A soft-throated rumble reached them from the car park where the blue and silver car was turning under the trees. Kerry stood up and slung her bag over her shoulder. Then she looked at the Chinese nurse with a serious expression and a twinkle in her eye. 'If your husband was an aerial taxi-driver, and you'd been married less than two years, and he was younger than you and hadn't yet got over the thrill of being able to stay up all night without his mother getting on his case, you'd want to spend the weekends somewhere a lot closer than Monte Carlo.'

BRIAN GRAHAM stood in the middle of the room, turning slowly on his heel and shaking his head. It had been described to him as a studio flat but Graham had been at teacher-training college: he knew a bed-sit when he saw one. 'You need more space than this just to empty your briefcase.'

'I shan't be working here. I shall be sleeping here. There's the bed, there's the wardrobe, there's the cooker, and the bathroom's through there. It's all I need. I shan't be here long.'

'How long?'

'I told you, I don't know,' said Liz. 'A fortnight, maybe a month. Until they get themselves organized. It's a big blow to a small division, losing a DI and having a detective sergeant put out of action in the same incident. All I'm doing is filling in till they can make a permanent appointment.'

Graham sniffed. 'It sounds a bit irregular to me.'

Liz smiled at his petulance. It wasn't like him. She thought with a warm glow of satisfaction that he was missing her already. 'It *is* irregular. At least, the way it was arranged was. But I've known Frank Shapiro for ten years, he's been more help to me than anyone else in the Force, it really isn't asking too much for me to step in and help him now. It's not as if I'll be missed. There are DIs coming out of the woodwork at Headquarters but Alan Clarke was the only one Frank had.

I can put up with'——lacking a word for it she waved a hand round the comfortless room——'for a month if it'll help him out.'

'But you'll be home weekends?' Inflected as a question, it was actually a statement of intent.

Liz sat on the bed beside him and linked her arm through his. She was a tall, good-looking woman with a lot of fair hair that for work she wore in a French pleat but which at present hung down her back in a thick girlish plait. 'Exigencies of service permitting'——it was the formula which said that effectively police officers were on duty any time they were needed——'I'll be home at the weekends.' Her smile turned impish round the corners. 'If not, you can always come up here on Saturdays for a bit of how's-your-father. You could sleep on the sofa.'

Graham looked at it. It was a typical bed-sit settee, two-seater if one was anorexic, an adequate put-you-up for a dwarf. Graham was six feet tall. He gave Liz a censorious frown. 'What, and miss the Middle School soccer friendly?'

Graham unpacked her things while she changed, then she drove him to catch his train——they'd left his car at their local halt——and went on to the police station. She'd promised to let Shapiro know when she arrived. She wasn't sure if she'd find him in his office on a Saturday but someone would give her a cup of tea and show her round.

Shapiro was not only in his office, he'd been watching for her. The desk sergeant showed her up but Shapiro met her on the stairs. His eyes were warm with welcome. 'Liz. I'm glad you're here.'

They had known each other for more than ten years. In another division, almost it felt in another life, she had served as DS to Shapiro's DI. He was the first to treat her as a police officer rather than a police woman. Everyone else complimented her on making sergeant not in Community Relations or Traffic Branch but in the male-dominated world of CID, but Shapiro encouraged her to take her inspector's exams, and to take them again when she was initially denied the promotion. He wanted her to show results that would shame the board into giving her her due. He knew she was a good detective: if the police force could not recognize a good detective when it saw one it wasn't as good a police force as it ought to be.

Liz blossomed under his tutelage but there were inevitable disappointments and she could not always swallow them cheerfully. 'It's hard,' she'd complained wearily to him one day.

'You think being a woman detective is hard?' Shapiro had said. 'You try being a Jewish detective.'

Now the Jewish detective was a chief inspector and the woman detective was an inspector, and but for the precise circumstances they would have been delighted to be working together again. As it was they settled for a warm handshake as Shapiro showed her to his office.

She was sensitive to the fact that the world had moved on since they'd last worked together: she waited for an invitation before sitting down. Then she said, 'I'm sorry about Alan Clarke. He was a good man, he'll be missed. Do you know yet what happened?'

Shapiro gave a distracted little shrug. He'd thought of nothing else for four days and three nights. There were blue rings under his eyes and tiredness was grained into his skin. Today for the first time Liz got a glimpse of how he would look when he was old.

He said, 'He was, yes. And no, I've no more idea

why he died than I had on Wednesday morning. I still can't say whether it was an accident or murder.'

Shapiro's secretary brought them some coffee.

'Wasn't there a witness?' Liz asked.

'Yes and no,' sighed Shapiro. 'Alan's sergeant was with him, it was his snout they were meeting. But the lad was hit too—head injury, he was unconscious six hours. He's told me what he thinks he remembers but it's hard to know how accurate his memory is and also whether there's more stuff locked up in it than he can get at. There may be: he came up with something yesterday that he hadn't remembered before. If it was how he thinks—' He shrugged, spooned sugar into his coffee.

'What?'

'Donovan thinks it was deliberate—murder. That may be colouring his recollection. But he thinks the man who hit them stopped the car, walked back to check them, and when he saw that Donovan wasn't badly hurt returned to his car to have another go at him. It was only the lights of an oncoming vehicle that made him change his mind. If it did happen anything like that we're not dealing with an ordinary hit-and-run.'

'Donovan,' said Liz, thoughtfully. 'Haven't I heard of him?'

'Probably. Oh, there's not a lot wrong with Donovan. Normally, I mean. He's a bit keen sometimes, and sometimes he's a bit unconventional, but he's a better copper than most people give him credit for.' Shapiro scowled then, wrinkling his nose as if he'd bitten into a lemon. 'Actually, Liz, there's something you can do for me. As soon as he's half-way fit Donovan's going to come in here wanting to be in on the investigation. I can't use him but I'd rather not have to fight him off.

Can you keep him busy? I want to run this enquiry but
you'll have Alan's caseload to cope with plus anything
new that comes up. Even if we get a quiet week or two
you'll still be shorthanded. I mean to get to the bottom
of what happened under the viaduct, and I'll need most
of the department to do it. Donovan could be useful to
you. If—'

'If?'

'If you can get him to concentrate on his job instead
of trying to do mine.'

HE WAS AT THE END of his strength and still he was
running. He couldn't feel the road under his feet. All
he could feel was the great wet patch on the front of
his shirt that was cold against his skin with the chill of
the autumn night. He no longer knew where he was
running, only what he was running from.

It was a clear, almost frosty night brilliant with moon-
shine so that although the road was not lit he could see
where he was going. Further back, stumbling among the
trees, he had fallen again and again: there was leaf-
mould in his hair and sticking to his shirt. Remotely, in
some portion of his brain where he could still think
coolly, he supposed that was why no one would stop
for him. Lurching along the road in his shirt-sleeves,
with a great patch of wet blood on his chest, he must
have looked like an axe murderer.

The water-meadows were a local beauty spot; this
road was busy on sunny Sundays in summer. At two in
the morning in mid-October it was all but deserted. He
must have run a mile from where they parked the car
but only two vehicles had passed him, one in each direction. Too much time was passing. He needed help.

He was about ready to drop when more headlights

slashed round a bend at him. Not a car; higher, further apart, maybe a lorry. Little old ladies out driving alone could be forgiven for taking one look at him and pumping the accelerator but lorry drivers should be made of sterner stuff. This could be his last chance: any time now exhaustion would sweep the legs from under him and roll him in the gutter and it would be morning before anyone found him.

It was a lorry and it wasn't wasting time: he could hear the big diesel bearing down on him. Desperation made him reckless. Shielding his eyes against the light with one hand he stumbled into its path, flagging it down. A long hollow siren of a horn warned him off and the lights moved into the far lane to pass him.

The driver must have cracked muscles to make it swerve like that, like a fast snake coiling across the road. The black bulk of the load swayed against the diamond-dusted sky as the wheels went one way and the weight the other. He watched it swerve and sway, and knew it could not stop before it reached him.

The front mudguard missed him by inches but the slipstream hit him a blow like a sledgehammer, pitched him off his feet and threw him down hard on the shoulder of the road. He rolled twice then hit the verge and lay still, face down, his limbs splayed like those of a rag doll.

Ray Bonnet the lorry driver had had a bastard of a day and it didn't look like getting better even now it was tomorrow. He'd had a breakdown, he was in trouble with his hours, now he'd run down some lunatic clog-dancing his way home from the local pub. It wasn't his fault. All he'd seen was the white shirt lurching across the dark road in front of him, spinning into the gutter behind. But it was scant comfort. He thought he'd killed someone.

As soon as he could he stopped the lorry and turned on the hazard lights. Snatching his torch he dropped to the ground and ran heavily back to where the flash of white had gone spinning in his mirror.

When he found the body spread-eagled by the side of the road, Bonnet looked for some moments and did not touch it. He was only a youngster: in his mid-twenties perhaps, his face still a boy's face, smooth and unweathered. There was a graze and a smear of road dirt on his cheek. As Bonnet leaned over him he opened his eye. The pupil shrank in the light of the torch, leaving a great blank blind-looking blue-grey iris. His lips moved.

Bonnet leaned closer. 'What's that, son?'

The young man seemed more stunned than injured. He got his hands under him, levering his face off the ground, and Bonnet gently eased him on to his side. As he twisted the great gory splash on the front of his shirt came into view.

The young man blinked his eyes into focus and fixed them on Bonnet's face. His voice was quiet and frail, breathy with effort but absolutely distinct, as if all his energies were directed into making it so, as if conveying this message was now the most important thing in his world and easily worth risking his life for. 'You have to help me. My name is David Page, and somebody's shot my wife.'

THREE

LIZ'S FIRST REACTION was to wonder why Page had run for help, up a deserted road miles from anywhere in the middle of the night, leaving a perfectly good car parked among the trees overlooking the water-meadows. When she saw inside she understood.

The bloody ruin that had been Kerry Page was in the driving seat. Her husband could have moved the body, and if there'd been any chance of saving her presumably he'd have done so and too bad if it complicated matters for the police. But Kerry had been hit at close range by a shotgun and the blast had taken her full in the face. All that was left of her above the waist was bloody garbage: he got her blood down his front when it toppled sideways against him. Moving her from the driving seat would have taken a strong stomach.

When Liz walked towards the blue and silver car one of the young constables who was having trouble holding on to his supper moved to intercept her. But Shapiro put a wary hand on his shoulder. 'It's all right, son, she's one of us.'

His face was grim, his greeting apologetic. 'Talk about being thrown in at the deep end! It's not always like this, you know. People in Castlemere do occasionally find something to do of an evening besides killing one another.'

Partly it was the shock talking. He had seen more and messier bodies than most men but the sight had never lost its power to appall him. Facetiousness was a defence.

Liz twitched a little smile and nodded. There were lights set up round the car. She tilted her head towards it. 'Let's see what we've got.'

A thinness in Shapiro's voice warned her what to expect. 'It's a bit of a shocker. We've designated that bush over there as a throw-up zone.'

In fact she did not find devastation on this scale as horrific as lesser injuries to living flesh. There was no question of Kerry Page having survived, even momentarily, the blast that took her face away. There was no need to wonder how much she had known, how bad the pain had been and how long it had lasted. One moment she was alive and well, the next dead meat. She was beyond reach of their help, beyond need of their sympathy. All she asked of them now was to find her killer.

The forensic pathologist was already on the scene, immediately identifiable by his composure amid the shambles. The police worked in the same surroundings, and many of them had seen things which would have been kept decently out of sight at a family butcher's, but they lacked this easy familiarity with the biological basics. To a policeman, a person was a person until another person tore the back of the watch to reveal the surprising mechanism. To a pathologist, a person was a cardiovascular system governed by a nervous system hung on a skeleton for mobility, and the surprise was that this intricate mechanism thought of itself as a unique individual.

The pathologist was a tall, rather plump man with ginger hair. He had been in bed when the police called: Liz glimpsed pyjama stripes in the neck of his thick sweater. Soon he would be going back to bed because he was almost finished here. Jars and envelopes, carefully labelled, ranged across the bonnet of the car. The pathologist straightened up with a sigh, absently wiping blood off his tweezers with his handkerchief.

Shapiro introduced them. The pathologist's name was Crowe.

Liz said, 'Both barrels?'

'No,' said Dr Crowe, 'just one. It was enough. He must have aimed at her face: the pellets thin out as you move down the body and some went over the top of her head, lodging in the lining of the roof. Some of her hair's up there too.'

'She died quickly?'

'Oh, yes.'

Most of the windscreen was gone but a crescent of crazed glass clung together on the passenger's side. 'He must have been close.'

The pathologist nodded. 'Yes, the spread's pretty dense. Just as well for the husband—a metre further back and the same shot would have taken his arm off.'

'The husband was in the passenger seat?'

'Apparently,' said Shapiro.

'And he wasn't hurt?'

'Not in the shooting. He collected some cuts and bruises going for help.'

The first officers on the scene had cordoned off the area in front of the car where the killer had stood. Liz walked round behind the car in order to peer in at the passenger seat.

Shapiro said, with just a trace of smugness, 'I already looked. No pellet holes.'

Liz smiled. 'So we can't say he wasn't in the seat.'

'And we can't say that he was.'

Dr Crowe sniffed. 'You're a suspicious lot, you policemen. Police persons,' he amended with a coy smile. 'It's not fair. I spend hours bent over a microscope trying to get my witnesses to give their evidence. Yours come straight out and tell you what happened, and half the time you won't believe them.'

'Half the time they're lying,' said Liz.

'You think he did it then—this boy, the husband?'

'Oh, come on,' complained Shapiro, 'it's a bit early for that. For one thing, I shall want your report on his clothing first. But you know as well as I do that most murders are family affairs, committed by someone close to the victim; and the other recurring theme is that people who report crimes are often the ones who committed them.'

Dr Crowe stood sucking his teeth. 'Well,' he said finally, 'if he staged it he made a good job. There are no splashes of blood on the passenger seat—if the husband wasn't sitting in it he must have covered it up first. Then there's this business of the body collapsing on to him.'

'What about it?'

'I haven't seen his shirt yet, I can't guess what it'll tell us. But the thing is this. If he was sitting beside her when she was shot he'd be spattered with her blood. The pattern's practically diagnostic. But if she immediately slumped on to him and covered him with the stuff then the splashes would vanish into the greater— um—' He couldn't think of a word and so left the sentence hanging. 'So the evidence that he was where he says he was is destroyed. By the same token, we can't point to a lack of spattering and say he must be lying.'

Liz's blood ran momentarily chill in her veins. She nodded at the corpse. 'You mean, he may have pulled

—that—on to him to erase an inconsistent blood-spot pattern?'

Dr Crowe gave an undergraduate shrug. 'Couldn't say, Inspector. All I can say is that if he did it would have had that effect.' The sudden amiable grin was engaging. 'My business is facts. Suppositions are your field.'

After the body was removed the mood lightened perceptibly. By now the first eastern palings of the false dawn were dimming the stars: in an hour it would be light enough to start a search of the woods around the car park. Liz organized a torchlight sweep of the immediate area and radioed in for more help as it became available.

It was not that she expected to find the shotgun in the long grass. Whatever had happened here that wasn't likely. If Page murdered his wife he had thought it out, planned it in detail, and executed it with care, and he wasn't likely to blow it by throwing the gun away afterwards. He could have taken as long as he needed to dispose of it, only leaving the scene to flag down a vehicle when he was confident it could not be found. On the other hand, if someone else murdered Kerry Page then he—conceivably she—left the scene while Page was running for help and there would have been time enough for an orderly withdrawal.

But if a search was unlikely to find the murder weapon it might provide information about the murderer. How he had reached the little scenic car park set in its copse of trees between the secondary road and the water-meadows of the River Arrow; if he had left the same way; if he'd had a vehicle, what kind of vehicle it was. There might be signs of more than one person. The murderer might have smoked while he was waiting for his victim. When he saw what he had done perhaps he staggered away to be sick among the trees. None of these possibilities was a likelihood but they had to look, they had to look thoroughly, and they had to do it at the earliest opportunity.

'And we'll need divers to drag the river,' said Shapiro, mentally ticking off a check-list. 'I'll get that moving. Why don't you go and talk to the boy?'

'The husband? All right.' But Liz was surprised. David Page was the only suspect they had so far, she'd expected Chief Inspector Shapiro would want to conduct that interview himself.

There was a sly quality to his grin. 'He's just a kid. Talk to him kindly and he might tell you things he'd only tell his mother.'

Liz remembered that he was her superior and resisted the urge to blacken his eye. She said sweetly, 'Rather than his grandfather, you mean, sir?'

OFFICIALLY, David Page was bereaved next-of-kin. A woman constable was sitting with him in the interview room, supplying him at intervals with cups of hot sweet tea. He had his hands round one when Liz introduced herself, his elbows braced on the table-top to stop him shaking and spilling it. He clutched it as if the warmth in his cupped palms was the only bit of comfort he could find. He did not appear to be drinking much. Two other cups, their contents gone cold and scummy, stood almost untouched on the table.

'She was so—kind,' he said, the words jerking out of him.

She had heard worse epitaphs but it struck Liz as an odd thing for a man to say about his murdered wife. Beautiful, perhaps, or sweet: 'She was so lovely, why would anyone want to kill her?' Alternatively, she was so alive, how could she be gone? Or she was so head-strong, so wilful, it was only a matter of time before something happened to her. But kind?

But perhaps that was why he'd married her. He was younger than her—not much, three years, though it may have seemed more. Page was twenty-six but Liz saw now why Shapiro described him as a kid. Knowing he did a responsible job she had expected someone mature and self-confident. Instead he seemed little more than a boy, a blue-eyed, fair-haired boy. He was a pretty thing, even with his face grazed and tracked with tears. Perhaps that was why Kerry, who was a nurse and may have been drawn to helplessness, had married him. It could have been a marriage made in heaven, one of those improbable pairings that succeed beyond all expectation because they give both parties what they need most.

The other possibility was that the partnership had failed so utterly that one of the parties to it had disposed of the other with a shotgun.

A possibility was all it was. Page did not look like a violent man, but if her years in CID had taught her nothing else they had warned her not to judge by appearances. Mild-mannered little men did occasionally murder their wives, and big hectoring bullies were capable at times of astonishing tenderness. Liz hoped she was a fair judge of human nature but knew it was more important to be a punctilious collator of evidence. So she asked him what happened.

His sky-blue eyes flickered. 'I—already—'

'Yes, I know,' she said, her voice reassuring. 'But it's helpful for me to hear it first-hand. There's no rush, take your time. Tell me what you did from, say, tea-time onwards.'

DAVID MADE their meal. He enjoyed cooking. When they were in town, between his flights and Kerry's shifts they had trouble making their off-duty hours match and tended to snatch food as and when they could. But at the cottage David assumed responsibility for their evening meal, immersing himself in recipes and ingredients.

This Saturday evening he made chicken paprika. When it was done they left the washing-up in the sink and sprawled, gently burping, in front of the log fire. They had no television at the cottage. At the end of an hour David suggested a little healthy exercise but Kerry thought they should go for a walk first. They drove to the local beauty spot, an elevated viewpoint in a bend of the River Arrow, and walked down to the water-meadows. It was dark but the night was clear, the moon painting the lush grass silver. They strolled for a time, then returned to the car and just sat, looking out over the river, watching the moon take a slow dive into the trees on the opposite bluff. Kerry had seemed half asleep, leaning against him with her head on his shoulder.

He did not know how long they sat there. Twice he suggested heading for home but Kerry was comfortable, enjoying the quiet and the moon-silvered view. So they went on sitting, hardly speaking, close and comfortable and happy.

Then, in a second or two, everything changed for ever. A man walked in front of the car and the waning moonlight gleamed on something long and slim cradled in his arms. He looked at them through the windscreen.

Kerry sat up. The man raised the gun and shot her in the face, and she toppled slowly sideways, resting on her husband's shoulder in death as she had in life.

He did not believe Kerry made a sound. He himself cried out in horror, and pushed his wife's bloody head aside as if it were something vile and alien, not someone he loved.

Beyond the crazed glass he saw the black eyes of the gun pan slowly across the car until he was staring into them. He knew nothing about guns except that shotguns commonly fired two cartridges. He was very afraid. He whimpered.

The gunman regarded him levelly, without speaking, for perhaps half a minute: thirty seconds, each of them spun out impossibly long and thin, in which David Page did not breathe, dared not move, felt the presence of death beat in his face like the wings of a bird, felt a scream building within him.

Then the man—it was a man's voice—said, quite quietly, almost gently, 'No, not you.' Then he walked away.

For minutes longer David sat paralysed in his car, behind his broken windscreen, beside his butchered wife. Then a little life began creeping back into his mind and, with it, awareness of having to do something. He edged carefully out of the car. The night air struck his chest where his shirt was wet. He looked round fearfully but there was nothing to suggest that anyone else was there. Nor, on the wrong side of midnight, was there much chance of anyone coming. What help he needed he would have to find.

BEFORE SHE SENT him home—to the flat in town, he would be handier there and the cottage would be knee-

deep in police for a while yet—there were a few questions Liz wanted answering. Before they were finished
there would be more questions, but a few would suffice
for now.

'Kerry was driving the car. Why was that?'

Page shrugged numbly. 'No reason.'

'You drive it sometimes?'

'Of course.'

'But this evening Kerry drove. Did she keep the
keys?'

'They were in the car. She got there first, she got in
behind the wheel. We were only going a few miles.'

'So you'd have driven if you'd been going further.'

'Maybe. Sometimes. Does it matter?' Page's voice
climbed, fluting and querulous.

Liz changed the subject. 'Was it a warm evening?'

Page stared. 'I've no idea.'

'You didn't have a coat on.'

'Yes, I did.'

Liz's eyebrows arched. 'Not when you picked a fight
with Mr Bonnet's lorry—all he saw of you was your
shirt. When did you take it off?'

Page shook his head. 'I don't know.'

'Before Kerry was shot or after?'

'I don't remember. For God's sake, my wife was in
pieces beside me—you think I noticed the cold?'

'Could you have put it over the back of your seat?'

His sky-blue eyes were mystified. 'I suppose so.'

'This man. How close to the car was he when he
fired?'

'Very close.' A tremor caught up the edge of his
voice. 'He was at the bumper. The barrel of the gun
was almost as long as the bonnet. The muzzle couldn't

have been'—he held up two fingers, both visibly shaking —'from the glass.'

'Would you recognize him again?'

'The voice maybe. Not the face.'

'Why not? It was a bright night—bright enough to go walking by the river. He was only a metre from you.'

'He had the moon at his back. I never saw his face.'

'Could you see what he was wearing?'

'A hat of some kind, a coat. I think there was a scarf over his face.'

'So he didn't think it was a warm evening.'

Anger kindled in Page's eyes. 'You don't think maybe he put all that on so no one would recognize him? You don't think that maybe, since he was going out to shoot someone, he thought that might be a good idea?'

Liz nodded calmly. 'Yes, that's probably the reason. Was there anything familiar about him—the voice, the way he moved? Could you have met him before?'

As fast as it had surged Page's temper subsided, leaving him frail and exhausted. 'I've no idea.'

'Someone Kerry introduced you to, for instance.'

'I don't know. I don't know.' Tears welled in his eyes. 'She had a lot of friends. She had no enemies.'

'She had one,' Liz said gently. But at the back of her mind another possibility was taking shape. She said nothing aloud but to herself she observed: Or else you did.

FOUR

LIZ WENT to the cottage but learned nothing except that Page had told the truth about the washing-up. It was still waiting piled in the sink for the couple to return from their drive. She was not sure when it would be done now.

At the police station there was a message for her to see Shapiro.

His office was like the man: lived-in almost but not quite to the point of shabby; not scruffy but with a pre-disposition to appear untidy; comfortable and without pretension. A pot-plant which had seen better days and a framed snap-shot of him with his ex-wife and their daughters at David's Tower in Jerusalem shared the windowsill. The desk was oak, more worthy than pres-tigious, and there were more papers stacked on top than was seemly for a Detective Chief Inspector. It was an office for working in rather than impressing people.

Shapiro waved her to a seat. The broken night on top of his other worries had taken its toll of him: he looked older every time Liz saw him. There was a greyness to his skin that suggested that if he pushed his health much harder it would start pushing back. DI Clarke's death had hit him personally as well as professionally. He'd lost a friend and a colleague; it was his job to find out why; now while the division was still in shock he had an extraordinarily brutal murder to contend with. In all the circumstances there was no chance of him taking time to get his breath back, but that didn't mean he didn't need to.

'You let the boy go, then?' he said.

'For the moment. He's not going anywhere. If he meant to skip the country he'd have done it instead of reporting the murder.'

'So sending him home doesn't necessarily mean he didn't do it.'

Liz smiled. 'Me thinking he didn't do it doesn't necessarily mean that either. But I wouldn't say I've formed an opinion yet. Have you?'

Shapiro spread a defensive hand. 'You're the investigating officer—I've got enough on my plate without this.' He glanced sidelong at her. 'But since you ask, no, I don't really see him as the type. It was a particularly bloody act. Someone stood close enough to that girl to see the whites of her eyes, then blew her face off with a shotgun. Most people couldn't do that. I doubt if he could. He's not what you'd call a hard man.'

Liz demurred. 'Maybe it didn't take hardness so much as anger. If he was furious with her, if he wanted not merely to kill her but to destroy her, to expunge her, he could have done it that way, and planned the rest to protect himself. He may look like a schoolboy but actually he's an intelligent man. He does a job that requires meticulous attention to detail. If he decided to kill her he'd have considered the consequences.'

'Such as?'

'Such as the blood spattering. His coat's missing. What if he put it over the passenger seat when he got out of the car? That would have kept her blood off where he was supposed to be sitting. Then he removed the coat, got back in the car, and pulled her on to him.

Then he disposed of the coat and there's nothing to contradict his account.'

Shapiro stared at her. 'You're talking as if he did it. Is that what you think?'

'Not particularly, no. But he could have done. We need to find that coat. If it got mislaid in the general mayhem the search'll turn it up. If it stays lost he'll have to be a bit more specific about where it got to.'

Shapiro regarded her with a new respect. He'd had a keen regard for her when she worked for him before, had tried to teach her all he knew. But he was beginning to suspect that it wasn't all *she* knew. 'So where did he have the gun?'

'Under the seat? It would be accessible without being on view. When they'd been sitting in the car for a while and Kerry was nice and drowsy he could have said he'd got cramp, he was going to walk about for a minute. He could have shrugged his coat over the seat, and got out and pulled the gun from underneath without her even noticing. Even if she saw, even if she guessed what he intended, sitting behind the wheel she'd have been slower to move than him. All he had to do was step in front of the car and shoot. Then he moved the coat, took his seat, pulled Kerry against him. Then he disposed of the gun and the coat—he may have had a hiding place ready, this was only four miles from their cottage, remember. Then he made his way up to the road and waited for someone to come along.'

'My God, you *do* believe he did it!'

'No, I don't,' she insisted. 'I believe he could have, and that's how. If I can find the coat or the gun, or pin a lie on him, or come up with some kind of a motive, then maybe I'll begin to think it was him. But so far it could have happened just as he said. The only finger-

prints we have are his and Kerry's, but he never said
the man touched the car and even if he did he was
probably wearing gloves. The grass in front of the car
shows someone was there but there's no clear impression, it could have been either Page or this mystery
gunman. I'm sorry, Frank, we're going to be walking
both sides of the street for a while yet.'

Shapiro sighed. 'What's your next move?'

'I want to talk to the people at the nursing home
where she worked. Get some idea what kind of a
woman she was, what kind of a marriage it was. She'd
been there four years, she should have made some
friends. They'll know things about her that even her
husband can't tell us.'

'You mean, *won't* tell us.'

'No, things he doesn't know himself. When women
work together they share their secrets.' She smiled.
'They talk. Sometimes they talk about things they
wouldn't discuss with their nearest and dearest. If her
marriage was in trouble, if she was in debt, if she had
a bit on the side, they'd know before Page would.'

Shapiro was looking bemused. 'I never thought of a
manfriend as being a bit on the side.'

Liz grinned.

The phone on Shapiro's desk rang. As he answered
it she went to get up but he waved her back to her chair.
His brow furrowed. 'What, now? Did you tell him I'm
busy? How does he look? Oh, you'd better send him
up.' He put the phone down, leaned back and gave Liz
a wry smile. 'You're about to meet Detective Sergeant
Donovan, who should have his feet up but is apparently
convinced we can't manage without him.'

When Shapiro called him in and he stopped just inside the door, plainly surprised to see his chief had com-

pany, Liz's powerful first impression was of a streak of
darkness in the corner of the room. The height of him,
the thinness, the dark clothes, black hair and olive skin
bled together to create a three-dimensional shadow. His
eyes narrowed warily.

Shapiro introduced them much as he might have introduced oxygen to a flame—cautiously, at arm's
length. Then he sat back to watch the result.

Liz stood up but did not offer her hand, judging that
Donovan would be reluctant to take it. 'I'm sorry about
Alan Clarke. He was a good copper. He was a good
man.'

'You knew him?' Donovan's voice was low, rising a
shade on the interrogative.

'Not well, but enough to know he'll be hard to re-
place.'

'That's the truth.' The way he said it, looking her up
and down and clearly finding her wanting, was just the
safe side of objectionable.

But Liz could bear his resentment. He was a young
man, the range and depth of his experience must necessarily be limited. This could be the first time he'd lost
a close colleague. He'd been hurt and was still hurting.
He would find it hard to accept whoever was sent as DI
Clarke's replacement. For now she could afford to be a
little tolerant.

Donovan hadn't been in the station since the night he
and Clarke went to meet his informant behind the gasworks. So he hadn't heard the rumour that Castlemere
CID was getting a female inspector. The first he knew
was when he opened Shapiro's door and there she was,
a tall woman in her late thirties with a calm, squarish
face and a lot of fair hair pushed up out of the way.
She was wearing fawn slacks with well-made brogues

and a burgundy tweed jacket: not the Oxfam look fa-
voured by most male detectives but not *Vogue* either.
The shoes had walked too many miles, the tweed had
gathered a little moss as she brushed by a tree, and there
was a damp spot on one knee where she'd got down to
look closely at something on the ground. Probably with
a magnifying glass, Donovan thought derisively.

In all honesty, Divisional Headquarters could not
have pleased Sergeant Donovan, whoever they had sent
to make up the numbers in Castlemere. He stood watching her truculently from under lowered lids and thinking
the lunatics had taken over the asylum if HQ thought
Alan Clarke could be replaced by a blonde bimbo with
a degree in computer science.

As he got used to the idea, however, he began to see
certain advantages. Inevitably a woman would do things
differently—spend more time behind her desk probably,
tell him what she wanted and let him get on with it.
That suited him. He was a loner by nature: the closeness
of his relationship with Clarke had been something
unique in his experience, something he had no wish to
try and recreate with someone else. Alan Clarke and
Cal Donovan: at their best they'd been unstoppable, the
terror of the criminal classes of Castlemere. While it
lasted it had been like being on a permanent high.

But he'd paid for it in the end. Rather, Clarke had.
The man should have known better. He knew Donovan
was bad luck: always had been, things happened round
him, not through any fault of his but just because he
was there. Clarke thought he'd beaten the jinx but it got
him in the end. Now the powers-that-be thought a Bar-
bie doll a suitable successor.

'Donovan, what are you doing here?' Shapiro said
wearily.

'I heard about the shooting. I thought you'd be short-handed.'

'Yes,' admitted the Chief Inspector, 'well, it could have come at a better time. But you're not fit to work.'

'I'm fine.' But Liz noticed the surreptitious easing of his weight against the door-frame.

'How's the head?'

'It's fine. It ached for a couple of days but it's all right now. I want to get back to work.'

'Well,' Shapiro said doubtfully, 'Inspector Graham's new to Castlemere—she could use someone who's familiar with the place. She's handling the Page murder.'

The sergeant's eyes flicked wide. A note of alarm sounded in his voice. 'Wait a minute, I've got a case—what Alan and I were working on, and what happened to him because of it. Sir.'

'Oh no,' said Shapiro with absolute certainty. 'I'm sorry, Donovan, it's not on. You're too close to it. And if it comes to trial you'll be a witness. You'll be more credible if you weren't in on the investigation.'

Donovan looked as if he'd been kicked in the face by someone on his own team. 'But—'

'I'm not arguing with you, Sergeant. I doubt if you should be working at all but we're stretched and I can use you. But understand this. If you report for work you'll be on Inspector Graham's enquiry, not mine.'

Liz watching discreetly, saw disappointment and anger in his eyes in the moment before he dropped them. She said quietly, 'The sooner we wrap up the Page case, the more resources we can devote to finding DI Clarke's killer.'

Shapiro waited for a response. When none was forthcoming he said tetchily, 'Well? Are you reporting for duty or not?'

To his credit Donovan didn't hesitate. 'Of course I am. I said so.' There was surprise along with the resentment in his voice, and he waited longer than usual before adding, 'Sir.'

Shapiro sighed and his shoulders slumped. Liz thought he was relieved not to have had more of a battle. 'All right. Good. Have you seen the doctor yet?'

Donovan shook his head negligently. 'No point disturbing him on a Sunday. I'll see him through the week sometime.'

The ghost of a smile was beginning to tug at the corners of Shapiro's mouth. 'By which time, presumably, you'll be feeling even more fine.'

'I hope so,' agreed Donovan fervently.

'Get out of here,' said Shapiro. As Donovan went he shouted after him, 'One proviso. Until you've seen him, stay off that bloody bike!'

Liz got up too. 'I'll go and see the people at the nursing home. I'll send Donovan to the airfield where Page works.' She twitched a grin. 'See if pilots and mechanics gossip together as much as nurses.'

Shapiro eyed her askance. 'As in: "Guess what I'm going to do tonight, fellers?—murder the wife"?'

Liz shook her head. 'More as in: "Why's Page going round so po-faced these days?—anybody'd think his wife was having it off with an air-traffic controller."'

She collected the address of the nursing home, found out where Rosedale Avenue was, and went out to the car park. She had to walk crabwise to avoid seeing Donovan ride out on his motorcycle.

LIKE DONOVAN, Sister Kim had heard the news on the radio. Her almond eyes and the saffron-tinted skin round them were red with crying. But she had recovered her composure by the time Liz arrived. They went to the office where they could talk without interruption.

'I'm trying to find Matron,' she murmured. 'But she went away for the weekend too and I'm not sure where. Unless she hears on the radio and calls in....'

'I'm sure you can tell me everything I need to know,' Liz assured her. 'Probably more than Matron could. I imagine Kerry talked to you about her private life more than to Matron.'

The Chinese girl gave a demure smile. 'You know Matron then?'

Liz smiled too and shook her head. 'I doubt if people become matrons by discussing man trouble round the coffee machine and that's the kind of thing I need to hear about Kerry. What worried her, what made her happy. How she was getting on with her husband. If she was frightened at all. The things you confide to friends rather than discussing with employers. You worked with Kerry for—how long?'

'Four years,' said Kim, 'I came here soon after she did.'

'Then you've known her longer than her husband has. I doubt if anyone knows more about her than you do.'

The Sister inclined her head with its little lace cap pinned to the coils of black silk hair. 'I will of course help all I can.'

There were no specific questions Liz needed answers to. She wanted a picture of Kerry Page and her marriage. She let Sister Kim talk for as long as she would about whatever occurred to her, and when she ran out of things to say set her off again with a well-judged prompt.

She reported, word for word, the last conversation they'd had before Kerry went off to her weekend cottage. It reinforced what Kim had believed all along: that her colleague was happy with her marriage, that she enjoyed her young husband physically and also liked his company, that she had left for her weekend in the country with no shadows on her horizon, that she didn't know she was in any danger and the last thing to cross her mind before a 12-bore cartridge rendered it unfit for further use would have been utter amazement.

'You don't think,' hesitated Sister Kim, 'it had anything to do with her work here?'

'I don't know what it was to do with yet,' said Liz. 'I'd have thought it unlikely. Why, do you think it could be?'

'Oh, no,' said the nurse hurriedly, 'I can't imagine that it was. Our patients are sometimes disturbed and often frustrated, it's not unknown for them to threaten us. But half an hour later they don't remember, and if they did they're not fit enough to do anything about it. It's not possible that anyone followed her from here to her cottage in order to kill her.'

'Sometimes,' Liz said carefully, 'people who work in medical facilities find themselves approached for drugs. I'm sure you've come across this yourself.'

A quick dip of the black silk head. 'I have heard of it.'

'Is it possible that Mrs Page was taking drugs from here?'

Kim shook her head decisively. 'No. We are most careful with drugs, anything taken would be missed. Also, Sister Page was not a foolish young nurse who might do such a thing without thinking of the consequences. She did not use drugs herself, I am sure of it. And I do not believe she would supply them to anyone else. Also....' She stopped then, with a little sideways smile at the detective.

'Also?'

'Is there much demand among addicts for heart pills and enemas?'

'Not that I've heard,' Liz admitted with a grin. 'Is that all you use here?'

'Not quite. We have sedatives and sleeping pills, and routine medications for various conditions. But we can't treat seriously ill patients, they're transferred to hospital, so we have no use for powerful drugs. We'd disappoint a junkie.'

Liz nodded. 'They won't be queuing up with their hypodermics at the ready, will they? I don't suppose Kerry had much contact with—I don't know—the general hospital maybe?'

'Castle General is where she did her training, she knew many people on the staff. But I don't think she saw much of them after she left. I think she was not very happy there.'

'Why not?'

'I don't know. It's a different sort of work to here— more pressure, more formality, and it's harder to specialize in the things that interest you.'

'Geriatrics? It's not the most glamorous branch of the profession: I'd have thought nurses who wanted to work with old people would get every encouragement.'

'Inspector,' Kim said gently, 'there are no glamorous branches of nursing. But you're right: nurses don't have to fight to do geriatrics. Of course, a private nursing home generally pays better. That's probably why she came here.'

Liz had gone to the Rosedale Nursing Home hoping for an insight into the Pages' life that would begin to

explain what happened in the car park on the Castlemere Levels. When she left, though, the darkness
seemed deeper than ever. It struck her as a little odd
that Kerry Page had lost touch with former colleagues
when they all still lived in the same town. But she'd
married since she knew them, the shape of her life had
changed. She had better things to do than see people
she used to work with. The Pages lived like everyone
else; better than some because they had two good wages
but essentially it was a picture of domestic normality.
Kerry Page had a worthy if mundane job and a happy
if unremarkable marriage. The only unexpected thing
she ever did was having her head blown off.

FIVE

BEECH TREES lined the road to the airfield. A blink of
autumn sun washed the copper leaves with light. Flame-
like, they flickered in the breeze of his passing. At least,
Donovan thought they were flickering. If he was wrong
about that then Shapiro was right and he shouldn't be
riding the bike yet.

Actually the ride in the sunshine and the fresh air
was doing him good. His head felt clearer than at any
time since the—incident. Shapiro insisted on calling it
that in the hope that it might have been an accident.
Donovan knew better. He'd been there. True, his memory was hazy and nothing he could recall labelled it
indelibly as murder. But he had been round stupid men
and drunken men, and he had been round killers, and
he knew the difference. He knew the difference between
a car out of control and one controlled very precisely
in order to crush men's lives out against a brick wall.

All he had seen of the man who had hit them was a
pair of feet. But he knew from the way they walked,
from the way one rolled him over—because it was
quicker and easier than crouching over him and less
likely to result in blood on his clothes—that there was
nothing random, nothing careless, about what had happened. The man had walked back to see if the job was
done. Donovan owed his life to the fact that an appren-
tice painter and his girl had done all they could think
to do in the back of a van reeking of turpentine and
wanted a take-away before the Chinese chip shop shut.

Now the clean air pouring through his visor blew away some of the black rage and other garbage that had been stuffing his head and he was finally getting the thing into perspective. He was sorry to be off the case but what Shapiro said made sense. And Shapiro, if cautious, was a good detective. If there was a way of having Clarke's killer he would have him; if he was a pro it would be obvious then. And Shapiro would have to listen to Donovan's theory as to who sent him and why.

In the mean time Donovan was better working on something than nothing and the Kerry Page case was indisputably murder. He had half expected to come back from sick-leave to find ten years' worth of files on his desk with a note from Shapiro to up-date them. He'd already decided he'd walk if that happened.

The sign on the road welcomed him to Castlemere Airport, a pretentious description of one runway, one hangar, a windsock, and a caravan posing as air-traffic control. Castle Air Services was the only business using the field regularly. Starting with an RAF-surplus DC3 Joe Tulliver spent ten years ferrying mixed freight round Europe for marginal profits before realizing that the way to make money was to specialize in low-weight, high-value cargoes. Like people.

With the motorways filling up people were looking for a better way to cover long distances. Businessmen, race-goers, hospitals needing urgent supplies, and factories waiting for spare parts provided him with a thriving trade. By the time David Page joined the firm in the late eighties Tulliver was running a four-seater, an eight-seater, a light freighter, and a helicopter. His turnover wouldn't have matched British Airways' but then neither would his problems.

Tulliver's office was a corner of the hangar glassed

in so that the telephone didn't have to compete with engine tests. An expansive Yorkshireman with a high pain threshold as far as checked jackets were concerned, Tulliver met Donovan at the hangar door. For a moment the detective was impressed by his courtesy; then he realized the man was watching his Skyvan taking off. When the boxy little freighter was a dwindling speck against the vast sky over the Levels they went inside.

'Bad business,' grunted Tulliver. He dropped heavily into the chair behind his desk, kicked another towards Donovan. 'How's the lad taking it?'

'About how you'd expect,' Donovan said, carefully noncommittal. 'Know him well, do you?'

'I've known David for fifteen years.' Tulliver spoke slowly. 'He used to ride out here on his bike after school: just to watch at first, then I gave him odd jobs to do. He got his private pilot's licence when he was eighteen or nineteen. Then he was coming out here after work—he had a job in the bank, spent most of his pay flying. When he got his licence up-graded I took him on. That's about three years ago.' He sighed. 'It was a mistake. Don't misunderstand me, he's a good pilot, when I've had enough of this business I'd like to see David running it. But I used to make a packet out of hiring him the Cessna. Now he gets all the flying he wants and I have to pay him.'

Donovan supposed it was a dour Yorkshire joke. 'You've had no problems with his work, then.'

Tulliver regarded him levelly. 'If I'd had problems with his work, lad, he wouldn't still be here. There's a word for unreliable pilots. It's Unemployed.'

'Funny,' murmured Donovan, 'my boss thinks that's the word for policemen who don't file reports.'

Tulliver gave a broad grin. 'I think I'd like your boss.'

Donovan wished he hadn't said it. 'Yeah, we all did, and it didn't do him a pick of good because now he's dead. But that isn't my case. The Pages: did you ever see them together?'

Joe Tulliver was a bluff man, unpolished, a man with little in the way of refinement. But he had not built a good business without learning something about people. He heard the grief still sharp in Donovan's voice and realized this was something that had happened recently; and noting the healing wound on the man's temple and the stiff way he moved he supposed this was the sergeant who survived and his boss the inspector who died in the incident behind Castlemere gasworks the previous week. The other thing he heard in Donovan's voice was that he didn't want to talk about it.

So he answered the question. 'All the time. She used to go with him sometimes if she wasn't working. She was a nice girl, and David's been like one of the family for ten years. Most weeks they'd drop by our house at least once.'

'This weekend?'

'No, not this weekend. They were at the cottage, weren't they? Mostly it was during the week they came to us. We didn't go there: you couldn't swing a cat in that flat of theirs. There's not a lot of David but she was a big girl, she damn near filled it on her own.'

'Why didn't they move somewhere bigger?'

'I think it suited them well enough. It was Kerry's flat before they were married, just round the corner from where she worked. It meant she didn't need a car, and she could get home for a couple of hours if she was on a split shift. But any time they had a day off they went to the cottage. That was where they were at home. The flat was just for convenience.'

'They liked the solitude, then.'

Tulliver raised one bushy eyebrow. 'They were only married two years. Of course they liked the solitude.'

Donovan twitched a saturnine grin. 'They were OK, then, were they? It was working out?'

Tulliver knew what he was asking. 'They were more than OK. They were very happy. David thought the sun shone out of her navel, and I reckon she loved him too. All their off-duty time they spent together: he'd go to the flat to be with her, she'd come out here to be with him. They weren't just in love, Sergeant, they liked one another. If you've got it at the back of your mind that maybe David Page blew his wife's head off with a shotgun, forget it.'

Donovan was still thinking about something Tulliver had said earlier. 'The car's his then. Did Kerry drive it much?'

The big man thought. 'Not really. I mean, she could drive. But David needed it to get to work so it was always here with him. No, David did most of the driving.'

'Only she was in the driving seat when she was shot.'

Tulliver shrugged. 'I suppose she liked to keep her hand in. If they ever gave up the flat she'd need a car of her own.'

'Yeah, maybe that's it.' Donovan was trying to picture them together. 'She was taller than him, was she? You said she filled the flat.'

Tulliver considered, shrugged. 'A shade taller, a bit broader. But you expect it the other way round, don't you? What's big for a girl is still small for a man.'

'So given the right circumstances—not much light,

say, and them sitting down, and her sitting where you'd expect to see him—you could maybe mistake one for the other?'

Tulliver's eyes narrowed as he thought about it. 'In the car? If whoever it was expected to see David driving? Well, maybe. If she had the collar of her coat up about her hair, say. She was fair too. Maybe in the dark you wouldn't notice that her hair was curly and there was more of it. Maybe, if you were planning on shooting one of them, you wouldn't be taking that long to weigh it up.'

Donovan was almost literally chewing it over. He found himself gnawing on the inside of his cheek and stopped. 'Do you know any reason someone would want to kill Page?'

Tulliver didn't answer immediately but when he did it was with conviction. 'No. David hasn't any enemies, he's not that kind of boy. He's inoffensive. He doesn't get into trouble.'

'You've never caught him making—oh, I don't know—unauthorized flights, landings he couldn't explain?'

Tulliver's eye was stern. 'I told you, laddie, I've no complaints about his work. I plan to make him a partner, all right? When he's ready to buy in this business'll be in both our names. You think I'd be doing that if I didn't trust him? Besides which, you seem to be confusing us with British Airways. Yes, we do international flights—Longchamps for the racing, Frankfurt for the Book Fair, that sort of thing. But he doesn't fly to the same places regularly enough to be of any interest to smugglers, say. I can't see it, Sergeant. I can't see David Page getting mixed up in anything crooked.'

Thinking was making Donovan's head ache. He

knuckled his fist into his eye. 'Then suppose it wasn't something he did that made him a target but something he saw or heard. They're pretty small, these planes, aren't they? I mean, the passengers are right up there with the pilot?' Tulliver nodded. 'So anything they were talking about he'd hear. You keep records of who's flown where, when, and for what purpose?'

'Of course.' The big man reached for a heavy black-bound ledger with the entries made by hand. 'How far back do you want to go?'

Donovan shrugged. 'Let's start on Friday and work back.'

He was expecting the job to take an hour and the results to be inconclusive at the end of it. He could hardly believe his luck when he found what he was looking for on the first page. And what he found filled him with a kind of unholy excitement that he had to keep the lid on until he could leave Tulliver's office.

He didn't want to waste time so he telephoned before leaving. Inspector Graham was in Clarke's office. 'I've found something. It could be important and it could be urgent. We need to talk to Page. Where is he?'

'I sent him home,' said Liz. 'To the flat.'

'Can you meet me there?'

'Now? Why, what have you found?'

Tulliver had taken himself out into the hangar so it wasn't that Donovan couldn't talk freely, more that he didn't want to. 'I can't explain on the phone but it's got to be significant. I can be there in fifteen minutes: will you meet me?'

'All right,' said Liz, and before she could ask for more detail he'd rung off.

SHE WAS PARKING her car in the avenue of slightly run-down Victorian houses, many of them converted into flats, a hundred yards from the nursing home, when a roar like a Harrier taking off preceded Donovan's motorbike round the corner. It slewed to a halt, spitting grit. Liz waited in the open door of her car while he took his helmet off. Then she said, 'What's all this about? What have you found out?'

His urgent stride carried him up the steps to the front door. 'Come on, I'll tell you inside.'

She didn't move. 'Sergeant.' When he looked back she tapped her finger on the roof. 'In the car.'

He frowned, puzzled and irritated. 'But—'

'The car.'

When he had folded his long legs inside, and shut the door because she made it clear she was waiting for him to do so, she said—quietly, without rancour, but also firmly: 'A few ground rules, Sergeant. You don't bounce me around. I'm happy for you to use your initiative but this is my case and I want to know what you're doing and also what you're thinking. When I know why you want to, I will decide if we talk to Page again, and what we say. But we're going nowhere until I know what you suspect and why.'

For a moment Donovan looked like a sparrowhawk who's been mugged by a sparrow. Then he blinked resentfully and explained. 'What if Kerry wasn't the intended victim? What if it was Page? Anyone who knew them would be expecting him to be behind the wheel. His boss says you could make that mistake—particularly if it was dark and she was wrapped up warm.'

Liz had considered the possibility without reaching any conclusion. 'Did Tulliver know someone who might want Page dead?'

'No. But I might.' Liz heard the electric thread running through his voice and wondered if it should be warning her of something. Clarke would have known, and probably Shapiro, but she didn't know him well enough. 'I looked at his flight log. Last Saturday week he flew a party up to Cartmel for the races.'

Liz knew the pause was for dramatic effect but did not mind humouring him a little. 'Who?'

'Jack Carney.' He said it with a kind of tight-lipped triumph. 'Maybe the name doesn't mean much at Headquarters but he's the closest thing we've got to the Godfather. What trouble we have with organized crime is down to Carney. It's always someone else does the time but Carney pulls the strings. He's an evil sod, and he'd buy a hit if he thought it'd keep him out of jail.'

Liz's eyes were searching his narrow face. She had not realized how ravaged he looked. 'So what are you thinking? That Page was running errands for this man, that he tried to cheat him—something like that?'

Donovan shook his head. 'Tulliver says not, reckons Page wouldn't do anything illegal. But suppose he overheard something—something that could put Carney behind bars? It's a two-hundred-mile flight, say three hours there and back. Maybe somebody got careless, forgot Page wasn't on the payroll.'

'So Carney waited a week and then shot his wife?'

'Even Jack Carney doesn't have a resident hit-man,' glowered Donovan. 'He's got muscle. If this was a broken arm I'd want to know where Terry McMeekin was last night. But McMeekin isn't a killer. He'd like you to think so but he hasn't the guts. Carney'd bring someone in from outside. A week is about what it'd take to get hold of a pro, brief him, and get him in place. Only he made a mistake and shot Kerry instead.'

Liz turned it over in her mind. It was possible. It

didn't stand out as a certainty but in this job not much did. You found something the rough shape of an answer and chipped away at the inconsistencies until a theory emerged. And the connection between David Page and the local gangster was surely more than a coincidence. At any event it warranted exploring.

'All right, we'll talk to Page. You can talk to him if you like. But don't spring any surprises on me. I'll go along with you, Donovan, but I won't be led round by the nose.'

The flat was two rooms on the second landing. By the time they reached the door Donovan was limping. He rang the bell and when there was no reply rapped with his knuckles. His face twisted in bitter disappointment. 'God damn, he's gone out.'

'Give him time,' she said softly.

The door opened. Page looked at the Sergeant blankly. Then he recognized Liz and something almost like hope kindled in his face. 'Is there some news?' As if she might tell him there had been a mistake, that it wasn't his wife whose flayed head fell in his lap after all.

'Not news exactly,' she said, 'but something we wanted to ask you about. It might help.'

Page took them inside. It was a very small flat. The other thing that was immediately noticeable was that it was Kerry's place. The decorations, the furnishings, the taste were all hers. After two years of marriage he was still a guest there. The cottage was different, a joint endeavour, but this remained essentially a single girl's flat.

Home ground and time to pull himself together had left David Page both calmer and clearer. His face was tired and grey, he'd missed a night's sleep and would

miss more before he started making it up, but Liz
thought he was regaining control over himself. He was
beginning to look like a man who routinely held other
people's lives in his hands and not so much like a
schoolboy accused of indecent acts behind the bicycle
shed.

'What is it? What have you found out?'

'Last Saturday you flew some people to Cartmel,'
Donovan said. 'Tell us about them.'

Page was taken aback, couldn't imagine what this had
to do with his wife's death. But he answered as best he
could. 'The booking was in the name of John Carney.
The other man, McMeekin, was an employee of his.'

'Did you know them before Saturday?'

'No. He's chartered the Beechcraft—that's the eight-
seater—a couple of times but it wasn't me who flew
him.'

'What did they talk about?'

Page blinked. 'Racing. There was a horse Mr Carney
had an interest in. He kept calling it his National prospect. He told McMeekin and me to put our shirts on it.'

Donovan gave a cheerless grin. 'What else did they
discuss? Business? It's a longish flight, they must have
talked about something other than horses.'

'I suppose so. I don't remember. Nothing interesting:
they weren't exactly great conversationalists, you
know?'

'But you could hear what they were saying? Even
when they were talking between themselves?'

'I could hear. I wasn't listening. Why would I? I'm
a bus driver, I get my passengers where they want to
go, I try to be civil to them, I collect my pay, and I go
home. I make small talk if they want to, I show them
which is the altimeter and which is the clock, after that

I do my job. I don't know what they were talking about last Saturday. I can't see it matters.'

Liz crossed her fingers out of sight in her pockets and hoped Donovan wouldn't tell him, but Donovan did.

'It matters because Jack Carney is a thug, and if he thought he'd said something or Terry McMeekin had said something unwise in front of you he wouldn't hesitate to send someone to shut you up.'

The little blood that remained in it drained from David Page's face as if someone had cut his throat. He had trouble finding a voice. 'You mean—?'

'I mean, if you'd been driving last night maybe Jack Carney would sleep sounder in his bed for knowing that nothing you'd heard would go any further, even at the autopsy, even when the pathologist opened your head up to see what you'd got inside.'

SIX

LIZ WAS OUTRAGED. This time she didn't wait to get Donovan in the car: as soon as Page's door was shut she turned on him. 'That was unforgivable! That young man is mourning for a woman he loved who was murdered in front of him. Who gave you the right to grind his face in it?'

Cal Donovan was a tall, thin man with all the features of his black Irish heritage plain about him. The olive skin was drawn tight so that his narrow face hollowed under the high cheek-bones. His dark, deep-set eyes held a primordial spark. Expressions flitted across his face too quickly to leave a mark on the underlying structure, which was sharply brooding like a dyspeptic hawk. His hair was too long even when he'd just had it cut. He looked like the hired gun in a cowboy film.

So he was not well equipped to feign injured innocence. But he gave it his best shot. 'Me? What did I do?'

'You told him two things he didn't need to know. You told him that the atrocities committed on his wife didn't stop when she was dead. And you told him it was his fault. He's never going to forget that, Donovan. When he's come to terms with the rest of it, when he's ready to believe the people who tell him he couldn't have saved her, you saying she died because of him will live on like a worm in his brain.

'He doesn't know you're no better than walking wounded yourself. He doesn't know your thinking has been affected by what happened under the viaduct. He doesn't know, and he wouldn't care if he did, that you feel responsible for that, that DI Clarke would be alive now if you hadn't put him on that street at that time. You feel guilty as hell and you want him to feel the same way.

'I won't have it, Sergeant. If you can't handle your feelings you go home until you can. Survivor guilt is a natural phenomenon but you deal with it: you *don't* try and dump it on some poor boy who's got enough of his own to carry without picking up yours as well.'

Donovan had taken enough tongue-lashings in his time to become more or less inured, but this was different on two counts and momentarily he was speechless. In the first place she was a woman, had seemed the sort of nice middle-class woman who would shy away from making a scene in a public place, didn't look like she had that kind of anger, that capacity for invective, in her. The way her eyes blazed into his from close range, her strong body blocking his escape down the stairs, startled him.

The other difference was that she was right. But he wasn't ready to admit that yet. 'I didn't tell him anything he didn't already know or wouldn't find out.'

'Yes, sure, if this comes to something we'd have had to tell him somehow. *I'd* have told him, and I'd have done it gently because he is not my enemy, he's a victim of this as much as she was. I would not have hit him in the face with it because striking out made me feel good and I couldn't get at the person I really wanted to hurt.'

Donovan swallowed and his eyes dropped. He did not know how much Shapiro had told her and how much she had worked out for herself but she'd made a good case against him. He wouldn't perjure himself by denying it. At the same time he was still too angry, with himself and with the world, to throw himself on the mercy of the court.

Liz saw his lips twitch as if the words had a bad taste. 'I'm trying to do my job, that's all. Some bastard blew Kerry Page to kingdom come when she had every reason to expect another fifty years' health and happiness. Now I'm pretty sure we know who and I'm pretty sure we know why, and even if Page doesn't know it the answer's there in his head—something he heard or something he saw—and if I have to shake him a little to get it out I think that's a price worth paying to take this murderous bastard off the street.'

'But it's not a trade-off you have any right to make,' Liz insisted. The temper was going from her eyes now but she wasn't ready yet to let him off the hook. 'If you can't get the guilty without hurting the innocent then you wait for another chance. If you're doing your job well enough another chance will come.'

'But maybe not before he blasts some other luckless sod who gets in his way,' Donovan retorted. 'What about Page himself? If Carney took out a contract on him, he still wants it done. While we're being nice and polite about this maybe the bastard's on his way here with his shotgun.'

Liz caught her breath. She should have thought of that. 'That's a point. All right. You stay with Page, I'll go and see Carney. Where do I find him?'

Donovan's eyes flared. 'You're not going alone.' It was a statement, not a question. 'Look, the last baby-sitter Page wants is me. You're right, I was out of line with him. Ask the station to send someone round. I don't know, maybe they should draw firearms. Then you and me can go question Carney. He's a different kettle of fish, he won't be upset if I get heavy with him.'

'You won't *get* heavy with him,' Liz said positively. 'If anybody's going to get heavy it'll be me. You're there to watch my back, nothing else: is that clear?' Donovan nodded. 'And another thing. The feminine form of sir is ma'am. Until I can trust you to remember I'm your superior officer, I think you'd better get in the way of using it.'

BECAUSE IT WAS Sunday Liz assumed that the Castlemere Godfather would be at home. Though she knew nothing of Carney she had seen enough career criminals in her time to know that, whatever their origins, they didn't continue living in back streets after finding that crime does pay. So she was surprised when Donovan directed her into the black Victorian heart of Castlemere, the narrow streets under the shattered fortress it took its name from. But she drove where he said, doglegging between the old buildings until an iron archway appeared ahead, the gates pushed back against the walls. It would have looked like any disused factory gate except that the iron had been recently painted and the lettering on the arch picked out in gold.

'Mere Basin?' said Liz, wishing she'd had longer to get to know this town. 'What's that?'

'The canal,' said Donovan. She had made him leave his bike outside Page's house and ride with her. 'All these buildings were warehouses in the last century. Castlemere was a canal junction; narrowboats travelled from here all over the country.' He paused then and she thought he was going to add some other nugget of information. But, staring ahead through the windscreen, he only added bleakly, 'Ma'am.'

Liz looked at him curiously. 'Are you some kind of a local historian, Sergeant?'

He did not return her gaze. 'I'm a detective, ma'am. In Castlemere it's important to understand the canals as well as the road system. We've had thieves use getaway boats before now. You also feel a bit of a prat when someone you want to arrest waves at you across twenty feet of water and you don't know where the nearest bridge is.'

She didn't blame him for trying to level the score a little. 'I'm going to have to do a bit of homework.' She drove under the arch. 'So Mr Carney's a canal buff?'

Donovan spared her a disdainful glance. 'Jack Carney? The only thing that interests Jack Carney is money. He's got an office down here. The council spent a fortune doing the place up. They wanted it to be like St Katharine's Dock in London, with boats and businesses and cafés and yuppie-hutches. Only when Carney moved in all the nice people moved out. So the cafés went up for sale and he bought them too; and the yuppies moved out and now half the flats are vacant. The boat-owners use it, of course, they've no choice. But the council could have saved its money. The place is more like Execution Dock than St Katharine's.'

Gold paint notwithstanding, Liz was already getting that impression. When the entry took a sudden steep dive it was like entering the underworld. 'Still, it is Sunday. Will he be in his office?'

'Fish don't stop swimming on Sundays,' Donovan replied grimly, 'politicians don't stop lying, and crooks don't stop turning blood into money. He'll be here.'

'Tell me about him,' said Liz. 'How did he get started? How does he work? What's he into, and for how much?'

Momentarily Donovan seemed taken aback by the question, as if startled to meet someone who didn't know all about Jack Carney, his life and times and crimes. Liz understood that. She too had worked on target criminals, immersing herself in their affairs so deeply that she'd found it difficult to return to the world of ordinary people, ordinary problems. It became a kind of obsession, necessarily so; it was a job that couldn't be done on a nine to five basis, but part of the cost to be paid for success was that police officers had to get down in the dirt with them to fight people like Carney. Donovan had been there. She could see the marks on him.

After a moment he got his thoughts organized. 'He started in the protection racket. No, before that he was in construction and somebody tried to put the frighteners on him. Boy, did they ever get it wrong! Carney not only didn't cave in, he took the firm over. They were only local lads trying to turn a dishonest penny, but by the time Carney had sorted them they were a major employer in these parts. All the usual victims—building firms, pubs and clubs, and just about any business run by immigrants. They're a soft touch: until they've been here a while they'd rather pay up than come to us. They don't like to make a fuss. Maybe they think it's part of the local culture,' he added disgustedly.

'Well, it's no great leap of the imagination from protection to drugs. Bouncers are always in the right place at the right time, unless they're dead straight they're an ideal outlet. You catch the odd one but Carney pays him to say he was moonlighting and when he comes out he's got a new car and a time-share in Spain.

'Another thing bouncers are useful for is reminding gamblers of their moral obligations. Illegal gambling's a big money-spinner'—Donovan acknowledged the pun with a grim smile—'so he's into that too. Ah, but he's clever. Nothing as simple as a room above the pub we could raid from time to time. He's used a boat on the canal, a caravan in a field, and a removal van in a layby before now. We get to hear about it afterwards, of course, when it's too damn late.'

'Has he ever been charged?'

'Sure,' said Donovan. 'Careless driving. Keeping a dangerous dog. Possession of an unlicensed firearm—it was a war souvenir, general consensus at Forensics was that it'd have blown the hand off anyone who tried to fire it. But for the real stuff, the protection, the drugs, the gambling, the hookers—did I mention them?—never. Had him in for questioning more times than I can remember but we never came up with evidence a pricey brief couldn't overturn. Except—' He didn't go on.

'Except?'

'Except we'd been working hard on him these last few weeks, shaking a lot of trees and watching what fell out. Maybe we'd have got him this time. Only then—well, it was Alan's operation.' He said no more.

'When this current mess is sorted out,' said Liz, 'someone'll take over where Inspector Clarke left off. Make sure of Carney then. Alan would appreciate that.'

It was the middle of the day but they descended through darkness. Liz turned her headlamps on. Then sunlight blinked ahead and they emerged into a magical place, a man-made cavern deep in the bowels of a man-made earth. Brown water glinted, and on the water boats painted like bathtub toys.

All around black warehouses soared to six storeys, their roofs framing a square of sky. Windows rose in ranks up the face of them, glazed and framed in cheery red brick which was the planners' compromise between dour authenticity and the sort of environment where people might want to live and work. Some of the windows were curtained, some had blinds. It was still impossible to gaze up at those looming heights without a sense of claustrophobia.

At ground-floor level, enclosing the pretty cobbled wharfs, the warehouses had been hollowed out to provide parking. The wall was scalloped into a colonnade and vehicles faded from view as they passed through it. Standing in front of the colonnade were the white furniture and gaily striped umbrellas of a pavement café, but none of the seats was occupied.

Mere Basin was the confluence of four canals. Each arrived under a masonry cliff, the buildings drawing up their skirts in a quartet of low-roofed tunnels. The water was peaty brown, glinting weed green where its surface was ruffled. Tied to the wharf by great shaggy ropes or chugging in and out under the black buildings were long thin boats with black hulls and gaily painted upperworks. Men in oily sweaters tinkered with engines or plied the long swan's-neck tillers; girls in peaked caps stood on the foredecks coiling rope. It was an extraordinary sight, charming and eccentric and quintessentially English, about as sinister as a conclave of bellringers.

Parking under one of the warehouses, between a primrose BMW and a Volvo estate with an outboard engine in the back, Liz was about to say as much when she saw that they were being watched. A well-built man of about thirty was perched on a bollard, looking not at the activity on the water but into the shadows where she'd driven. She might have dismissed it as the curi-

osity of a regular spotting a strange car but for the fact
that he was wearing a suit. It was Sunday afternoon,
everyone else here was in jeans and jumpers, but this
well-built young man was perched on a mooring bollard
in a well-cut charcoal-grey suit.

Donovan had seen him too. 'Terry McMeekin,' he
growled. 'Carney's muscle. He'll follow us inside. He'll
crowd us but he won't start anything. But when you
decide to lift Carney, he's the one to watch.'

'It's a bit early to think of arresting him!' exclaimed
Liz. 'Can I talk to him before you send for the Black
Maria?'

Donovan sniffed. 'Just looking ahead.'

Access to the flats and offices above was via lifts and
stairways also parked discreetly out of sight behind the
colonnade. The business users were on the lower
storeys; a phone controlled the residents' lift.

Carney Enterprises had offices on the first floor: a red
arrow directed Liz to a staircase. The glass door at the
foot of the stairs was locked. 'I don't think there's anyone here.'

She turned and caught Donovan breathing heavily.
'The BMW's here, McMeekin's here, therefore Carney's here. Tell you what, I'll go outside and throw
stones at his window.'

The offer had the desired effect. As he turned back
to the basin the man in the suit came to meet him, taking
keys from his pocket. 'Sergeant Donovan? Looking for
Mr Carney, are you?' Liz could not see his face for the
shadows but heard the lilt of mischief in his voice.

'However did you guess?' Donovan said flatly.

'He's upstairs. We're sorting through some paperwork—the only time you can do it's when the office is
closed, there's too much going on during the week. I

just stepped out to check on the motor. It's a new one, do you like the colour?' He rubbed a sleeve appreciatively across the primrose bonnet. 'I locked the door. You don't want all sorts wandering round up there, do you?'

Liz smiled at him. 'How very security-conscious of you, Mr McMeekin. I'm sure Mr Carney appreciates the care you take of him.'

McMeekin's eyes warmed on her. He knew who she was, had known about her before Donovan did, was confident enough to engage in a little banter. 'I like to think so, Inspector. I like to think I do a good job.'

'Don't we all? Would you tell Mr Carney I'd like a word?'

'He'll be pleased to meet you.' He unlocked the glass door, fastening it again behind them. 'That was a bad business about Inspector Clarke, by the way. We were all very shocked.'

'I just bet you were,' Donovan said in his teeth.

The broader man turned to him with every appearance of concern. 'That's right, you were involved in that too, weren't you, Sergeant? How are you feeling now? I hope you get the stupid sod. The way some people drive, nobody's safe.'

Donovan's lips were tight as he and Liz followed McMeekin up the stairs.

If they'd had an appointment Carney would not have received them more courteously. He ushered them into his office, helped Liz to a chair and cleared files off another for Donovan who studiously ignored it. Folding his hands together on his desk and leaning over them he enquired, solemn as an undertaker's clerk, 'And how may I help you, Mrs Graham?'

Liz had long ago learned not to judge by appearances,

so she was not disturbed by the fact that Jack Carney
was a small, plump man in late middle age with the
faintly rosy complexion associated with good diet, good
health, and a clear conscience: more grandfather than
Godfather. She knew that no conscience at all is even
better for the digestion. Still she had to make a small
effort to remember that this neat man with his glowing
skin and silver hair and caring eyes, and the suggestion
of an all-embracing *bonhomie* was certainly a criminal
and possibly a murderer.

She said, 'I'm investigating the murder of Mrs Kerry
Page early this morning in a car park on the Castlemere
Levels.' And she said nothing more, waiting, watching
him, hoping to learn something from his reaction.

He blinked. He looked surprised, then perplexed.
'And you think I can help?' The puzzlement in his voice
could have been genuine or a skilful forgery. He didn't
deny anything; but then she hadn't accused him of anything yet.

'I hope so,' said Liz. 'You knew Mrs Page, didn't
you?'

'Did I?' Carney seemed to be searching his memory
without success.

'You certainly know her husband.'

So far as she could tell the man was genuinely confused. He wasn't rattled, not yet, but he didn't like being
at a disadvantage. 'I'm sorry, Inspector, I don't think I
know either of them. Page? What does he do?'

'He's a pilot.'

The penny dropped. Carney beamed with relief. 'Oh
yes. Page—he's one of Tulliver's men, out at the airfield.' He shook his head. 'I couldn't honestly say I
know him. He's flown me, only the once I think: last
Saturday, to Cartmel. A horse I have a little interest in

was running. I'd know him to see but I couldn't have told you his name.'

'David Page.'

He nodded slowly. 'And his wife's been murdered, you say? What a terrible thing. Just last night?' Understanding dawned. 'My God, you think it was Page! You want to know—what?—if he said anything on the flight?'

'Yes, all right,' said Liz. 'What did you talk about?'

Carney shrugged. 'We didn't really. I mean, he was civil enough, we didn't fly two hundred miles in silence. But I don't think he was interested in racing. We talked mostly between ourselves, didn't we, Terry?' This to the man who was standing to one side of the door as Donovan was standing to the other.

McMeekin nodded. 'Pretty much, Mr Carney.'

'He certainly didn't talk about his wife.'

'No, I suppose not.' Liz gave a solemn smile. 'If he'd been planning to murder her he'd hardly have discussed it with clients he'd never met before.'

Carney was looking puzzled again. 'Then how *do* you think I can help you?'

'Were you in town yourself last night, Mr Carney?'

The caring eyes in the cheery face recoiled as if she'd hit him. 'Me? You want to know where *I* was last night? You want to know where *I* was while Mrs Page was being murdered?'

'Yes, please,' Liz said calmly.

Then the sheer effrontery of it seemed to disarm him, whittling away at his sense of outrage. He blew out his cheeks in a huff of mild indignation. He looked at McMeekin, glanced at Donovan, then looked back at Liz. 'I was at home.'

'With your wife?'

'With my wife.'

'And?'

'And Terry here.'

'Really?'

'Yes. He's a useful chap to have about the place when you're throwing a party.'

Liz tried to keep the reaction out of her face and voice, doubted if she'd been successful. 'A party?'

Carney made no effort to disguise the fact that he was now enjoying himself. 'Yes, it's something we do a couple of times a year. I see a lot of people in the way of business—councillors, professional men, even the odd policeman—it isn't always easy to thank them properly as individuals so we throw a bit of a do every six months. A buffet and a band. It's not exactly Saturday Night at the London Palladium but I think everyone enjoyed it.' He couldn't keep from beaming. 'It was damn near breakfast time before we wound it up.'

Liz nodded steadily, waiting for her mind to process the information, made herself smile. 'And Mr Mc-Meekin was helping.'

'Oh yes. Master of Ceremonies, that's Terry. Filling a glass here, passing a canapé there; dancing with the Mayoress while I interest the Mayor in an idea or two... Oh yes, Terry's the life and soul of these things. Everybody'd miss him if he wasn't there.'

Liz was a realist. Short of getting themselves arrested for streaking in Castlemere High Street at the relevant time the two men could hardly have a better alibi. Either Donovan was wrong or Carney had timed the attack precisely so that he was covered. It didn't make him fireproof, but before she could tie him to the murder she'd need concrete evidence. It would mean finding the mechanic first. If there was a mechanic. If this wasn't all a figment of Donovan's bruised imagination.

'Not everyone,' Donovan said, not quite under his breath.

McMeekin squared up to him, the broad shoulders of his suit swinging like the yards of a sailing ship. There was a braced note in his voice like the twang of straining cordage. 'It was a good night, Sergeant, you should have been there.' He snapped his fingers. 'Sorry, I'd forgotten—you were busy yesterday.'

Donovan showed his teeth in a wolfish travesty of a grin. 'Your turn'll come, McMeekin. I'll not only go to your funeral, I'll dance at it.'

'Unless you take more care crossing roads, Donovan, your dancing days are numbered.'

'Saturday night at Wormwood Scrubs is nothing to write home about either.'

They were like a couple of pitbull terriers straining their leashes to get at one another. Liz sighed, turned to Carney. 'If I call off mine will you call off yours?'

The small man chuckled, tapped his knuckles on the desk. 'Terry, leave the policeman alone. He's had a hard week.'

'And you,' Liz said, spearing Donovan with her gaze as she stood up, 'and I have some things to discuss, so we'll be on our way now.' She looked at Carney, who had also risen. 'Thank you for your time. I'm sure we'll meet again.'

'I do hope so, Mrs Graham.' The little gangster smiled, for all the world as if he meant it.

SEVEN

SHAPIRO HAD BEEN out of the office when Liz called for someone to baby-sit Page but he was back now and wanting to see her as a matter of urgency. The pointed discussion she wanted with Donovan would have to wait. She left him in her office with strict instructions not to leave it, not even for help if he was dying.

The Chief Inspector started up at her entry with a fraught expression that drove from her head the things she'd intended to say to him. 'You've been to the basin? You've seen Carney? Whatever possessed you?'

She didn't understand, either the reproach or the worried look in his eyes. 'We found a link between him and David Page. I wanted to ask him about it, that's all. What's the problem?'

'Who found the link? What link?'

'Page flew him to Cartmel races last weekend. Donovan found it in the flight records at the airfield. Frank, what's this all about?'

'Donovan!' Shapiro exploded. 'God damn it, girl, don't you know—?' Then he stopped, made himself breathe deeply, made a wry apologetic gesture with his hand. He sat on his desk and gently shook his head. 'No, of course you don't. How could you? I haven't told you and I'm damn sure Donovan hasn't.'

'Told me what?' She took the chair he indicated.

'It's my fault, I should've had the guts to send him home. He's not fit to work, his judgement's shot to hell.

You may find it hard to believe but he doesn't usually behave like this.'

'Like what?' asked Liz. She still didn't know what it was Shapiro thought had happened.

'Donovan blames Carney for what happened under the viaduct. There's no evidence, but that doesn't mean he's wrong. Alan had been working up a case against Carney and he wasn't far from a break-through. All it needed was for someone to take his nerve in both hands and decide he could get Carney off his back for longer by putting him behind bars than by paying him off.'

Jack Carney started in the construction industry, he knew its weaknesses. He knew that when a builder had a crew going all out to meet a stiff completion date with the threat of a penalty clause hanging over him he needed luck on his side. He simply couldn't afford unexplained accidents, predatory vandalism, or people beating up the nightwatchman and making off with the next day's supplies. Get such a man at the right time and put it to him in the right way—as a suggestion that understaffing was causing a lot of his problems and with more people, supplied by someone who understood the construction industry, the job would run like clockwork—and he'd go along with it.

He'd sign them up. No matter that they give their names as Michael Mouse, David Duck, and Charles Windsor. No matter he'd never see them carrying a hod, wielding a saw, or pouring concrete. No matter that he'd never see them at all except on pay-day. The accidents would stop, the vandalism would stop, even the thefts would drop to the usual level of shrinkage. All right, so ten per cent of his payroll would be going to men who redefined the whole concept of casual labour. But the job was getting done and it's cheaper to pay a few phantoms than to run into penalty clauses.

'It's just another form of protection racket,' said Shapiro. 'But it works because the victim's able to hang on to his self-respect. He can convince himself that the extra manpower on the site, even if you can't see them most of the time, is making the thing run sweeter. He knows better really, but he has a vested interest in believing it. As long as the financial burden doesn't become too heavy, he'll pay.'

'That's what Carney's been doing?'

'He's been doing more than that,' said Shapiro, 'but that's what Alan was working on. He picked up word that one of the builders—Jim Potter, a local man, he was being hit for this time and again—was getting angry enough to do something about it. Of course, he didn't want to be the one to stick his neck out for everybody else's benefit. He'd give evidence against Carney—well, McMeekin actually, all the arrangements went through him—but only if some other people would as well.

'So that's what Alan was doing: talking to builders and persuading them they'd been taken for a ride long enough. It was coming together—slowly, you know how it is, nobody wants to be the first. Then all at once the thing died on him. Nobody was talking any more. Nobody was in when he called, and nobody'd say why.'

'They'd been got at.'

'They'd been got at,' agreed Shapiro. 'Specifically, Jim Potter, who'd been just about ready to talk. Now he'd clammed up. It seemed safe to assume that Carney had put the frighteners on him but he wouldn't say so. All we knew was that when Alan first approached him he had two children and an Alsatian dog he thought the world of.'

Liz felt herself paling. 'And now?'

'Now he just has the two children. That's what Lucy called Donovan about. Lucy's a tramp, she spends a lot of time around building sites and the like, and she keeps her ears open. If she hears anything he could use she calls him. It's her main source of income; I also think she's sweet on him.'

Liz tried to imagine anyone being sweet on Donovan, even a tramp, and failed. She gave a little shake of her head. 'What did she hear?'

'We never found out. She said she knew why Potter had suddenly lost his nerve. She said she knew where the dog was. Donovan and Alan were on their way to meet her when they were hit by the car. We looked for Lucy afterwards but nobody's seen her since that night.'

Liz drew in a long, soft breath, understanding how Donovan had used her and why. 'I see why Donovan thinks he was set up.'

'Oh, so do I,' said Shapiro. 'There's every chance he's right—you can't conduct an investigation in total secrecy. If Carney got wind of it he'd be prepared to take action, and maybe that's the action he'd take. Hit the victims and you risk frightening them so much they go to the police. If you show you can hit the police, where do the victims turn then?

'So yes, it's a real possibility. But I won't prove it's what happened by doing what Donovan wants: giving Carney the third degree in the hope of extracting a confession. What I'll get for that is a phone call from the Chief Constable and a writ from Carney's brief, and that'll be the end of it. This fish I have to play carefully. But Donovan thinks I'm afraid to tackle him. He was always going to make an excuse to go round there himself. I'm sorry, I should have warned you.'

She found herself defending Donovan. 'The link he found is real enough, Carney confirmed it. It doesn't seem to lead anywhere, and both he and McMeekin have an alibi for last night.'

'What did Donovan say? Has he dropped us in it?'

She shook her head. 'He got a bit stroppy with McMeekin, that's all.' Her eyes widened. 'I suppose, if he's right about this, it was McMeekin who was driving the car.'

'No, this would be out of his league. Carney'd bring in a hired man with a stolen vehicle, both of them long gone by now.' Shapiro gave a thin smile. 'Or of course it could still have been an accident, in which case some local worthy's leaping out of his skin every time his phone rings.'

The more Liz thought about it, the more annoyed she became. 'That's why he wanted me to meet him at Page's instead of here. That's why he wanted to go straight to the basin instead of coming back here first. He didn't want to risk running into you. The crafty sod.'

Shapiro nodded ruefully. 'Well, we didn't make him a detective sergeant for his simple, open nature.'

'You didn't make him one so he could run the division either,' growled Liz. 'He set me up, deliberately, knowing he could use me to do things you wouldn't let him do. I won't have that, Frank. If I can't trust him, I can't use him.'

'It's not that you can't trust him.' Shapiro tried to explain. 'You could trust him with your life. It's just that—always, but more right now—Donovan thinks with his instincts instead of his head. He's a good copper, he cares about the job and he'll put himself out on a limb to do it, but he can't seem to grasp that making an arrest isn't worth a damn if you can't get a court to uphold it.'

'He's a detective sergeant,' Liz echoed, not without some irony. 'If he hasn't grasped that yet, when are you expecting him to?'

Shapiro didn't answer directly. He pressed his hands together and spread his fingers in a curious gesture of supplication. 'Liz, it's up to you, but—you don't think maybe we could haul him in here, drag him over the coals, threaten him with everything up to and including public flogging, then—well—let him off? He was out of line with you, I know that. But he's had a rough time. Maybe he shouldn't be back in harness yet but that's my mistake, not his. He's a good detective, he's done some good work. If he's earned a bit of tolerance he'll never need it more than now.'

Liz frowned, fighting the urge to accept his argument just to please him. 'But police work is not about what policemen need. It's about what the paying customers need: protecting the innocent, apprehending the guilty—all that stuff. In the last hour he's distressed a bereaved husband, put at risk the case against a target criminal, and made his inspector and his chief inspector look like a couple of idiots. I'm sorry for him, Frank, but either he's responsible for his actions or he isn't. I can't have a loose cannon rolling round the deck.'

'No,' agreed Shapiro. 'You're right, of course.'

He said nothing more. Liz said nothing more. But she felt first her resolve and then her face beginning to crack. He had done too much for her in the past for her to refuse him a favour now. 'God damn it, Frank,' she exploded softly, 'you make sure he knows this is positively his last chance.'

Shapiro grinned. 'Thanks, Liz. You won't regret it, I promise.'

But when they went together to Liz's office, grim expressions tacked firmly in place, the room was empty. Donovan had left his warrant card on the desk and gone.

ON MONDAY morning, while Shapiro was juggling the available manpower, Liz went back to the house in Rosedale Avenue. The motorbike was gone from the street, she noticed. She didn't ring Page's bell. She was looking for someone who had been a neighbour of Kerry's for long enough to know her the way Sister Kim knew her, to have celebrated triumphs and drowned miseries with her, to have shared her gossip.

There were six flats. One was the Pages', one was empty; she worked her way from the art student in the attic to the man in the basement who'd been thrown out by his wife but none of them had been in the house more than eight months. They knew the Pages only casually; they knew nothing against them but they didn't know much about them either.

Then Liz had a little luck. The man in the basement, who wanted to get rid of her because he was going to be late for work, remembered that Kerry Page used to work with a nurse in the next house, that they had been friends for ten years. She went next door, found the buzzer labelled J. Perrin, and managed not to look surprised when Julian Perrin came to the door.

He was Kerry's age or a little older, of medium height, delicately built, with slender hands and a pale sensitive oval face. He had finely textured mid-brown hair but didn't look as if he'd have it much longer. His eyes were softly hazel, red-rimmed from crying.

Liz said gently, 'You've heard about Kerry then.'

Perrin sniffed and nodded. He took her inside. His flat was almost identical to Kerry's, but decorated simply in the Japanese style.

Liz sank on to a low settee and wondered if she'd be able to get up again. 'I understand you were friends for a lot of years.'

'I loved her,' the pale man said simply. Liz realized that he did not mean the same by that as David Page meant, but he meant it sincerely.

'You worked with her?'

'Kerry Carson and I trained together. We went on the wards together. Until she went to Rosedale we never went more than a few days without seeing one another, if only for a snack in the canteen.'

'When did you come to live here?'

Perrin smiled, a sad and tender smile. 'Soon after she did. She moved here when she left the hospital and I followed as soon as I could. I didn't want us to lose touch. She never came back to Castle General, not once, not even to say hello. I couldn't get a job at Rosedale so I came to live near her.'

'Did it work?'

'Oh, yes,' he said happily, remembering, 'it wasn't me she wanted to get away from. We stayed friends. Even after she was married we'd eat together whenever she was alone. Usually she came to me. If I went to her flat I always started cleaning it, which drove her up the wall.'

'It wasn't you she was getting away from, you said. Was it someone else? Was there some reason she left the hospital? More than a change of scene or a better salary, I mean.'

'I don't think so. Why?'

'Only that you're the second person who's told me

she cut herself off from the people she knew at the hospital. That's a little odd when she was still living in the same town.'

'Well...' Perrin said it so slowly that Liz knew there was something he wasn't saying and went on regarding him levelly until he felt pressured into saying it. 'In fact I think she did keep in touch with someone from the hospital. A doctor. He came looking for her once, a year or so ago, and only about a month ago I saw them going into a restaurant. I don't think he's at Castle General: he looked vaguely familiar but I couldn't put a name to him. But there was a doctor's sticker in his car window.'

It was the first mention Liz had heard of another man in the dead woman's life. She wanted to be sure what he was saying. 'You think they were having an affair?'

Perrin shook his head in quiet conviction. 'No, I don't. Maybe he was someone she used to know; maybe he was offering her a job. I don't believe she was unfaithful.'

'People are,' Liz reminded him. 'Why not her?'

'She was happy.' Liz was watching him carefully so that she would not only hear his reply but know how to interpret it. But Perrin's response could not have been less ambiguous. He wasn't jealous of David Page: Kerry's friendship was all he wanted and he'd had it. 'She loved her husband. She was happy with her life. She wouldn't have risked spoiling it.'

Liz nodded. 'Would she have been interested in a new job, do you suppose?'

The nurse shrugged. 'Perhaps, if it was a good offer.'

'Was she short of money then?'

Perrin looked startled. 'Lord, no. They had two good salaries coming in, enough to run two homes and that big car. With no children they'd really more than they knew what to do with. They put the surplus into a life assurance scheme.' He smiled again but his face started to break up. 'She used to joke about how much they were worth dead.'

THE MOTORBIKE which Liz had missed from Rosedale Avenue was propped outside the Fen Tiger in the centre of Castlemere. Propped in a dark corner between the door and the dartboard, Donovan, with his dark clothes and his dark eyes and his black helmet thumped down on the table in front of him, was a brooding presence that put the other customers off their beer. He looked as if he was drinking hard and might soon become violent. More than one of them, thinking he was under surveillance, finished his drink quickly and left. Among them were regulars who thought he was still a policeman.

After half an hour of this the barman quietly lifted the phone and called his boss.

Donovan wasn't watching anybody. He knew the regulars at the Fen Tiger as well as they knew him, could make a good guess at what nefarious activities each was involved in and why each left when he did. He didn't care. Donovan was a private citizen again. They could have sold drugs, compared knuckledusters, and pored over obscene photographs with complete impunity. Probably he wouldn't have noticed. Donovan wasn't watching, he was listening.

He was listening for a voice. He'd only heard it once and hadn't been firing on all cylinders then. But it had become of vital importance to him to find the owner of that voice, and he believed the way to do it was by haunting all the places where Jack Carney met people.

So he was drinking in Carney's pub—or rather Carney's wife's pub: Carney himself would have had problems convincing a magistrate of his suitability to hold the licence. He'd had a long coffee break—actually it was breakfast and lunch combined—at the Spotted Dick, Carney's canal-side café. He'd been to enquire about membership at the Castlemere Country Club (prop. John Carney), and he thought tomorrow he'd ask Carney Motors about spares for his bike.

Sooner or later one of three things would happen. He'd hear the voice of the man who got out of the car that killed Alan Clarke. Carney would get rattled enough by his hanging round—you couldn't call it harassment, pubs were for drinking in, cafés for eating in, and anyway it was hard to prove harassment by someone who was not now a policeman—to make a mistake: to threaten him, perhaps, or set McMeekin on him. Or another car would come speeding out of the night and leave Donovan's blood smeared along a wall and his body broken in a gutter, and Shapiro would have another crime to investigate. If he couldn't nail Carney for anything else, maybe he could nail him for that.

LIZ TOOK what Perrin had said back to her office and mulled it over. She found him a credible witness. He had no axe to grind. Another man might have hated Page for marrying the woman he loved but not Perrin. He was so clearly homosexual she'd hardly felt the need to ask; but when she did, for the record, he confirmed it without hesitation or rancour. He had loved Kerry without the desire for possession; he was content for her to be happy with Page. He had no reason to accuse the man of killing her.

Nor had he done so. Liz doubted if the possibility had occurred to him. But Perrin had supplied Page with a motive; they had always known he had an opportunity, and he might have had the means. It was time to talk to him again, at the police station this time.

WHEN HE FOUND himself the only customer left in the Fen Tiger Donovan gave up. Nothing more was going to happen today. He'd come back tomorrow, at lunchtime, when the place was full of people talking and he could pass unnoticed for a while. He was somewhere, the man who'd killed DI Clarke and tried to kill him. He was somewhere, he probably took a drink and he wasn't a Trappist monk. Some day, somewhere—in this bar or another one or another of Jack Carney's little earners—Donovan would hear his voice again.

But not today. He was ready for home. It was only mid-afternoon but his bones ached. He'd made a start. Carney would know by now what he was doing. Today he would be puzzled, tomorrow amused, when it was still going on the next day he'd be getting irritated and some time after that he'd have to act. A man like Carney couldn't work in a spotlight. If Donovan watched every move he made, the people he needed to see would be either avoiding him or laughing at him, both fatal to his authority. Whether or not he wanted to, Carney would have to deal with Donovan sometime.

Outside McMeekin was waiting for him, his suited backside resting casually on the seat of the motorbike, his legs crossed elegantly at the ankle. He wore a mildly pained expression. 'Sergeant Donovan, what are you doing here?'

Donovan eyed him for a moment longer, then looked up at the hostelry sign hanging out over the street. 'Having a drink.'

'You're frightening the customers away.'

'I noticed that,' said Donovan. 'Touchy, aren't they? Anyone'd think they had something to hide.'

McMeekin spoke carefully. 'I think they're afraid of being pinned in a corner and told some rambling tale about crossbows and albatrosses.'

Donovan grinned at that. He quite saw himself as a character invented by a poet on opium. He thought it would explain a lot. 'Who is he, McMeekin? You know, don't you?'

'Who?'

'The driver. The mechanic Carney hired to take out DI Clarke. And old Lucy. Did he kill Lucy as well? Why? What was it she knew, what was she going to show me? And how did you hear about it? Or—wait a minute.' His tone quickened with understanding. 'She didn't know anything, did she? She was just the bait. You had your hit-man in place, all you needed was to get Alan and me to where he could get a clear run at us. Lucy was just the means. But you still killed her. Did they let you do her, Terry? Practice on an old bag-lady so maybe you could manage a man next time?'

McMeekin shook his head sadly. 'You're raving, Donovan. That knock on the head. You want to go home, put your feet up, take some time off. You could end up back in hospital if you don't let it heal properly. You could end up dead.'

Donovan grinned wolfishly. 'You threatening me, Terry?'

McMeekin was disdainful. 'Be your age, Donovan. But we've all heard of it happening. You get a knock on the head, seem to make a good recovery, then a week later you run after a bus and your brain explodes. Very nasty.'

Donovan looked at the pub again. Since he'd left a

couple of people had strayed back. 'Well, don't count on it happening to me. I won't be running anywhere for a while. I'm going to be doing a lot of sitting round. Pubs, cafés, round the canal: places like that. It's time I caught up on the local gossip.'

It was meant as a threat and taken as one. The veneer of concern fell from McMeekin's eyes and his voice dropped a tone. 'You've got nothing on us, Donovan. But try to stir up trouble and we'll return it with interest.'

'What you going to use next time then—a steamroller?'

McMeekin came up off the bike with the easy fluid motion of well-trained musculature. He regarded Donovan with dislike. 'If you think that Mr Carney had something to do with Inspector Clarke's accident, try to prove it. And if you can't, leave him alone.'

'And if I can't do that either?'

'Why then,' McMeekin said bleakly, 'I suggest you watch your step, Sergeant.'

'I intend to.' Donovan's lip curled in a vicious smile. 'And yours. And Carney's. Every single one you take.' He threw a long leg over the machine, started up, and rode away satisfied with the exchange. The gauntlet was down now: Carney had no choice but to pick it up.

ON HIS WAY home he found himself turning off the main road. He'd driven half a mile before he realized where he was heading.

The man with the pushchair was there again, tidying his wife's grave. He looked up as Donovan passed like a shadow on the gravel paths. But the young man with his darkly brooding face seemed to be in no mood for conversation so he only paused long enough to say something amiable and not requiring an answer to the dull-eyed child in the pushchair before resuming his work with fork and trowel.

Donovan had told Shapiro he had no use for formalities, in death as in life, and for the most part it was true. A dour Catholic upbringing in the north of Ireland had left him with an abiding mistrust of ritual. He believed devoutly that religion was humbug, that good and evil were artifacts of the human state needing no supernatural explanation, that the only afterlife a man could hope for was in his children and the memories of his friends. Alan Clarke's future was assured on both counts, but still Donovan wasn't here seeking communion with the dead man but because he used to work through his ideas with Clarke when he was alive and had nowhere else to take them now.

He stood for a long time, his hands in his pockets, his chin on his chest and his shoulders hunched round his ears, looking at the oblong of raw earth where the grass-seed had yet to sprout. But Marion must have been here because there were fresh flowers in the vase. The headstone was still being cut: for the moment a plain wooden cross carried the name and dates.

He didn't know what he was waiting for. He didn't know why he was here. Alan Clarke had been his superior, his mentor, and his friend; and Donovan's trust in his informant had cost him his life. Clarke couldn't absolve him of that, and Marion wouldn't, so all he could do was stumble on in the dark groping for something he needed but could not have described.

The graveyard was quiet on Mondays. Most people visited on Sundays, little family parties strolling flowers in hand along the neatly raked gravel between the stones. The flowers were on the graves now: because it was autumn mostly they were chrysanthemums, white and yellow and bronze. But there weren't a dozen people scattered across the whole forty acres and the only sounds were the occasional murmur of conversation, the crunch of a step on gravel, and the steady distant snipping as a groundsman trimmed away at a yew hedge.

So there was something immediately disturbing about the new sound that made both Donovan and the man with the pushchair look towards the stile in the wall where a couple of cars and Donovan's motorbike were parked. Four young men in motorcycle helmets were climbing over the wall. Since he'd have heard four motorbikes Donovan thought they must have come in the van that was turning round, so the helmets were not for protection or only in a way. The sound was the chime of chains as they vaulted the stile. As he watched they began to run towards him.

Tersely, out of the corner of his mouth, he said to the man with the pushchair, 'Get out of here. Now!' Then he looked for a good big block of monumental masonry to put at his back.

II

ONE

ACROSS THE INTERVIEW room table Liz regarded the young man with his choir-boy haircut and sky-blue eyes and tried to see him as the perpetrator of a clever and brutal murder. It was coming. It had seemed impossible the first time she talked to him. But Page was a professional pilot, trained to operate under stress. A man who could make the calculations necessary for an emergency landing with five different sorts of flame leaping from his engine could plan a murder, carry it out, even seem to be in shock afterwards. It didn't mean Page killed his wife. But it meant that he could have done.

'Tell me about the insurance you had on Kerry.'

Under formal questioning she had watched the flesh fall from his face, his smooth cheeks hollow, his eyes recede into shadowy pits. Liz couldn't judge whether it was the reaction of an innocent man unjustly doubted or one who had thought till now that he'd got away with murder.

'Insurance?' he stammered.

'You had a policy on Kerry's life. Tell me about it.'

'There are policies on each of us. I arranged them about a year ago. We had some surplus income, it seemed a sensible thing to do. If I'd died first the money would have made sure Kerry had no financial worries.'

'That was a good reason to insure you. Why insure Kerry? You don't need her income to meet your obligations. I don't imagine you'll keep her flat, will you? Presumably you'll either move to the cottage or get somewhere nearer the airfield. Why did you need to insure Kerry?'

He was flustered, his eyes flickering across her face. 'I told you, it seemed sensible. And—we did everything that way. Split down the middle. Not her money and my money but our money; not her future or mine but ours.'

'Even when it made no sense?'

'It *did* make sense. I didn't expect her to die now, for God's sake! She was twenty-nine years old, she should have lived another fifty years. The policies would have given us a pension!'

Liz's eyes flew wide with derision. 'You're twenty-six, Mr Page! Nobody your age wonders how he'll get by when he's seventy!'

'Well, we did,' he insisted. 'For one thing, pilots don't always work to retirement age. You have to make your money while you're medically fit. For another, Kerry worked in an old people's home: she saw what time does to people, how things can go wrong, how they can think they've got enough to see them through but ill-health or bad luck or just a lot of years being old run through it till there's nothing left. Neither of us wanted to be worrying about money when we got old. It would have been crazy when we had more than we needed now.'

'You've no current use for the money then?'

'What?'

'The insurance money. There's nothing you need it for, nothing you're wanting to buy.'

'No.'

'I see.' She lowered her eyes to the papers on the table before her, glancing through them. When she found what she was seeking she looked up again, holding him steady in her gaze. 'Then Joe Tulliver hasn't offered you a partnership in Castle Air Services when you can get the capital together?'

Page's mouth opened and shut several times before anything intelligible came out. 'No! Well, yes. I mean yes, but—' He was clutching the arms of his chair as if it was moving. For a moment he really looked ready to crack. Then he disengaged his eyes, dropping them into his lap, and breathed deeply until he had a grip on himself again. Then he looked up. 'Inspector Graham, you don't believe I shot Kerry because I'd rather have a share of Joe Tulliver's firm. You can't believe that.'

Liz declined to answer. 'But he did make the offer.'

'A couple of months ago. It wasn't a take it or leave it thing. Joe said if ever I fancied working for myself we could work something out. He didn't expect an answer there and then. We didn't even talk about money. I said I'd give it some thought, talk to Kerry about it, and he said no rush but when the time came for him to retire he'd like to leave the business in good hands. That was all. There was no question of having to lay my hands on big money at short notice.'

'Did you talk to Kerry about it?'

'I never got round to it. I didn't want to disappoint her if it didn't come to anything. I wanted to be sure Joe meant it. I wanted to be sure it was what I wanted, that I wasn't making a commitment I'd regret later. And I wanted to be sure we could—' He stopped, leaving the sentence unfinished.

Liz finished it for him. 'That you could afford it. What about all this surplus money that was going into insurance policies you didn't need?'

A spark of temper kindled in his eye. 'Fifty quid a month is one thing. Twenty thousand pounds down is something else. It was a big step. I had to be sure it was what I wanted.'

'Have you decided yet?'

'No, I haven't,' he snarled. 'All at once it doesn't seem very important.'

Liz nodded mechanically, giving nothing away, wondering if it was time to hit him with the other thing. The prospect gave her no pleasure but the results might be revealing. She said, 'Did you know your wife was seeing another man?'

She thought he might leap to his feet, hurling denials and abuse. She was ready to defend herself if he hurled more than words. She knew she had stripped away so many of his skins that he must be close to losing control. Whether he was a cornered killer or a young man driven to the edge of reason by the events that had overtaken him, she had to be ready for violence.

Instead he began to cry. His shoulders slumped, his slim hands slipped from the arms of the chair into his lap and great tears began to roll down his cheeks. His lips trembled like a child's. 'That isn't true. It isn't true.'

'It is true,' said Liz. 'She went to a restaurant with him only a month ago. Before that he'd called at the flat.'

'No. No.'

'When you weren't there,' she added unnecessarily. Perhaps all of this was unnecessary. If he was guilty he was a hell of an actor; if he was innocent she was putting his heart through the wringer.

'Who?' His voice was a mere breathy ghost.

'A doctor.'

'She was seeing a doctor?' A note of hope elevated the last word. 'Someone she knew, someone she worked with. A friend, that's all.'

'Wouldn't she have told you?'

His face fell again. 'Yes,' he admitted softly.

The time was coming, Liz was aware, that she was going to have to come down off the fence and decide—innocent or guilty. Did she believe him? The evidence against him was circumstantial but couldn't be ignored. He had insured Kerry's life. He'd been offered a partnership in a business he loved when he had the money to buy in. If he learned that Kerry was having an affair, in a fury of cold rage because he'd loved her and she'd betrayed him, could he have decided to realize his investment in her and put it into something more reliable—the planes he'd hungered after since he was eleven years old?

He might look like a broken child but he was a grown man with a man's passions. If Kerry hurt him enough he was capable of exacting revenge. But would he have done? Everyone who knew them said they were in love. If he'd found her with her doctor friend he might have brained her with the iron. But was he a man who'd resort to careful, clever, cold-blooded murder? She hoped she wasn't being swayed by his tears, but Liz was about ready to wager that he was not.

She began to say, 'Mr Page, you must see how it looks—' Then there was a sharp rap at the door of the interview room and Shapiro's head appeared briefly, beckoning her with a terse nod. She announced her departure to the recording equipment and went outside with him.

'What is it?'

Shapiro indicated the door. 'How long's he been here?'

Liz checked her watch. 'Something over an hour. I can get you the exact time.'

He shook his head. 'An hour's more than enough. There's been another murder. Another nurse, another shotgun. David Page didn't kill his wife and it doesn't look as if Jack Carney did it either. It's just turned into a serial killing. That means we're looking for someone with no motive outside his own mind.'

THE KILLING took place outside the nurses' home adjacent to Castle General, in broad daylight, with passersby twenty yards away and probably thirty people close enough to have seen something. And none of them had seen anything.

Or rather, they had all seen the same thing: a woman in a lime-green track-suit jog across the park then ease back to a walk as she reached the pavement. She traded a word with two young men who were just entering the park. Someone else saw her look at her watch and shove an unruly mass of dark red hair back into the knot it was escaping from. Then it seemed everyone lost interest in her and got on with their own pursuits—playing with dogs, exercising children, feeding ducks, sailing model yachts—until the sound of the gunshot brought them snapping round like soldiers called to attention.

If Maggie Board had been less profoundly injured she might have survived. Not only because the hospital was just a hundred yards from where she was shot but because a good half of those enjoying the autumn sunshine in the park that Monday lunchtime were doctors or nurses. They didn't freeze at the sight of blood. They ran to her, crouched over her, hunted for vital signs, hunted for bleeding points in the welter of chewed-up flesh. One of the joggers sprinted for the casualty entrance.

But in the event nothing they could do would have

saved her. The blast from the shotgun hit her in the chest and throat and if she wasn't dead when she hit the pavement she was already beyond saving. It would have been better if fewer of the on-lookers had been experts and more had been helpless bystanders. For while everyone in the immediate area was trying to render medical assistance no one was looking to see who left the scene in a hurry with a wisp of smoke curling from under his raincoat.

Liz had spoken to a dozen people before somebody mentioned the yellow car, and he wasn't sure if it had anything to do with the shooting. But it was parked close to where Mrs Board was shot, and it seemed odd that it should drive away while people were on their hands and knees round the woman on the ground, trying to drag her back from the abyss although in reality she had already fallen.

'What sort of a car was it?'

The witness was an elderly man who had been walking his elderly dog as far as the duck-pond. Neither of them was up to running when the shot was fired so they watched while others acted. The man didn't have his glasses on: all he could say of the car was that it was yellow, and he didn't see the driver. If the dog saw anything more it wasn't talking.

The other thing which they learned, which served to confuse the issue more than it illuminated it, was that Maggie Board wasn't a nurse. She had a room in the nurses' home, she worked in the hospital, but she wasn't a nurse. She was a surgeon.

'WHAT DO YOU MAKE of that?' asked Shapiro.

The neat division of effort which Liz's arrival had made possible, which had come under stress almost immediately with the murder of Kerry Page, had now collapsed entirely. The only way Castlemere police could get through at all was for everyone—CID, uniform, Traffic Branch, and dog handlers—to turn their hands to whatever needed doing most urgently. Liz had not needed to tell Shapiro this: he had gone with her to the scene of the latest outrage as soon as she'd sent David Page home.

The only one missing was Donovan. Liz thought privately they'd manage well enough without him but Shapiro was disappointed. 'I thought he'd have been here. He knows the state we're in. He could have offered to help.'

'Make of what?' Her head was spinning. She knew from experience that when there had been time to reduce the information they had into a series of reports she would be able to pick up the threads and get a cohesive picture of events and chronology. But just now it was like swimming in a kaleidoscope, words and images exploding at her from all directions. She was sure she should know what Shapiro was talking about but she didn't.

'Maggie Board wasn't a nurse,' he explained patiently. 'She lived in the nurses' home—she'd taken a spare room while contractors were dealing with damp at her house, apparently. And off duty she looked rather like a nurse—you don't see many women of her age out jogging in fluorescent track-suits. She could easily have been taken for a nurse, particularly if you weren't talking to her. But she wasn't. She was a surgeon.'

'Yes,' said Liz. 'Er—so?'

'So,' he went on, still patiently, 'did the killer think she was a nurse or did he know who she was? Did he make a mistake or does he hate all medical personnel equally?'

Liz was sure that it mattered but just for the moment she couldn't quite see how.

Shapiro peered into her face with puzzlement turning to concern. 'Good grief, girl, you're wrecked! Did you get any sleep last night?'

She sighed. 'Not much, no. I'm sorry, Frank, I'll try and get my act together.'

He sniffed mournfully. 'I wish I could afford to send you home. But I can't. Even the walking dead are indispensable just now. But listen, get back to the station, wash your face, get some coffee, and put your feet up for ten minutes. Then you might be some use to me.'

She raised a hand helplessly. 'I can't leave—'

'Do as you're told,' he said firmly. 'We're just about finished here anyway. I'll talk to a couple of people at the hospital, then I'll be back there myself. You can run a murder enquiry from a pavement for just so long.'

She accepted the wisdom of what he was saying, still felt she was letting him down. 'Yes, all right. The coffee: I think maybe I'll buy a fresh jar on my way in. A big jar.'

The police station was almost empty. The desk sergeant, the RT operator, a couple of constables to deal with anyone who couldn't resist having an accident while their colleagues were interviewing people who had seen nothing outside the nurses' home, that was about it. When Liz went upstairs to the CID offices it was like being on the *Flying Dutchman*.

She put the kettle on—Shapiro's secretary was helping to man the switchboard—kicked her shoes off, dropped her forehead on her arms on the desk and shut her eyes for a moment.

Five minutes later she woke with a start, roused not by a sound but by a smell—the aroma of strong coffee. She blinked round her, looking for an explanation. When she found it she didn't know whether to be glad or sorry. 'What are you doing here?'

Donovan had his back to her and for a moment he didn't answer. He was pouring boiling water carefully into a mug. Then he put the kettle down and picked up the mug with the same hand. When he passed it to her she saw why. His other hand was in plaster from the knuckles to half-way up his arm. His face looked as if he'd lost an argument with a lamppost.

His voice was low and his eyes avoided hers. 'I heard about the incident at the hospital, wondered if I could help.'

'You, Sergeant?' Liz asked testily. 'I thought you'd resigned.'

His head jerked but he didn't look up. 'That was—stupid. Petty. I wouldn't have done it to Alan Clarke and I'd no business doing it to you.' He gave a little lop-sided shrug. 'It's up to you. I gave you my card, keep it if you want.' His eyes travelled slowly up to meet hers. He looked as weary as she felt. 'But if you want to get the work out of me before I go, maybe I can be some use. I can man the phones. I can take statements, there's nothing wrong with my right hand...' He ran out of things to say and fell silent.

He handed her the coffee a little as if it were an olive branch. She sipped it speculatively. 'What happened to you?'

'I got mugged.' He risked a fractional grin. 'In a graveyard.' He told her how he'd spent his day.

'Carney's doing?'

'Probably McMeekin's.'

'What do you want to do about it?'

He shook his head. 'Nothing. I asked for it and I got it. His time'll come. There's more important things to do first.'

Liz thought a moment longer before answering. 'Donovan, get yourself a coffee, sit down, and listen to what I have to say. And listen good because I won't say it again. I'm tired of you behaving like Tintin the bloody Boy Detective. God knows I need all the help I can get on this investigation, but if I have to wonder whether you're assisting in the same enquiry or pursuing some vendetta of your own I'd just as soon you stayed at home.'

'I'm sorry,' he muttered. 'I—'

'I haven't finished yet,' Liz interrupted fiercely. 'It's this simple, Sergeant. I need to be able to rely on my officers. I expect their loyalty. You took advantage of the fact that I'm new here and don't know all the background, and you used me to have a go at Carney even though you knew we were putting an important investigation at risk. I won't tolerate that kind of irresponsibility. I've no room on my team for a prima donna.

'Maybe Alan Clarke allowed you a certain leeway. I know Mr Shapiro thinks you're a good copper. But, Sergeant, your problem is that Alan is dead and you answer to me, not Mr Shapiro. I can use your help, but if you're going to work for me you have to work with me. I'm not going to let you get on with it and rubber-stamp the results, however sure you are that you're in the right. I don't work that way. Unless you're prepared to fit in with me you'd better take a long leave, starting now.'

This time he waited until she indicated she was ready to hear him. 'You're right, I was out of line.' He spoke in a low voice. 'It won't happen again. I don't want to go on leave. Tell me what to do: I'll help out any way I can.'

She'd been ready for more of a fight. By backing down he left her with nothing more to say. 'Right. Good.' As a parting shot she added tersely, 'But next time you slap your warrant card on my desk I'll feed it to the pencil-sharpener.'

After she'd given it back to him she said, 'You've been to the hospital? What's the damage?'

'A cracked bone in my wrist, cuts and bruises. That's all.'

'Four of them, you say—with chains?'

He nodded. 'Chains.'

'You fought them off?'

He smiled at that, a rueful smile that was much less fierce than his grin. 'Jesus, no. I was on the ground behind a gravestone with my hands over my head, I couldn't have fought my way out of a wet paper bag.'

Liz smiled back. Something—it may have been the beating—seemed to have done him good because he was calmer now than at any time since she'd met him. 'Then how come you aren't in a teaching ward in Castle General with medical students walking round you then sitting their finals?'

Donovan thought for a moment. 'You know Superman?'

She stared. 'Pardon?'

'Well, he isn't a reporter with glasses after all. He's an antiques dealer with a kid in a pushchair and a First World War pistol in his glove-compartment.'

IT WAS A PISTOL in appearance only, incapable of being fired: a legitimate antique. George Swann kept it in his car because he regularly carried valuables and wanted something to scare thieves off that couldn't be snatched and used against him. The Luger looked deadly serious but was actually no more lethal than anything else with which one man could hit another.

His first instinct when thugs with helmets and chains came storming over the wall was to get his son to safety. He pushed the buggy at a dead run up the gravel path to the main gate where his car was parked. The stile was no use to a man with a pushchair.

But when Danny was in the car and he looked back to where the four men had cornered the other against a Victorian marble angel he knew he was the only one close enough to help. If he went looking for a phone they'd be finished before the police could get there. So he grabbed the seventy-five-year-old pistol and ran back as fast as he could. He was not a young man anymore, and he was afraid, but he made himself run.

When he was within thirty yards—close enough for them to see what he was holding, far enough that they wouldn't jump him before weighing up the risks—he shouted a challenge. The four of them were in a knot at the feet of the angel, arms flailing, boots swinging, but they looked up at his shout, the helmets turning like the heads of giant insects. The scene froze.

If they'd called his bluff he could have done nothing to save himself. But one of them yelled in a thick local accent, 'Holy God, he's got a gun!' They were running towards the stile and the waiting van while Swann was still wondering what to do if they came at him.

He felt his outstretched arm begin to shake and put the gun in his pocket before he should drop it. Then he stepped round the angel to see how much damage they'd done.

Donovan was having trouble getting his face off the ground without using his left arm. Every inch of him hurt. He'd taken a thorough beating and if it had gone on five minutes longer he'd have been pounded to a bloody pulp.

Swann had helped him to his car and taken him to the hospital. When he'd asked timidly what it was all about and Donovan said he was a policeman, the Castlemere Superman had turned the wrong way up a one-way street.

TWO

DONOVAN'S RETURN put new life into Liz. Partly it was an extra pair of hands—well, hand—at a time when it was most needed. Partly it was knowing that, exhausted as she felt, she couldn't possibly look as bad as he did. And partly it was because he represented a small success, the only problem she had resolved satisfactorily since coming here. Three days ago she was a bright confident detective inspector from Headquarters sent to hold the fort while DCI Shapiro discovered what happened behind the gasworks. Now they had not one body but three, at least two killers on the loose—one possibly a drunk driver, the other a psychopath with a nurse fetish—and Liz felt she'd gone five rounds with Frank Bruno. But she'd got Donovan back on the rails, at least for now.

Returning from the hospital and seeing the distinctive figure stooped over a phone, Shapiro did a double-take. He stuck his head round Liz's door to see if she knew. 'Er—?'

'Oh yes,' she said, almost breezily, 'all sorted out. He made the coffee.'

'Oh—good,' said Shapiro doubtfully. 'That's all right then. Um—why is his arm in plaster?'

'He was mugged.'

'Was he?'

'In the cemetery,' Liz added.

'R-i-g-h-t,' said Shapiro, understanding less with every word. 'So now he's back at work?'

'It seems to have knocked a bit of sense into him.'

'And he's—er—he *is* fit to work, I suppose?'

'I wouldn't think so,' said Liz candidly. 'He looks like death warmed up, but we can't afford to be picky. I thought he could work here, then if he flakes out it won't be so obvious.'

Shapiro nodded. 'I always said we should encourage women in the police force. The compassionate face of criminal investigation, I called it.'

'You never told me to be compassionate,' she remembered. 'You told me I'd have to be as hard as nails.'

'Could have saved my breath, couldn't I?'

As he left her office for his own Donovan came in. He'd been gathering vital statistics about the dead woman. 'She was forty-five, divorced for eleven years, no children, no contact with the ex-husband as far as anyone knows. She'd been at Castle General since then; she trained in London but wanted a change of scene when the marriage broke up. She lived in one of the alms houses in Cottage Row, backing on to the canal.' He glanced up from his notebook. 'Sorry, you wouldn't know. Midway between the castle and the basin, off Milne Road. She had a damp problem, the workmen have been in for a fortnight. There were some vacant rooms at the nurses' home so she rented one of those till she could get back in the house. She was older than the rest of them but she was on good terms with the nurses—they'd go for a drink together, sometimes go jogging in the park. Unless you knew her there was nothing much to mark her out from the others. Someone looking for a nurse could have easily picked on her.

'One thing, probably not significant but you never know. She and Kerry Page—Kerry Carson she was then—worked together before Kerry went to the nursing home.'

Liz shrugged. 'I suppose any nurse and any doctor are likely to have worked together in the local general hospital at some time.'

'No, it was a bit more than that. Kerry was Staff Nurse in theatre for about a year. Then she switched to geriatrics and left the hospital soon after.'

'So they haven't worked together for—?'

'About four years,' said Donovan.

'Any suggestion that they've seen one another since?'

'Apparently not.'

'Four years.' Her face went in thoughtful wrinkles. 'It can't be significant now, can it?'

'I wouldn't think so,' said Donovan. 'It might be worth asking Page, and this friend of hers next door—Perrin?'

'When I get the time,' agreed Liz. 'Right now I'm up to my eyes with Mrs Board.'

'And Page's jacket has turned up.'

'Has it?' That was more interesting—at least, it would have been earlier today when he was still a suspect. 'Any blood on it?'

'None.'

'Where did they find it?'

'In the water-meadows beside the river, half a mile from the car park.'

'How did it get there?' asked Liz, exasperated. But still it was mostly a rhetorical question.

Donovan chose not to interpret it as such. 'Maybe I should go ask him,' he said, watching her from under hooded lids. 'I can call on Perrin too, see if either of them knows if Kerry had seen Board recently.'

Liz frowned. 'You can't drive like that. And I can't spare anyone to take you.'

'I'm not a cripple,' he exclaimed, 'I can walk that far!'

She eyed him with amusement. 'Now there's a word I thought had disappeared from the detective's lexicon. Lord, that takes me back!'

'What?' His dark face was suspicious.

'I remember when policemen used to walk. And ride bicycles. I bet you didn't think I was that old, did you?' He preserved a careful silence. She chuckled. 'Yes, all right, have a word with them. If Kerry and Mrs Board had kept in touch perhaps we should know.'

HE WASN'T SURE what kind of a welcome Page would give him. Their last meeting had been less than amicable. But Page had more on his mind than remembering which police officer had said which beastly thing to him. He greeted Donovan without enthusiasm but without anger either. Like all of them he seemed more tired than anything else.

'We found your jacket,' Donovan said. 'I'll have someone drop it back to you.'

'Thanks,' Page said automatically. 'Where was it?'

'Down on the riverbank.'

Page frowned. 'How——?' Then he stopped abruptly. 'Oh.'

Donovan waited for a moment, then prompted. 'So how did it get there?'

'I told you. I told someone. We walked by the river, then we went back to the car and sat for a while.'

'And you took your jacket off and dropped it in the grass?'

Page looked at him. The blue eyes were luminous,

caught between tears and laughter. 'Sergeant, it was a beautiful night. The moon was up, there wasn't a soul for miles. We walked for a while, then I spread my coat on the ground, and we lay down and made love. OK? I made love to my wife, and afterwards I forgot to pick my coat up. That surprises you?'

Donovan shook his head. 'Not even slightly.'

'You're right.' Page accepted the compliment with a faint smile. 'She could make you forget anything—where you were, who you were, that the sun would rise come morning...' His voice was turning bitter. 'With her, like that, I was ten feet tall. I'd have gone through fire for her. And half an hour later some mad bastard who knew nothing about my wife except that she was a nurse pointed a shotgun at her, and I never even yelled at him to stop. I didn't raise a hand to save her. She might as well have been alone for all the use I was.'

Donovan recognized the mood. He'd been living it for three days longer than Page. He shook his head. 'He had a shotgun. You couldn't have saved her, you could only have died with her.'

'Even that would have been something!'

'No,' said Donovan. 'No, it wouldn't. You saw this man. You heard his voice. Sooner or later we'll get him and you'll identify him. You couldn't have saved her, but you can do that for her.'

Then they talked about Maggie Board. Page had heard about her before he left the police station, had been listening to the local radio since. But he didn't know until Donovan told him that his wife once worked with the dead surgeon.

'They hadn't stayed friends, then.'

'She had almost no friends from the hospital,' said Page. 'Julian next door, but only because it mattered so much to him. She wouldn't have cared if Castle General had turned into a steamboat and sailed for Africa.'

'Why was that? OK, she'd moved on, but why make the break that complete? Could there have been something she wanted to get away from?'

'Maybe.' Page's voice quiet, almost too calm. 'I don't know what, she never talked about it. But geriatrics wasn't her first choice. It was a—' He stopped, lacking the word.

Donovan pressed him. 'What?'

'A refuge, I think. She said once, it's the only branch of medicine where the relatives send thank-you letters instead of writs when a patient dies.'

Donovan frowned. 'She got upset at losing patients? Then why specialize in the one department where all the patients die sooner or later?'

Page shrugged helplessly. 'I don't know. It didn't make sense to me either but like I said, she wouldn't discuss it. I wondered once—'

Again he stopped. Again Donovan had to prompt. 'Wondered what?'

'If she'd had a fright in theatre. If she'd made a mistake sometime. I mean, if I made a mistake that could have killed people I'm not sure I'd want to go on flying. However much I'd miss it, I wouldn't want to take the risk again.'

'She did choose to move into geriatrics, I suppose? She wasn't sacked from the theatre, anything like that?'

'Oh no, she chose to leave. She moved first on to the hospital's geriatric wards, then when the job at Rosedale came up she went there.'

'So if she made a mistake it couldn't have been a big one.' He meant, not big enough to die for four years later.

'I don't think so. The people at Rosedale pay enough to be choosy, they wouldn't have hired Kerry if there'd been a black mark on her record. Maybe somewhere less prestigious or in another town, but not so close to Castle General. If there'd been a problem they'd have heard.'

BUT IF THE PEOPLE at Rosedale hadn't perhaps Julian Perrin had. Donovan tried his flat, found it empty, was walking back up Rosedale Avenue when he saw the man DI Graham had described parking a banana-coloured Citroën Deux-Chevaux. 'Mr Perrin?'

The nurse glanced at Donovan's plaster and his battered face and said politely, 'I'm sorry, we don't do house-calls.'

Donovan grinned. 'You should have seen the other guy.'

'Not a mark on him?' asked Perrin sympathetically, and Donovan shook his head.

'Not a scratch.' He introduced himself.

Inside Perrin's flat he said, 'You've heard about Mrs Board, I suppose.'

'I *know*,' said Perrin, shocked as anyone might have been by an act of mayhem but not personally upset as he had been by Kerry's death. 'Whatever's going on? Is it the same man, do you think?'

'Hell of a coincidence if it's not,' said Donovan. 'Didn't they work together, Kerry and Maggie Board?'

'That's a long time ago,' said Perrin. 'Kerry did theatre for about twelve months, and yes, she did work on Mrs Board's crew. But she packed it in about four years ago and moved to Rosedale.'

'Why did she quit theatre? It's a good job for a nurse, isn't it?'

'It's what she wanted to do since we started training. She loved it. It's the sharp end: things happen quickly in surgery, you have to be on your toes. There's a lot of pressure—if some guy's bleeding rivers surgeons don't have time for 'please, Nurse' and 'thank you, Nurse'. You have to be able to take the rough with the smooth and still do a professional job. The pay-off is when someone comes into theatre with his drawer in the morgue already booked and leaves it neatly zipped up and mumbling for his mother.' He grinned boyishly. 'The credit goes to the surgeon, of course, which is all right because he carries the can when you lose one, but actually everyone in theatre is doing life and death work. The surgeon, the anaesthetist, the nurses: none of us can afford to have off days. It suits some people better than others.'

'It suited Kerry for a year and then stopped suiting her?'

Perrin looked uncomfortable. The skin round his eyes creased and he looked at Donovan and then out of the window at the small, delicate garden. 'There was a bit of unpleasantness. I don't know the details. One day they ran out of miracles and the relatives threatened to sue. It didn't come to anything but I think maybe it soured it for her.'

'Was Kerry responsible?'

'Oh, no. No one was to blame: they did their best and it wasn't enough. I don't even know if that's why but about that time she became—disenchanted. Maybe she'd just had enough. She transferred to geriatrics and I don't think she ever regretted it.'

'She didn't keep in touch with people from the hospital.'

His eyes dropped. 'No.'

'How about Mrs Board? Would she have seen Kerry recently?'

'I doubt it. Kerry didn't go to the hospital and I can't see Mrs Board taking the trouble to look her up. Don't misunderstand, Sergeant, she was a fine surgeon. But she didn't make personal friends of her staff. She expected the highest standards of professionalism. I think more people respected her than liked her.'

'She seemed to get on with the girls at the nurses' home.'

Perrin smiled. 'Most of them weren't working for her. Also, she was a guest in their house.'

'Could she have been mistaken for a nurse?'

Perrin shook his head. 'I really can't judge. I knew her, maybe that colours it. But I'd have said a man would have to be a long way off to think Maggie Board was an Indian rather than a Chief.'

Donovan was leaving, half-way down the outside steps, when Perrin threw after him—quite casually, without import—a snippet of information that hit him like another speeding car. 'You know, of course, it was Mrs Board who operated on your colleague last week. The policeman who died.'

He had the walk back to the police station in Queen's Street to marshall his thinking. It was just as well. If he'd burst into Inspector Graham's office in a hot sweat and claimed he could pin this one on Jack Carney too she'd probably have fed him to the pencil-sharpener.

His first thought was that this connection between the two cases was hugely significant. As he walked, breathing the cool air, the significance seemed to diminish. By the time he turned into Queen's Street he didn't know if it was significant at all.

Liz looked up at the rap on her door, saw it was

Donovan, prepared to go on working, then caught as a kind of visual echo his odd ambivalent expression and looked again. 'What is it?'

His voice was improbably diffident. 'You know when Kerry Page was killed, and I found a connection between her and Jack Carney, and it wasn't much of a connection but it might have meant something only it turned out it probably didn't?'

Liz's head reeled with his syntax but she knew what he meant. 'Yes?'

'What would you say if I told you there was a connection between Maggie Board and Carney, and it's even less of a connection but it still might mean something?'

IF CIRCUMSTANCES had allowed them to stick to the original plan this would have touched on Shapiro's case, so when Liz heard what Donovan had found out she took him to the Chief Inspector and had him say it again. By the time she'd heard it twice she was even less sure what it meant.

Shapiro hadn't got to be a DCI by being slow on the uptake. He said shrewdly, 'It's a bit of a self-fulfilling prophecy, isn't it?'

Twenty-four hours earlier Donovan would have slapped down his warrant card again. It was a sign of his returning equilibrium that he only wrinkled his lip and nodded. 'Well, it is if I'm wrong about Carney. If I'm right about Carney then it's a hell of a coincidence.'

'Why are you so sure that Carney had DI Clarke killed?' asked Liz. 'I mean, suspicious, yes, we're all suspicious, I can see he's odds-on favourite. But you don't suspect him, do you, you think you know. Why?'

Donovan stood his ground. 'I know the man. We

were on his case for three months, for the last month we weren't on very much else. That's a lot of hours talking to people about one man. You learn how he works, how he thinks, what he's capable of. You begin to see what he'll do next, how he'll react in a given situation. What we were doing put him under pressure. He was always going to push back.'

He paused a moment, marshalling his thoughts. 'This man is bad news, all right? It's not just that he's a villain. There are other villains in Castlemere, they don't give us too much grief. When we catch them at it we put them away, when we miss them we think: Never mind, we'll get them next time. I mean, it's a job, all right?—that's all it is. It's their job to steal and deal drugs and demand money with menaces, and it's our job to stop them. Sometimes we win, sometimes we lose, but we don't take it too personally either way.

'Carney's different. He doesn't think he can get away with breaking the law, he thinks it doesn't apply to him. He runs his scams like a business empire, and he does it under our noses and dares us to do something about it. He probably has the biggest payroll in town and he thinks that entitles him to respect. Dear God, he even gets it in certain quarters. Half the council would tell you Jack Carney can't be the villain the police make out because of the annual party he runs for the local orphanage.

'He sits in the middle of his web like a spider in a Savile Row suit, juggling money through a battery of accounts like some city tycoon, smiling his smug little smile and thinking he's fireproof. He's clever, and he's cautious, and he's powerful, and he thinks we can't touch him. We might pick off the odd foot-soldier from time to time but he thinks he's safe. He thinks he's too big for us.

'So when Alan went after him—not his scams, not even his organization but him personally—he wasn't so much worried as outraged. He couldn't believe someone had the gall to do that. And when Alan started getting somewhere with the investigation Carney had to stop him. Not only to protect himself but to protect his authority. In this town you don't mess with Jack Carney, not even if you're a detective inspector. That was the message he had to put out, and what might have been a nasty accident but everybody would assume was an assassination was the ideal way. I don't believe in a drunk driver chancing to run down the one man in Castlemere Jack Carney had to see dead.'

He shook his head. 'We should have been more careful. We knew what we were dealing with. I should have known there was something wrong with the message I got from Lucy. She always met me at chip vans so I could buy her a meal, why would she suddenly want to see me behind the gasworks?'

'And there's been no sign of Lucy since?'

'I think she's probably dead,' said Donovan evenly. 'Maybe Carney settled for scaring the wits out of her and she'll turn up in time, but my guess is they killed her. Maybe she did have something for me and Carney found out. Or maybe McMeekin leaned on her to set us up. She specifically told me to bring my boss, so I'd guess she had Terry at her elbow all the time she was on the phone. We'll never know for sure. Old bag-ladies like Lucy, they're almost more spirit than substance anyhow. When they die and the spirit drifts away you could dump what's left on a rubbish tip and never know it was once a human being.'

Liz found herself staring and dropped her eyes quickly before he saw. She knew how Clarke's death had affected him but was frankly astonished to learn he was also mourning a tramp. In a blaze of understanding, suddenly she recognized him. She should have seen it sooner, he was practically a national emblem: the Irish warrior-poet, the minstrel gone to the wars. Now soldiering was a business of machines and critical-path analysis, and the only battles the Irish fought these days were against one another, policing was perhaps the last refuge for a man with the blood of Feagh MacHugh O'Byrne in him.

'Still, it's a better reason for thinking it *could* have been Carney than for thinking it was.' Frank Shapiro was the latest in a long line of Jewish philosophers. It gave him a genetic advantage in sticking to the point. 'And if Carney didn't have Alan killed, then the rest of it has to be coincidence.'

Donovan wasn't letting go. 'But suppose it was Carney. We'd pushed him and pushed him until he had to start pushing back. Suppose he used Lucy to set us up and brought in a mechanic to take us out. OK, I can't prove it, but suppose. Only the mechanic botched the job and Alan was still alive when he reached hospital.

'Suppose Carney knew Maggie Board. If he did, maybe it occurred to him he could still walk away from this with a smile on his face. Alan was all broke up, it wouldn't have taken much to make him let him go. She wouldn't have had to *do* anything, just not try too hard. Let him bleed a bit longer than necessary. He was on the edge already, she could push him over without anyone noticing. I don't know why she'd do such a thing. For love, maybe, or money. One way or the other Carney bought her. Only afterwards maybe he didn't like being that much in her debt. Maybe she wanted more than he wanted to pay; whatever, it was another loose end. He got the mechanic back.'

'Do you see Mrs Board as a woman who'd risk everything for love?' asked Liz. 'Or money, come to that. It's a hell of an allegation to make about a surgeon: that she'd let a patient die to get a friend off the hook. We don't even know if she knew him.'

'People will do just about anything for love,' argued Donovan. 'It doesn't have to make sense. I grant you, Maggie Board wasn't a woman to fall in love at the drop of a hat. All the more reason why, if she was in love with Carney—and it's not that unlikely, if you didn't know he was a thug you could think he was a charmer—she might do something that stupid, that out of character, to hold on to him.'

'And where does Kerry Page fit in?' Shapiro asked softly.

'Two possible ways. She really was shot by mistake because Carney thought David Page had overheard something. Or else Page killed her for the insurance, or someone else did for some other reason, and Carney's mechanic used the same MO to persuade us Board was another victim of a serial killer and keep us from looking for the real motive.'

After a long moment Shapiro gave a little grimace. 'I don't know, lad, there's an awful lot of ifs and buts to it.'

'Yes,' admitted Donovan, watching him.

'But it's not impossible, is it? It could have happened. Mrs Board really didn't look much like a nurse, not from the range she was shot at. We'll have to find out somehow—find out, or rule it out.'

'Where do we start?' asked Liz.

Shapiro ran the ball of his thumb pensively along his jaw, smoothing a beard he didn't have, a race memory of a beard. 'We need to know if they knew one another. Carney's a married man, if he was seeing Board he wouldn't be doing it openly. And she wouldn't see him at either the hospital or the nurses' home. Show a picture of him to her neighbours in Cottage Row, see if they'd been seen together. And ask the people she worked with about the operation. If she was considering killing a patient she'd be disturbed, anxious. In a surgeon of her experience that should have been obvious.'

'She might well be anxious,' said Liz. 'If she refused to do as Carney asked he wouldn't want her round to talk about it. But doing it would give her a power over him that he couldn't tolerate. She was caught between a rock and a hard place.' She saw the flinch in Donovan's eyes and wished she'd put it some other way. 'If this is more than just an imaginative hypothesis, of course.'

Donovan scowled at his shoes but said nothing.

Shapiro nodded slowly. 'I have my doubts too. But if it's not a conspiracy then it's a striking coincidence, and I don't believe in those either. I think we have to follow it up, if only for my peace of mind.'

THREE

IT WAS GETTING SILLY, the amount of time Donovan was spending in this hospital. He'd been here for three days after the episode in the viaduct, on Monday afternoon he'd been back to get his wrist plastered; now it was Tuesday and here he was again.

The chief administrator, with a courtesy that hardly hid his disapproval, allocated him a room where he could conduct his interviews and arranged to have the team who assisted at DI Clarke's surgery sent to him as they came out of theatre.

He anticipated a lengthy wait but they must have been doing piles or tonsils that day because the senior nurse, still in her greens and with her mask round her neck like a cowboy's spotted handkerchief, joined him while Donovan was still wondering what it was that had come out of the drinks machine when he pressed the button marked coffee.

Staff Nurse Petrie, he surmised, would have been fourteen years older than Kerry Carson when she was doing the same job. Her experience sat on her in added authority. She was a woman of rather small stature, thickening at the waist so that soon she would be a sturdy column from broad shoulders to padded thighs. Under her cap her hair was pinned up in a thick chestnut coil unashamedly touched with grey, and the third finger of her left hand was pinched in, a constant reminder of the ring she left off when she was working. She had a rich contralto voice, almost a singer's voice, and her grey eyes were stern, humorous, and confident all at once. If something had gone wrong while Clarke was under the knife Staff Nurse Petrie would know.

The question was whether she would talk about it or whether loyalty to the dead woman would inhibit her. They'd been colleagues, perhaps friends: even if Petrie thought Board had been less than deft on this occasion, could he persuade her to say so? All her instincts would be to insist she had seen nothing.

Try as he might Donovan could think of no subtle way of asking, 'By the way, did your boss kill my boss last Wednesday?' While he was pondering it he showed her the photograph of Jack Carney. But the Staff Nurse didn't recognize it, and didn't expect to. 'She didn't bring her private life to work.'

'Did she have a man friend?'

'I really don't know, Sergeant.'

It was cards on the table time. Petrie wouldn't like what he had to say but he thought she'd answer if he put it to her straight whereas pussy-footing round would only get her cross. Donovan wasn't the first six-footer to hope he could avoid getting Staff Nurse Petrie cross. So he said, 'You were assisting when Mrs Board operated on Inspector Clarke last week?' He wasn't sure it was the correct phraseology but the nurse nodded, once, briskly. 'He was a bit of a mess, wasn't he?'

Again she nodded. 'Yes.'

'But there was still a chance for him? I mean, he'd hung on from when he was hit by the car, he must have had a chance.'

'Oh, yes,' agreed Petrie. 'If they're alive when they come into theatre they've always got a chance. We don't let them get past us without a struggle.'

'Staff Nurse, you've seen a lot of surgery, a lot of

patients—most who lived, some who died. What did you think about Alan Clarke? Did you think he was going to make it?'

She hadn't been sure before but the way he talked about the dead man confirmed her suspicion. This was Clarke's sergeant, the young man who'd been hit by the same car. It made her tolerant of questions that would otherwise have caught the sharp edge of her tongue.

'I hoped he was going to make it,' she said. 'We worked hard on him for eighty minutes, and when we closed him up and sent him to ICU I thought he probably would. He was certainly in a better state than when he came in. But you don't get any guarantees, Sergeant. You do your best, and some of them surprise you by recovering and some of them surprise you by dying.

'With all the hype you can be forgiven for thinking otherwise, but surgery is a craft rather than a science. There are too many variables. You could do a better job by spending more time inside, stopping all the bleeding, locating every sherd of bone, every trace of damage. But the patient's in shock, his heart's weakening, and he needs you out of there. So you compromise. You do the best you can in the time you think you have available. If you spend too long doing nifty needle-work you can lose him on the table. But if you cobble him up too quickly he can bleed internally after you've parted with him and maybe there'll be time to get him back and maybe there won't.

'Sometimes you guess wrong. That isn't negligence, it's the nature of the thing. Surgeons are only human, they can't always work as fast as patients bleed. They have to take short-cuts; usually it pays off but sometimes it doesn't.' She gave him a steely smile. 'An autopsy's a wonderful thing, you know. You can find out all sorts when there's no longer any urgency.'

Donovan nodded. 'Like a police review.' He spoke softly. 'Where some chinless wonder who's made his name streamlining the Photofit procedure looks over his glasses at you and says, "But Sergeant, you must have realized it was an imitation firearm—the real Mk IIa has the gunsmith's stamp on the *other* side of the barrel."'

They were on the same wavelength. Petrie's bosom lifted on a bleak sigh. 'Don't you just love an armchair critic.'

It was the only opening he was going to get and Donovan took it. 'So tell me, Staff Nurse—one poor bloody foot-soldier to another: did Alan Clarke die because his injuries were too bad, because his luck ran out, because somebody working under pressure made one judgement when with more time to think about it she'd have made another? Or did he die because his surgeon didn't try hard enough to save him?'

For a moment he thought she was going to slap him. His bruises saved him: by the time she'd weighed up how to land a blow between them the urge had passed. But her gaze was frosty and ice cracked in her voice. 'Young man, I know Mr Clarke was your superior, your colleague, and your friend, and his death was a shock to you. But I'd like you to remember that for four years I enjoyed the same relationship with Mrs Board. I don't think you'd stand for someone accusing Mr Clarke of incompetence now he's unable to defend himself, and I won't have you slandering Maggie Board. She was a fine surgeon. To the best of my knowledge she never did a bad day's work. No one suffered neglect at her hands. No one ever had less than the best work she could do for him.'

It made for a curious stand-off, the tall thin young man and the dumpy middle-aged nurse. There were chairs and a table in the room but both of them were standing, emphasizing the physical differences. Donovan looked down, his face wrung by the urgent personal and professional need to know the truth, and Petrie's eyes blazed up at him with anger and, so far as he could tell, absolute honesty.

And it was because he believed her—found her a credible witness, accepted that what she said was what she believed—that he pressed her. 'There's no doubt in your mind? You couldn't have—I don't know, seen what you expected to see? It suited somebody for Alan Clarke to die here. If he had a way of making sure— some kind of hold over Mrs Board—he'd have used it. And if that's what happened the same guy killed her.'

As her anger wore off Petrie was able to consider the suggestion more calmly. The fire died from her eyes and for a moment she was pensive, making herself re-live that one operation among so many others, distinguished only by the lateness of the hour and the fact that the patient was a local CID officer.

After a minute she shook her head. 'No, Sergeant, you're wrong. She did all she could for Inspector Clarke. She didn't make any mistakes. She didn't make any questionable decisions. I'm not a surgeon but I've seen a lot of operations and I know the difference between a good one and a bad one. Everything that could be done for Mr Clarke was done, he was just too weak to benefit from it. I'm sorry we couldn't save him. But the only one responsible for his death was the man who ran him down. Find him. Charge him.'

As she was leaving she turned in the doorway and Donovan saw a pain in her eyes that mirrored his own. She said quietly, 'And then find the bastard who robbed me of *my* friend.'

DONOVAN WAITED for the anaesthetist but only because he'd said he would. He believed Staff Nurse Petrie had seen what she said she'd seen. The only chance now was that Dr White, with his different training, his different angle, might have seen something which Petrie had not.

White was an amiable young man with curly fair hair and a nose that could only have got that way on the rugby field. He took a chair and waited amiably to learn how he could help.

In the light of what he'd heard from Petrie Donovan found it harder to repeat what half an hour ago had seemed a reasonable question. He expected Mrs Board's anaesthetist to react as vigorously as her nurse, and indeed when he got to the point he saw the amiability leach out of the doctor's face and resentment stiffen his muscles.

But Donovan was tired of playing the villain of the piece. Three people had died, the murderer or murderers were still at large, it was impossible to rule out further attacks, and the man most likely to be behind it all was still merrily running his empire from his office over the canal. If anyone had a right to be angry it was Donovan.

So he didn't wait for Dr White to protest but let his own irritation flood over. 'Don't tell me it couldn't happen. It could happen. It would be very easily done. It would be easily covered up, too: a handful of friends working together in a closed room, who's going to volunteer the information that one of them cocked up?

Maybe it goes on all the time, I don't know—you cover up my bungled hysterectomy, I'll turn a blind eye to your botched heart valve and we'll all pretend the instruments never got dropped on the floor. It doesn't happen? It didn't happen last Wednesday morning? Convince me, Doctor. Convince me that Mrs Board didn't let Alan Clarke bleed his life out on your operating table, and the rest of you didn't stand by and watch her do it because of the times she'd covered for you.'

Like Staff Nurse Petrie, White realized who Donovan was and made allowances accordingly. He drew a deep breath and kept his voice mild. 'You're right, it *could* happen. Maybe it's a wonder it doesn't. Or maybe it's a reflection of the standards in operating theatres.' He glanced down at his unappealing working clothes. 'What do you think people do this job for? The glamour? The money? The hours? Sergeant, I can only think of one less attractive job in the whole field of public service and that's yours.

'There are only two reasons why people work in hospitals. Everyone in Castle General could make more money more easily in private medicine, and most of them could walk out of here straight into a better job. The two reasons for staying are (a) the experience—no one in the private sector will see as many operations on as many different conditions as someone in a general hospital—and (b) the fact that you can do more good for more people here than anywhere else.

'I'm not saying that makes us a bunch of halo-headed philanthropists incapable of a tawdry act. What I am saying is that the chances of finding on the same surgical team three or more people prepared to put personal interests ahead of their duty to the patient are microscopic. I've never known anything like what you describe. I can't imagine it happening. It sure as hell didn't happen on Wednesday morning when we had Inspector Clarke on the table. Now, is that any help to you?'

By the time he had talked to Petrie Donovan had been pretty sure he was on a fool's errand. Now he knew. He nodded. 'In a way. I can't afford to go chasing wild geese, you know, I've enough to do without that. If Mrs Board wasn't killed because she was Alan Clarke's surgeon then it looks like we have a serial killer on the loose and we need to find him before somebody else from this hospital gets shot.'

Dr White was already regretting his lecture—not the contents, perhaps the delivery. 'I'm sorry. I suppose we're all a bit tense over this. Of course you have to find who's responsible. If I knew anything more I'd tell you. But you are wrong about Maggie Board. It'll sound pious but she genuinely was dedicated to the relief of human suffering. She wasn't the easiest woman to work with because of it. She wouldn't tolerate anything but the highest standards.

'You work with some surgeons and, unless it's actual life-and-death stuff at the time, it can be a bit of a chimps' tea-party. I don't mean we're careless, just that the mood's not that solemn. Maggie wouldn't have it. Even for routine work she insisted on total concentration. She used to say, Never forget you're dealing with the rest of this man's life. Ninety per cent success isn't good enough if it leaves him with ten per cent more sickness, disability, or pain than necessary. Accidents happen easily enough: if you invite them by letting your attention wander they're not accidents, they're negligence.'

'Why was she such a perfectionist, do you know?'

White shrugged. 'I suppose because she was a

woman. Even now it's hard for a woman surgeon to be taken seriously. When Maggie was training she'd have to have been twice as good as any man in the department. If anyone else made a mistake it was "That damn fool White" or "Why won't Cummings wear his glasses?" If Maggie did it was "Always said the job was too much for a woman." In that situation either she had to accept the limits other people put on her or she had to make damn few mistakes. Being a perfectionist was a form of self-preservation.'

His mind not altogether on Mrs Board, Donovan said, 'I hope she knew how much her colleagues respected her.'

'I think she did, Sergeant.' White smiled gently. 'Hard as she was to work with, people queued for the privilege. You can't take that as anything but a compliment.'

'You weren't the only anaesthetist she worked with, then, or Petrie the only nurse?'

'Oh, no. You work different shifts, different theatres; somebody goes down with flu and throws the whole rota. At the same time, you do tend to make up regular teams. Maggie, Petrie, and I were one.'

'For how long?' The question sounded casual.

'Oh, er—' He did calculations that involved the use of his fingers. 'Four years now.'

As far as Donovan could judge, Maggie Board was in the clear. But before he left the hospital he asked to see the chief administrator again. Mr Hawley, not knowing him, thought it was mere politeness, to say thanks before he went. When he realized he was being questioned his attitude changed. He stood erect and his chin drew in like a tortoise retracting its head.

'How long have you been here, Mr Hawley?'

The administrator didn't need to use his fingers. Donovan thought he could have said to the nearest week. 'A little over eight years.'

'So you were here at the time of the mass extinctions.'

Hawley stared at him and his grey moustache gave a quiver of disfavour. 'I beg your pardon?'

In the circumstances it wasn't the most tasteful remark ever made. Still Donovan was struck by the way one era had given way to another four years ago. 'Like the dinosaurs,' he explained. 'One minute—geologically speaking—you see them, the next you don't. It must have been a bit like that here when Kerry Carson left to do geriatrics, Staff Nurse Petrie took her place, Dr White joined the team, and presumably the last anaesthetist left. That's not normal, is it? What was going on?'

Hawley's moustache bristled with outrage. 'I don't know what you're suggesting, Sergeant Donovan. Going on? Nothing was going on. We had some staff changes. It happens all the time. This is a big hospital.'

'But that's one small surgical team and the only member of it to survive the purge was Maggie Board. And now she and Kerry Page are dead, both murdered by the same sort of weapon inside two days. You're not telling me that's par for the course?'

'What I will tell you, Sergeant,' the administrator said stiffly, 'is that I resent your attitude. We've had a tragedy here. A double tragedy, if you like—though Mrs Page was no longer on staff there are plenty of us who remember her. From where I stand it's obvious what's going on: there's a madman roaming Castlemere with a shotgun and a grudge against medical staff. Why, instead of finding that person and putting him where he can do no further damage, you're asking me about staff changes here four years ago I cannot imagine.'

Donovan's eyes were scornful. 'Oh, come on. Four years ago a girl who'd wanted to be a theatre nurse since she was in pigtails suddenly decided to jack it in. At the same time a vacancy arose for another anaesthetist. Something happened, didn't it? Something happened, and because of it Maggie Board the perfectionist wouldn't have them on her team again. What was it? And how was Kerry able to get a good job a couple of months later that wouldn't have been offered her unless there'd been a cover-up?'

Hawley's voice had gone bleak, grey as the little grey moustache jutting over his lip. He was a spare man of about fifty with thinning grey hair clipped ruthlessly to a bullet-shaped head. He wore a grey suit that would have run a mile from a puking child. Of course, he was not a doctor.

'You're fantasizing, Sergeant. I appreciate that you have to explore the possibilities, and this matter is urgent enough to justify any approach which might yield results. But you're barking up the wrong tree. If Mrs Board had been let down by her colleagues, do you imagine she'd have permitted a cover-up? Even if I or anyone else had been prepared to sanction one?

'No, Sergeant. Dr Saunders, who was Mrs Board's regular anaesthetist before Dr White, left Castle General because of an attractive offer from the Feyd Clinic, and Staff Nurse Carson transferred to geriatrics because theatre work turned out to be more stressful than she expected. That's all. I'm sorry it's so mundane. The truth often is.'

'Yeah,' agreed Donovan. 'And sometimes it's so bloody incredible nobody'll believe it till it's too late.

Who's this Dr Saunders? Maybe I should have a word with the only surviving member of the team before our madman mistakes *him* for a nurse and blows his head off too.'

FOUR

LIZ PUT THE PHONE down and looked up at Donovan, who was standing sullenly beside the door, leaning his shoulder against the wall, cradling his plaster with his good arm. She said evenly, 'How long have you been in Castlemere, Sergeant?'

His eyes were guarded. 'Five years.'

She nodded thoughtfully. 'And is there anyone left of rank or substance in the town whom you have yet to offend? I don't want to interfere with any ambitions you have in that regard.'

He indicated the phone. 'Hawley?' He'd come in midway through the call, tried to leave, and been firmly waved inside.

Liz breathed heavily. 'Yes, that was Mr Hawley. I think he'd like your body for medical research. Soon.'

'He's hiding something,' said Donovan.

'He said you were under that impression. He said that if I thought there was a hospital connection he'd co-operate in any way he could. He offered to show me his records for the period when Mrs Board and Kerry Carson worked together with this anaesthetist—Saunders? For a man who's hiding something it was a good impression of someone with a clear conscience.'

'Cunning bastard,' growled Donovan.

Liz sighed. 'There are two types that look like an innocent man, Donovan. One is indeed a cunning bastard. The other is an innocent man.'

Donovan levered himself off the wall. 'Look, this

isn't about my nasty suspicious mind, or a hospital administrator who was damn reluctant to answer a couple of questions until he'd had time to think about it. It's about Kerry Page and Maggie Board being murdered in the same way in the same week. That's either a cosmic coincidence or it's because of something they have in common. That time four years ago when they worked together, and then all at once the anaesthetist was off in one direction and the nurse in another, seemed a good place to look. Now, as a line of enquiry, what is *wrong* with that?'

'And where does Jack Carney fit into it?'

Donovan shot her a hunted look. 'He does, I know he does; I just don't know how. Neither the anaesthetist nor the nurse saw anything wrong when Board was working on Alan, they'd have said if they had. But if she didn't know Carney, why did he kill her? Or if he didn't, who did? There's something going on at that hospital. I just don't believe in a serial killer who could see well enough to distinguish Kerry Page from her husband in a car on a dark night but thought Maggie Board was a nurse. And if he went to the trouble of following the Pages to a country car park late at night, why was he so casual about his second victim that he shot her in the middle of town in broad daylight?'

It was a valid point. The trouble with Donovan, Liz was discovering, was that most of his points were valid: it was his conclusions that had to be treated with caution.

'All right,' she said. 'So we've three possibilities: that these murders are the work of a psychopath with a nurse fetish, that Carney's behind them, or they're connected with whatever split that surgical team four years ago. Who's the killer, then?'

'Depends what happened and who it happened to.'

'Yes, quite. But someone who—what, considered himself their victim? Someone whose operation was bungled?'

Donovan's eyebrows were sceptical. 'I've heard of sleeping on a decision but not for four years.'

Liz agreed. 'It doesn't sound too likely, does it? Unless for some reason this was his first chance. Could he have been in hospital till now?'

'Four years is a long time to be laid up. I don't think most people leaving hospital after four years would be fit to commit two murders.'

Liz nodded slowly. 'So who else would want to kill an entire surgical team?'

'Next of kin? If he's been looking after the victim, maybe he was too busy to do anything till now.'

Liz continued the thought almost seamlessly. 'If he cared enough about that person to kill those he blamed, he couldn't do anything that might result in him being put away while he was still needed. Suppose what changed after four years was that he wasn't needed any longer: his dependent either went into residential care or died. So our man was free to do what he'd been itching to do for four years.'

Donovan was watching her with genuine respect. 'That could work. How do we find out?'

'You go see Dr Saunders,' decided Liz. 'Forget what I said about not bullying people: bully him as much as you like but find out what happened in the theatre that made those three people split up. And ask him why he was seeing Kerry Page.'

The Sergeant looked surprised. 'Do we know he was?'

'She was seeing a doctor, not professionally. If it was Saunders it must be something to do with this.'

'Could she have been blackmailing him? If he was responsible for the incident that split them up?'

Liz frowned. 'It doesn't altogether fit with what we've been told about the girl. But yes, if Saunders made a mistake and Kerry covered for him it would give her a hold on him. Especially now he's doing nicely in the lucrative world of private medicine.'

'Blackmailers don't have lunch with their victims. They don't invite them to their homes while their husbands are out.'

'Which makes him sound more like a lover. But maybe not. He knew her, there was no point setting up an elaborate blind if he knew where to find her. Perhaps she misjudged him. Perhaps she thought he'd pay up quietly and instead he killed her.' She scowled. 'But why then did he murder Mrs Board?'

'Maybe he reckoned he had to. When she had time to think about Kerry's death she'd guess who had a reason to kill her.'

Liz wasn't happy with it. 'We hit the same problem: why would Kerry Page wait three years to put the screw on? Perrin first saw her visitor a year ago. And why would he pay up for twelve months, then take her out to lunch, then kill her?'

'Maybe she asked for more money.'

'Why?'

'If she knew about Page's partnership.'

'She was blackmailing Saunders to buy her husband a share in his firm?' Her voice wavered on the edge of doubt. 'Hell, Donovan, I don't know. That's an awful lot of guesswork.'

'It would work,' Donovan said slowly, 'if Kerry Page

wasn't the sweet kind girl we've been told she was and if Dr Saunders was a man who'd commit murder rather than give up a life style he was fond of. We'll have a better idea about that when I've seen him. Then maybe I should talk to Page again.'

'And I'll take Mr Hawley up on his offer and go study his records,' said Liz. 'This whole blackmail business is pure conjecture. If Kerry and Saunders turn out to have been lovers we're back to looking for someone with a grudge. In which case his name, or that of someone he loved, should appear on the theatre list shortly before the team split up.'

'Modern surgery's a production line,' objected Donovan, 'there'll be dozens of them. How will you know which one they cocked up?'

'I'll ask Mr Hawley,' Liz said.

ALMOST THE FIRST thing Shapiro had done after he left his detective inspector dead and his detective sergeant drifting in and out of consciousness in the hospital was interview Jack Carney. That time he had gone to the man's office, and had been received almost as courteously as Liz Graham would be four days later. He had, as Shapiro expected, a sound alibi: not so much Mrs Carney, who might have been willing to lie for him, as the doctor she summoned when Carney suffered palpitations in the middle of the night. As he was leaving the house the doctor, a locum with no known connections to either the Carney empire or the surgical department of Castle General, also saw McMeekin, half-dressed and apparently half-asleep, disturbed from his bed in the staff wing and anxious about his employer. It wasn't as good an alibi for McMeekin as for Carney but it was probably as good as it could have been without exciting suspicion.

This time Shapiro didn't go to Carney's office, he
went to his house, and the welcome was measurably
cooler. It became downright chilly when he announced
the purpose of his visit. They were in Carney's study:
just the two of them, for once McMeekin was occupied
elsewhere. The little man went a livid greyish-pink colour—perhaps the palpitations were not an invention—
and his voice sank to a viperish rasp.

'You've come here—to my house, to my wife's
house—to accuse me of—what? Having an affair with
this woman, this Mrs Board? You and I have had our
disagreements before this, Mr Shapiro, but I never expected that kind of vindictiveness from you. With all
your unwarranted interest in my business concerns,
you've never sunk to attacking my family life before.'

'I've no wish to be vindictive,' Shapiro said stolidly.
'But I do want an answer to my question. Did you know
Maggie Board, professionally, personally, or in any
other way? I should warn you I have other officers out
making the same enquiry in places where Mrs Board
was known. If it's true you'd be better telling me now.'

Carney came to his feet behind his writing table,
spilling his chair in his fury. 'God damn you, Shapiro!
You've got people going round this town—my town,
the place where I live—making an allegation like that
about me?'

Shapiro, who had watched Jack Carney field accu-
sations of vice, corruption, racketeering, drug dealing,
and having people's legs broken without flickering an
eyelid, without ever letting the confident little half-smile
slip from his lips, was surprised at the violence of his
reaction. In another man it might have signalled a guilty
conscience. But guilt was Carney's natural state, something he was at ease with. Shapiro rather suspected that

if it was true he'd have been better prepared for the question, would not have betrayed his feelings like this.

'Making enquiries,' he said, pedantically. 'We do it all the time. Sometimes our enquiries lead to allegations, sometimes they don't. It depends on the answers we get.'

'I'll give you my answer now,' said Carney, fast and hard. 'I have never had an affair, with this woman or any other. As far as I know I've never met Mrs Board. I've certainly never spent time with her. And in case that's your next question, I didn't have someone blow her head off with a shotgun.'

Shapiro sniffed. 'It wasn't my next question. But I'd have got there eventually.'

'Then I'm glad to have saved you the trouble,' spat Carney.

They weren't making a great deal of progress, but Shapiro was aware of having Carney rattled and wanted to press the advantage. Even if there was nothing between Carney and Board there was so much else the man might say if he was angry enough.

'You see my position,' he said. 'Three people have been killed in this town in the past week. As you and I very well know, you'd good reason for wanting Alan Clarke dead. And the other victims were the surgeon who operated on him and the wife of the man you hired as a pilot. Coincidence? Convince me.'

'Convince you?' It came out midway between a sneer and a snarl. 'I don't need to convince you of anything. Who are you that I should care what you think? I suppose there's a certain novelty value in a Yid detective, all very Opportunities for the Ethnics I'm sure. But if I decide I've had enough of this I'll break you. Then you'll find out how many friends you have, in and out

of the Force. The only thing that'll save you then'll be
an emergency induction into the Masons. And I don't
think you're eligible for that, are you?'

Frank Shapiro had been insulted more subtly and
therefore more effectively than that in his years as a
policeman. He'd met prejudice from colleagues as well
as from criminals, and found that infinitely harder to
deal with. When a man was very probably a murderer
it seemed silly to add, 'And what's more he's anti-
Semitic!'

But he didn't have to like it, and he didn't have to
take it sitting down. He too came to his feet, his thick
body looming over the little Regency desk. 'Shall I tell
you something about coppers, Mr Carney?' He made it
sound like a very quiet threat. 'A lot of them don't like
Jews. A lot of them don't like blacks. Quite a few of
them don't like women, and almost none of them like
the Irish. But the one thing they have in common, and
this applies to every member of every police force in
Britain, is that none of them will put up with dirty little
toe-rags who think they're immune to the law and they
can grind other coppers into brick walls—even Irish
coppers, even Jewish coppers—with impunity. You
want to take me on, Mr Carney, go right ahead. But
don't think you can take me on alone.'

He left then. He hadn't learned very much more
about Carney. But perhaps Carney had learned something about him.

DONOVAN WENT to the Feyd Clinic first thing on
Wednesday morning. Liz arranged for a young constable to drive him. The constable stopped feeling this was
an honour before they'd gone the first mile. Donovan

was a terrible back-seat driver and leaned into the curves.

The clinic occupied a choice spot overlooking the Levels, a green sea touched with bronze. The expensive rooms at the front enjoyed a view all the way to the same River Arrow which, miles further up its course, wandered through the water-meadows where Kerry Page made love and died. The cheaper rooms overlooked the car park, the road, and an electricity substation.

It was a smaller establishment than Donovan had expected, a low concrete box designed along minimalist lines, apparently by the same man who thought of nouvelle cuisine and charging more and more for less and less swimwear. In town it would have looked like a Social Services office. Out here amid the green, in an odd way it worked rather better. It was simple enough to slot into the landscape instead of imposing on it.

Whatever money was saved by leaving the outside plain had been spent in the foyer. There was money on the walls, on the floor, in the furnishings, and behind reception. The effect was discreet, professional, reassuring. You could tell from the spring in the carpet that the people here would give you a nose job you'd never forget.

The Feyd Clinic was owned by the same group as the Rosedale Nursing Home. It was to the field of cosmetic surgery and other fashionable treatments what Rosedale was to the care of the elderly: Rolls-Royce provision carrying a happy few up the fast lane while the National Health Service bus trundled along behind. The group offered top jobs and could afford to handpick its employees; indeed, could hardly afford not to.

Any suspicions about Dr Saunders couldn't have reached the ears of the appointments committee.

Donovan asked for Saunders at the desk. The expensive receptionist rang his office but his secretary wasn't expecting him. 'He was in his consulting room until six o'clock last night,' she said, quite breathlessly, as if this were a marathon session by Clinic standards. Perhaps it was. They wouldn't do many emergency face-lifts.

The receptionist wrote Dr Saunders' home address on a card. 'Shall I phone and see if he's in, Sergeant?'

'No, thanks.' The less time Emil Saunders had to think what he would say to the police the happier Donovan would be.

CASTLE GENERAL was everything the Feyd Clinic was not: a rambling metropolis of a hospital, the oldest buildings of smoke-blackened Victorian brick with additions of every period since—substantial stucco from between the wars, worthy red brick from the fifties, a poorly conceived and worse executed tower-block from the seventies, and a dear little Arts and Crafts dentistry department—all dropped on to the campus as if from a height, landing at odd angles and with no regard for the relationship of one to the next. An accident victim with both burns and fractures could have such a journey between clinics that it was expedient to hail a passing ambulance. Someone on a geriatric ward who still had enough teeth to visit the dentist could die in transit.

After the tower-block went up the site was full. Apart from the odd angles between the buildings, used for car parking, there was no room for further development. So when the next round of cottage-hospital closures increased the need for maternity, geriatric, and casualty beds at Castle General, patients were housed in the car parks, in prefabricated shells with consultants' BMWs and nurses' 2CVs for company.

Liz, appalled by the scale and confusion of the site, hardly knew where to start. She stopped a man in a white coat and asked where the chief administrator's office was, and the man pondered a moment and said he thought it was in the Victorian part though he once heard a rumour about it being in a red-brick annexe behind the tower-block. Then he asked if she knew the way out. He said he'd come here for his holiday jabs and been trying to leave ever since. Liz guessed then that he was joking, but clearly she was not the first person to have been overwhelmed by the chaotic architecture.

Mr Hawley's office was indeed in the Victorian core of the hospital. He greeted her with a formal inclination of the head. 'I'm not sure what you're looking for but my secretary and I will give whatever assistance we can.'

Liz smiled disarmingly. 'I'm not altogether sure what I'm looking for either. But it does seem a coincidence. In view of what's happened, and the possibility that it's not over yet, I think we have to explore every avenue.'

Even Castle General had been computerized for more than four years so the records she was interested in were on disk. Hawley eyed the hardware as if he still didn't quite trust it and said, 'Are you familiar with the equipment? Miss McNair will operate it if you'd rather.'

'Thanks.' If there was one thing Liz's time at Headquarters had fitted her for it was extracting information from computers. But it's a rash policeman who turns down an offer of help. She would take over when the answers started coming.

Hawley excused himself and went to withdraw to his

inner sanctum. But Liz, almost without seeming to move, barred his way, slipping her jacket on to the back of a chair. She was as tall as him and her eyes caught and held his frosty gaze—Donovan was right, however polite he might seem he resented her being here, even at his invitation. She said, 'Mr Hawley, if you knew why Mrs Board's team broke up four years ago—even if it couldn't have anything to do with what happened to her and Kerry Page—you'd tell me, wouldn't you?'

His eyes didn't flinch. 'Naturally.'

Liz nodded slowly, still watching him. 'It's a matter of priorities, isn't it? In normal circumstances a degree of discretion about colleagues' failings would be appropriate. But different circumstances put a different complexion on it. If there's any chance at all of people being hurt, no responsible person would put loyalty to a colleague above their duty to prevent that. I'm sure you'd agree, Mr Hawley.'

Hawley seemed to swell with indignation but retained a rigid control of his voice. 'I hope I know my duty as well as you do, Inspector. I will tell you again what I told your sergeant. I don't know who shot either Mrs Page or Mrs Board, and I don't know why. If there are any clues in our records I hope you'll find them. I've given it some thought, without success. But then, detection is your job. Mine is running a hospital.'

She learned nothing from reading the records, but then she had not expected to. She had Miss McNair print out details of the operations carried out by Maggie Board, Emil Saunders, and Kerry Carson in their last month together. If a mistake had occurred the consequences might not have shown at once. Also it would have taken time to arrange new schedules. Even a surgeon of Board's eminence could hardly have thrown her anaesthetist and nurse bodily out of her theatre without explaining why, which plainly she had not done.

Liz wanted to talk to the chief administrator again. She didn't believe that he knew nothing of what must have been a significant upset within his period of office. But she needed a name to throw at him, and while that name was probably there in the records she had no way of recognizing it yet.

She wondered how Donovan was getting on with Dr Saunders, if the anaesthetist was any more forthcoming. He might be. If he was not himself the killer he must have noticed that he was now the only survivor of the surgical team. Liz was sure of one thing. If Saunders hadn't yet thought that he might be the next victim, Donovan would make sure he thought about it now.

IN ITS HEYDAY Castlemere was one of the most prosperous small towns in England. It stood at the junction of canals connecting London with the growing industrial centres of the Midlands and those feeding westward towards the ports of the Bristol Channel. This brought the world to its door and the small traders of Castlemere developed first into larger traders and then into genuine merchants to take advantage of the fact. They built warehouses and mills, iron-works and tanneries. They cornered the boot and shoe industry. When the first railway cast a cloud over the thriving canals they hedged their bets by bringing in the railway too.

And when their prosperity was assured, they built houses. They built rows of little millworkers' houses under the shadow of the great mills they served. They built a neat greystone house for the canal superintendent and a red-brick one for the station-master. They built rows of pretty alms cottages to show that they had hearts of gold beating under their Albert chains.

For themselves they built mansions. They were Victorian mansions to be sure, solid and comfortable but less grandiose than the country seats with which earlier merchant princes had equipped themselves. For the most part these Victorian entrepreneurs had risen from humble roots and took a perverse pride in their lack of breeding. Their homes were still big enough to house a dozen millworkers' families in unaccustomed luxury.

When the canals stagnated in the second half of the nineteenth century, and a hundred years later the railways met a similar fate, the factory owners' families moved on so that many of their mansions stood empty and derelict. Some were demolished, others were converted to hotels, to offices, and to flats.

Emil Saunders had a penthouse flat in the most prestigious of these surviving mansions, an ugly but imposing square-built edifice of iron-black brick called Fairbairn House. It had a small park set with mature trees and sweeping lawns which, since the lease included the employment of a gardener, could be enjoyed without labour. Because of its elevation, Dr Saunders' flat had a stunning view down the lawns and between the trees to the glint of a small lake close to the boundary.

But Dr Saunders was not enjoying his view today. There was no answer to Donovan's rap at his door. Donovan tried again but heard no sound of stirring. Irritated, he went back downstairs. A man was passing a desultory rag over the communal brasswork in the hall. 'Do you know when Dr Saunders'll be back?'

The hall porter glanced at the grandfather clock under the stairs. 'Depends how much he's got to do. Five minutes if he's only gone for his paper, an hour if it's his weekly shop. You only just missed him.'

For five minutes it wasn't worth coming back. Donovan thought he'd spend the time gathering background information. 'Known him long, have you—Dr Saunders?'

'He's been here about five years. Most days I say "Good morning" to him once and "Good evening" to him once. Does that constitute knowing a man?'

Donovan recognized the hall porter as a philosopher. 'Had any problems with him?'

'No. Well, you wouldn't expect to, professional gent like that. He meets his obligations, he's polite to his neighbours, he remembers the staff at Christmas. What else is there to say? Once Miss Duke's car wouldn't start and he gave her a lift into town. She asked how she could repay him, and he said she could return the favour some day when the Porsche wouldn't start.'

'And?'

'The Porsche always starts.'

'Funny,' said Donovan, 'I had the idea he was a bit of a ladies' man.'

If the porter felt any reluctance to gossip about his residents he didn't let it hinder him. 'Dr Saunders? You've got the wrong man, squire. Or if he is he never brings them home. Doesn't bring anybody home much. Not one of the world's great socializers. He has his colleagues round for a party every New Year, otherwise he doesn't get many visitors. I don't think he rates stars in anybody's little black book.'

It had been ten minutes and there was no sign of the Porsche. 'OK,' decided Donovan. 'I've another call to make down the hill. I'll be back here in an hour, that should give him time to pack his freezer. If he looks like he's going out, ask him to wait—otherwise don't bother him.' He meant, and the hall porter knew he meant, Don't tell him I was here.

FIVE

IT DIDN'T TAKE AN HOUR. Page had nothing to tell him; indeed, found it difficult speaking to him at all. Donovan was no psychiatrist and had no bent for social work, but he was becoming uneasy about David Page. He seemed different every time Donovan saw him: one day tears, the next rigid control, now depression so deep it was like talking to a man down a well. Donovan thought he'd warn DI Graham: if Page was coming apart somebody should be looking after him.

The flat was quietly mouldering under a layer of dust and neglect. Page wasn't eating much. Mostly the meals he had made had gone cold virtually untouched; they sat around the flat as if somebody else might tidy up if Page left it long enough. He was sleeping on the couch with a quilt over him. The edge of the quilt was thrown back as if he'd just got up and his clothes looked as if he'd slept in them. Donovan was no slave to housework but even he could smell the faint musty miasma of decay.

It wasn't so much the pots and the dust and the quilt: they could be tidied away in half an hour and the windows flung wide to a cleansing breeze. The real problem was Page's inability to cope with what had happened to him. No breeze could aerate his foundering spirit.

Page looked at him as if through layers of gauze. His voice was a low monotone. 'Any news?'

Donovan gave an apologetic shrug. 'It's got awful

complicated, this. There's one idea we're looking into. Did Kerry ever mention Dr Emil Saunders to you?'

Page couldn't summon any interest. 'Who?'

'He was the anaesthetist when she worked with Mrs Board. He left about the same time she did.'

He might have been thinking, he might just have switched off for a minute. Then he shook his head apathetically.

'The name means nothing?'

'No.'

Donovan steeled himself to go on. 'We think he may have been the man she was seeing.'

Page looked up at that. His eyes were bottomless with misery. 'I don't believe that.'

'There's the possibility that she'—he shrank from saying the word *blackmail*, looked for a euphemism— 'that he may have lent her some money. Did she seem to have more money than you expected? In the last year, particularly in the last month?'

Page's face creased up in weary irritation. 'Money? She'd all the money she needed. She'd no need to borrow money. And why—?' But he didn't finish the question. Perhaps he had an inkling what the answer might be.

'So she never talked about working with Dr Saunders?' Page shook his head. 'Or seeing him, or borrowing money from him?'

'No.'

Donovan was getting nowhere, and he didn't think he'd get any further by pushing harder. Either Page knew nothing or the state he was in prevented him from communicating. He went to leave. But at the door he paused. 'Look—are you all right?'

Page's head went back in a silent bark of a laugh.

'My wife's been murdered. First you thought I did it because she was seeing another man. Now you think she owed him money so maybe he did it. I can't get her body released for a funeral. And my boss thinks I should take some leave: nobody wants an emotionally disturbed pilot. Can't altogether blame them, can you? Am I all right? I'm fine; and I bet Mrs Lincoln enjoyed the play too.'

Before he left Donovan put a note through Julian Perrin's door asking him to look in on Page when he could and call if he needed anything. He didn't know what else he could do.

HE RETURNED to Fairbairn House. A charcoal-grey Porsche was parked outside. He nodded to the porter as he went through the hall. 'He's back then.'

'You hadn't been gone five minutes,' the porter said cheerfully. 'He wasn't shopping, just his paper and some stamps. The other chap had more luck, arrived right behind him.'

Dononvan frowned. 'Who's that then?'

'I've never known Dr Saunders have two visitors in one day. You know what did it, don't you? Me telling you he never sees anyone. Mind you, family's fine but it's not a social life. And a brother-in-law's only just family.'

All the hairs down Donovan's neck stood up under his collar. He had to remember to breathe. 'His brother-in-law? You know him, do you?'

'Never seen him before. He didn't stay long—just returning Dr Saunders' shotgun. Funny, I'd never have taken him for a shooting man. Either of them, actually.'

But Donovan wasn't listening. He'd snatched the pass-keys out of the porter's hand—he'd been jingling them absently while they talked—and was haring up the staircase as fast as his long legs would carry him.

DR SAUNDERS was being cautious. Two women he used to work with had been murdered: he wasn't blind to the possibility that he was next on the list. He knew a sort of reason why he might be. If he'd been sure he'd have gone to the police for help. But that would mean explanations, an end to his career, probably criminal charges as well. He hesitated to act while there was a chance that he was wrong, that it was a coincidence, that he was in no danger.

So when his doorbell rang he was careful how he answered it. But it was a policeman. 'I don't know if you're aware of this, sir, but we have reason to believe you're the intended next victim of a man who's shot two women you used to work with. I'm here to arrange protection for you.'

So they knew. They knew of the connection between him and the women—not just that they'd worked together but about the thing which made them targets for a madman. Saunders let out a sigh, half trepidation, half relief. He was not an evil man, he was a weak man. He'd never intended to do harm. In a way he'd be glad to have light shone in the four-year-old shadows, whatever the consequences. Also, though he faced legal sanction at least he was now safe from violence.

'You'd better come in,' he said, opening the door.

He didn't look like a man around whom mayhem revolved. He was not far short of forty now and not bearing the years particularly well. He had few interests outside his work and his home, and since he drove between the two in a charcoal-coloured Porsche he'd put on weight. It showed in his face and round his middle, and his lack of height made it hard for him to carry it with dignity. His light brown hair was thinning alarmingly. When he gave his hall mirror more than a passing glance he couldn't help notice how little remained of the young doctor who with his ready charm and boyish good looks had put a twinkle into female eyes the length and breadth of Castle General.

When the policeman came inside Saunders saw the long gun-case he carried and shuddered. It was serious, then. They were expecting an attempt on his life. After four years of playing it carefully, of nursing his relations with the two women who could ruin him—roses on Maggie Board's birthday that she never acknowledged, to remind her how things had once been between them, an occasional lunch with an uncomfortable Kerry Page to remind her that she owed her present job to his benign influence—it seemed he hadn't got away with it after all. Seeing no point in further evasion he said, 'How much do you know?'

And the man in the tweed jacket said, 'I know it all, Dr Saunders,' withdrawing from the case not a police rifle but a double-barrelled shotgun.

Slowly Saunders' plump face fell apart, his eyes and the corners of his mouth sinking in the wreckage. When he spoke it was only a breathy whisper. 'I know you.'

SIX

THE MAN WHO WAS NOT a policeman nodded pleasantly. 'Good. Then you know why I'm here.' His eyes on the gun, Saunders stood mute with fear. Seeing what he was thinking the man shook his head. 'Oh, no, Dr Saunders, I'm not going to shoot you. Not unless you make me. I want to tell you about my family. How things have worked out for us since we last met. I don't want to be holding this thing all the time, so I hope you'll forgive me—?' He'd brought a length of clothes-line. The chair at Saunders' desk was a substantial oak piece with padded arms that could have been made for the job.

Saunders lacked the courage to struggle. Anyway it would have done him no good while the man had the gun. Better tied and alive than free with a hole through his middle.

When he was fixed securely in his chair the man put the gun aside, settled himself on the desk and began to talk. While he was talking he took some items out of his pockets and put them on the desk beside him. The sharp knife sent a quiver through Saunders' veins, but the thing he couldn't take his eyes off was a box of wax ear-plugs.

'You see before you,' said the man, still calmly, still pleasantly, 'someone whose life you have destroyed. Perhaps not by choice but not accidentally either: wantonly, without regard for the consequences. Even if I was disposed to forgive you, which I'm not, if I let you get away with it sooner or later you'd destroy another family the same way.

'I know what happened. I talked to Staff Nurse Carson, remember, before you corrupted her. You shouldn't have done that. She was a decent young woman. If she'd stood by what she told me, as she would have done except for your weasel promises, she'd be alive today. Mrs Board too, if she hadn't lied to protect you. Why did she do that?' He waited for an answer.

Saunders whispered, 'She—we—' and could not go on.

The man raised an incredulous eyebrow. 'You were *lovers*? My God. For all the questions I asked, I never heard a whisper of that. She was years older than you. What could a woman like that—a clever woman, a surgeon at the top of her profession—possibly see in a little toe-rag like you?'

This time the question was rhetorical because he went on without pause. 'I was telling you about my family. Danny made more progress than you might have expected. He can sit up and play with his toys. He can eat normally, if I allow an hour to feed him. He can make a sort of howling noise to let me know he's uncomfortable. He won't be going to school, of course—not this year, not ever. He's not a vegetable but he'd have trouble out-thinking a goldfish. That's my son and heir.

'My wife was a teacher. Head of the English Department: she had a good career until she gave it up to look after Danny. That wouldn't have mattered so much if she hadn't lost everything else as well. We had to sell the house, I spent the money on lawyers. It's not cheap, trying to prove negligence by a doctor—particularly when his colleagues close ranks round him. The

Legal Aid stopped when we couldn't get the evidence we needed. You're not allowed to waste public money, you have to waste your own.

'My solicitor—my last solicitor, after I'd exhausted all the more respectable ones—kept going till my money ran out too, then closed the file and sent his bill. That was about a month ago. Of course, you know—he wrote to tell Hawley the action was withdrawn and I'm sure Hawley told you. I imagine you all went out for dinner together, to celebrate.' For a moment Saunders looked as if he was going to say something, then he changed his mind.

The man shrugged and continued. 'All I had left to sell was the shop, which meant losing the last of our income and our flat as well. For four years, all the time she needed my support and I was trying to bring you to book, I never heard a word of complaint from Mary. Then a fortnight ago I came home to find Danny in his playpen and Mary in the bath with her wrists slit. She didn't leave a note. She didn't have to.'

He looked round the room then as if seeking something. 'When I leave here I'm going to kill Danny, then myself. You're a doctor—an anaesthetist, a man with a comprehensive knowledge of drugs. I'm sure you have something here I can use, something quick and painless. Remember what you've done to that child already, don't make him suffer any more.'

There were drugs in the bathroom cabinet. In a barely audible whisper Saunders described one and the appropriate dosage. When the man had found it Saunders, feeling that any last words he wanted to utter he'd better try and get out now, half-said, half-sobbed, 'I'm sorry.'

'Sorry?' echoed the man. He returned to his perch on the desk and picked up the box of ear-plugs. 'You've destroyed five people's lives and you're sorry? You went into an operating theatre to anaesthetize a baby knowing you were intoxicated, and you tell me you're sorry?'

'I was tired,' muttered Saunders, his eyes desperate. 'It was only a whiff of nitrous oxide. But the oxygen tube blocked and I didn't notice. It was only when Maggie said he was turning blue… And I panicked. God help me, I panicked.'

'Another minute and he'd have died on the table; you'd have had to face the consequences then. But Mrs Board got the oxygen flowing again and finished off. Then she saw Mary and me. She lied to us. She said Danny wasn't coming out of the anaesthetic as he should, that they were monitoring his condition, that we shouldn't worry too much but she'd felt she should inform us. But it was nothing to do with the anaesthetic. He'd been starved of oxygen. If she'd told the truth she'd still be alive. She did her best for Danny, but her lies cost me my wife.'

He was rolling the pink wax cylinders between his fingers, warming them, kneading them, making them malleable. Saunders watched his hands as if mesmerized. He didn't know what they were for, but he knew enough to be terrified.

The man took a woman's headscarf out of his pocket. 'This was Mary's. She looked good in blue.' He folded it lengthways and, stepping behind the chair, tied it as a gag through the doctor's mouth. 'Can you breathe through that? You should be able to breathe a little.' Then he reached for the soft pink masses of wax and cotton-wool and, holding the doctor's head steady, carefully thumbed them into his nostrils.

Emil Saunders was not a powerful man but he fought

for his life. His jaws worked frantically as he tried to gnaw through his gag; saliva frothed at the corners of his mouth and the silky fabric began to fray. His eyes bulged with fear, with effort and with the mounting pressure as his heart tried to get enough oxygen to his brain.

The man sat on the desk watching him. His eyes were without sympathy, his voice without mercy. 'Not a nice experience, is it, Dr Saunders? Not a thing you'd wish on your worst enemy, let alone a baby. But this is what you did to Danny. You destroyed his brain because you hadn't the decency to stay sober while you did your job.'

The air Saunders could drag in at the corners of his mouth was not enough to keep him conscious, only to delay the inevitable. For some minutes he continued to fight the growing weakness, the gathering dark. Wet with saliva the gag admitted less and less air. The chafing of his jaws grew slower, more ponderous. Spots of blood from his gums specked the silky blue of the scarf. Over the bulging, desperate eyes the lids grew heavy. Twice his head tipped forward and he struggled to lift it. The third time it stayed on his chest.

The man got down from the desk, walked behind him and untied the headscarf, easing the fabric out of Saunders' mouth with a careful finger. The doctor's starved lungs sucked in air with a sound like wind in a drain.

If he'd had the choice perhaps Saunders would have chosen not to bother, to go then when he was already so close to death. But his lungs had their own imperative and could not refuse air. With the oxygen awareness returned, with awareness the knowledge that he was still alive, still captive, still at the disposal of a man with no mercy. Lawyers and doctors argue over the definition of madness but Emil Saunders knew he was in the hands of a madman. He had never meant to cause the suffering that had consumed this man, chewed him up, and spat him out quite transformed and able to wreak unthinkable vengeance on a helpless victim. But that was what he had done: sown the seeds of a terrible obsession. Saunders had never been a Bible-reading man but he knew the bit about sowing the wind and reaping the whirlwind.

The gag that he'd chewed in his frenzy lay wet with his spittle on his chin, cool on his throat. The membranes of his mouth and throat were fiery with the effort to breathe, his tongue swollen and bruised. Dragging his eyes up to the man's face he whispered thickly, 'Please—'

'Please?' echoed the man, frowning. 'Is there something you want?'

'Please,' whispered Saunders again. 'No more.'

The man looked at his watch. 'Danny's had four years. I think you owe him a little longer.' His fingers, strong with his sense of mission, parted Saunders' jaws, forced the gag back into his mouth.

Dr Saunders' ordeal continued. To the man in the chair, his throat burning and his lungs bursting and the blood filling his eyes, it seemed an eternity. He gnawed at his gag until the darkness swamped him, and when the pounding head fell on his chest and the sight went from his eyes and the consciousness all but left him, his fading thought was that this was it, he was dying. But twice more the scarf was loosened, his starved lungs gulped air and oxygen stirred his senses again.

Three times in fifteen minutes Emil Saunders was choked to and brought back from the point of death. At last terror gave way to resignation. He was going to die, he was going to die here, and soon, and in this way, and there was nothing he could do about it. When hope was gone, much of the fear went too.

When Emil Saunders accepted the inevitability of death his eyes dulled and he ceased his frantic efforts to gnaw through his gag. He would have slipped away then as easily as the feathered seeds blowing off a dandelion clock. But the man perched on his desk watched him with growing unease.

He had planned this so carefully. For hours past counting he had contemplated, almost as a philosophical exercise, the relationship of crime and punishment. For the last ten days he had thought of almost nothing else. He'd wanted it to be right, to be apt, had been pleased with what he'd thought of. He'd expected a little difficulty in carrying it out—he was not a brutal man—but once he had steeled himself to it he expected to feel a kind of release. This was the monster who destroyed his family: he expected catharsis in accomplishing his end.

Instead he felt soiled, curiously humiliated. Dr Saunders wasn't a monster: he was a man—a man who had done something dreadful but still only a man—and stripping his life from him by shreds was a demeaning thing, not a triumph. He had expected to fill up with the music of mayhem, a Valkyrie's choir celebrating his awful deed. Instead he found within him the seeds of pity for his victim, a mounting sense of loathing for himself.

It was too late to turn back. Two people, less guilty than Saunders, had already paid for his actions: weakening now would make their deaths meaningless. But he wished he could start again, that he had not allowed spite to sully his revenge. He should have kept it clean.

Executing Saunders was one thing. Torturing him was another.

He couldn't undo what was done but he could finish it. He loosed the gag a last time. A last time he watched awareness, and disappointment, crawl back into Emil Saunders' eyes. He needed him to be conscious for just a moment. His lips formed words: 'I'm sorry.' Then he pulled Saunders' head back by a handful of hair and cut his throat.

He left the shotgun reared in a corner of the flat. He was a responsible husband and father: the last thing he wanted was for a dangerous firearm to find its way into the wrong hands.

SEVEN

'Do you suppose that means he's finished?' Shapiro was looking at the shotgun, reared tidily in a corner of Dr Saunders' study.

Liz nodded. Her voice was bleak. 'He's got all three of them. What else does he need it for?'

'He must be pretty sure it can't be traced to him.'

'Perhaps he doesn't care.' She jerked her head towards the desk, at a slight angle because she'd already seen as much as she wanted to of the face of Emil Saunders. 'That was personal. Vendetta. He's got what he waited four years for. Perhaps he doesn't care now if we get him.'

Donovan returned from using the hall porter's phone. He shook his head. 'It's not his gun.'

'How do you know?'

'It's been on the stolen list for six years.'

In all probability the stolen gun had been travelling round the criminal strata since then, taking part in a holdup here, being brandished in a demand-with-menaces there. A laboratory examination and test-firing might or might not link it to earlier offenses; anyway it must have changed hands many times. As a clue to the identity of the man who killed Kerry Page, Maggie Board, and Emil Saunders it was of marginal value. Even if he'd left his fingerprints all over it.

The Scenes of Crime officer, a middle-aged man with a glum face and flattened patches in the corduroy of his trouserlegs from kneeling, was kneeling in front of the gun, puffing powder on it. He said with satisfaction, 'He's left his prints all over it.'

Liz nodded slowly. 'So he isn't a pro—not someone on Carney's payroll. At least we know now: there are two cases and this one's about something that happened four years ago, not last week. He's an amateur, we won't have his prints on file.' She turned to Donovan. 'What did the porter say?'

'A yellow car. No make. Mid-range yellow hatchback, several years old. No idea of the registration number.'

Shapiro nodded resignedly. 'And the man?'

'Middle aged, medium height, medium build. Brown hair, clean shaven; tweed jacket. Educated type.' For a moment a ghost of a frown crossed his face, as if that meant something to him. Then he shrugged. 'That whittles it down to every third man in Castlemere. The porter said he was very calm.'

Shapiro was looking at the body again. 'You mean he came to do this and he hadn't even the grace to be nervous?'

Donovan shrugged. 'That's what the man says.' Later than usual he remembered to add, 'Sir.'

'He wouldn't be nervous,' said Liz. 'Not once he'd come this far. The only thing he was afraid of was being stopped.'

'The cold-blooded—'

'Not so much cold blooded, more—dedicated. He was doing something he believed in. Something he owed to someone. An injustice was done and he wanted—retribution.' As she spoke she could feel the man they were looking for like a shadow in the room with them. Without knowing the reasons, she could sense how he had come to this. He wasn't a wicked man. He'd been eaten up by what happened to someone he loved, as much a victim of events in that operating theatre as the others—the nurse, the surgeon, the anaesthetist, the patient.

'He had plenty of time to think about this: he'd come to terms with what he was going to do. He wasn't nervous because he didn't care what happened afterwards. That's why he left the gun. He doesn't need it again, and he doesn't care what we learn from it.'

'Why do you suppose—?' Shapiro cleared his throat to start again. 'I mean, the others, the women—at least it was quick. No warning, one shot and they were dead. This time he didn't even use the gun. Why the difference?'

To Liz it was obvious. 'Because Saunders is the one he blames. It was the anaesthetic that went wrong. The surgeon and the nurse covered up, but the mistake was Saunders'. If it was a mistake. It might have been unavoidable, an ana—ana—'

Donovan, expressionless, supplied the word she was groping for. 'Anaphylaxis.'

She nodded and carried on, almost without pausing, without noticing the twitch of a smile in the corner of Shapiro's mouth. Talking to Clarke and Donovan had been like this. They fed each other words and ideas almost without being aware of it. 'Anaphylaxis. But our man didn't believe that. He believed it was negligence, and when the rest of the team wouldn't confirm it they were closing ranks. He was probably right. If it really was no one's fault why did they split up over it? Why would Mrs Board have made such an issue of absolute professionalism at all times if it hadn't been a lack of care that caused it?

'So when he was free to do so he found those responsible and punished them. He didn't hold the same grudge against the women: he felt it necessary to kill them for their supporting role but not to make them suffer. Saunders was different. He wanted Saunders to know why he was dying, what it was for. He'd waited four years for this, he wanted to do it right. I bet he rehearsed it at home first, to make sure it would work.

'Saunders was an anaesthetist, any mistake of his would affect his patient's ability to breathe. Our man wanted him to know what that felt like. With his nose blocked and a scarf in his mouth he'd be fighting for air, and losing.' She turned to Donovan. 'How long did the porter say he was up here?'

'About twenty minutes. He arrived just after I left, and ten minutes before I got back he came down and drove off.' His voice was tight, his face pinched. 'If I'd waited... But I thought I could save some time, maybe learn something to get him talking.' He shook his head in bitter disbelief. 'Ten minutes, for God's sake! If I'd even got back ten minutes earlier—'

'There was no way you could have known,' Shapiro said quietly. 'It was a reasonable judgement. It's not your fault Saunders was out when you called and in when a man came to kill him.' He hadn't even had time to open his paper. It lay, neatly folded, on the desk in front of him where he'd dropped it when he went to answer the door.

'Twenty minutes,' echoed Liz. 'It was time enough. He watched Saunders suffer until he'd seen enough, then he cut his throat.'

An edge of bitterness had crept into her voice. It was almost the first loss of professional detachment Shapiro had detected in her. He murmured, 'Perhaps we should adjourn to the office.'

Liz frowned. 'What?' Then she realized he wanted to get her away from the disturbing corpse with its twisted face and gaping throat, and raked up a wan smile. 'I'm all right. It's just— It makes me so angry. I know Emil Saunders was no saint. He did something stupid that ruined somebody's life, and traded on the loyalty of his colleagues to bail him out. He wasn't much cop as a doctor. But he didn't deserve to spend his last minutes like that, having the life choked out of him an inch at a time.'

'Of course he didn't,' Shapiro agreed mildly. 'Nobody ever deserves to be murdered, any way. That's what makes us the good guys—we catch people who, whatever the circumstances, have no moral justification. And we'll catch this man. We already have his name— it's somewhere in those records you got from the hospital, we'll track him down if we have to follow up every case.' He looked at the gun in the corner. 'At least we have some time now, he's not going to be shooting anyone else.'

'We may not have that much time,' said Donovan. 'The lock on the bathroom cabinet's been forced. I don't know what was in there to start with but now there's only gaps and aspirin.'

'God damn!' said Liz in her teeth. 'So when we find him he's going to be only a corpse with a smile on its face.'

'Depends how quick we are,' said Shapiro, suddenly brisk. 'All right, there's no point us all standing round here. Liz, you and Donovan get to work on those files. The answer has to be there. If you can find it quickly enough, maybe we can get to this chap while he's still wondering whether to mainline the morphine or have a paracetamol sandwich for lunch.

'And while you're doing that I'll go talk to Mr Hawley. If this is about a medical accident that happened in Castle General during his term as administrator, he has to know about it. If he guessed who killed Kerry Page, and let Mrs Board and Dr Saunders die rather than face a scandal, I'm going to have him.'

Liz drove. Donovan refrained from giving instructions but still leaned into the corners. 'What *is* that you're doing?' she exclaimed, exasperated.

He straightened up with a guilty start. 'Sorry. All bikers do it.'

She stared at him for a moment. 'Really?' Then she chuckled. 'Do you know what horse-riders do?' He looked sidelong at her, not knowing and not daring to speculate. 'We lean forward over hump-back bridges. As if they were jumps.'

His first thought was that he couldn't imagine her doing anything as glamorous, frivolous, and unproductive as riding a horse. His second thought was that he could imagine her riding but not doing all the less glamorous bits like falling off and mucking out and hauling bales of hay. Finally he decided he was wrong, that she'd be in her element in gumboots and armed with a shovel, that as an antidote to a week in CID keeping a horse might be nearly as good as running a motorbike. Harder to park, of course. 'Do you have a horse?'

'Yes,' she nodded. 'At home. My husband's looking after her till I get back. He won't be enjoying it. He's an art teacher. He likes the look of horses more than the reality.'

'My grandfather,' Donovan offered unexpectedly, 'was travelling head lad at one of the top racing stables in Ireland.'

'Really? Is he still alive?'

'Nah,' drawled Donovan. 'One of the bastards kicked his head in after a bad day at Fairyhouse.'

They travelled the rest of the way in silence.

THE LIST OF OPERATIONS performed by Board, Saunders, and Carson in their last month together was longer than Liz had expected. If the surgical team had been doing heart transplants it would have been easy. But they had been working through a backlog of minor corrective procedures that took thirty or forty minutes each: there were several names on each day's list and seventeen days in the month when the team was working together. The print-out ran to four sheets densely packed with names and addresses, a digest of the problem in each case, the treatment, the outcome, and dates of admission and discharge.

Liz had also obtained a copy of the register of deaths in the Castlemere area in the last month, a record of admissions to residential homes, and even—a long shot, this—prison discharges in the same period. She hoped to find a name from the operating list recurring in one of the others. She was looking for someone with an abiding hatred for the surgical team, who could do nothing about it for four years, then suddenly could. It meant scanning through a lot of information with no guarantee they'd recognize the match when they found it.

Even if they were now working along essentially the right lines the family might have left the area in the last four years so that the name would appear in the hospital list but be registered as a death in another district. If the patient was still alive, he or she might have been admitted to a specialist unit in another part of the country. Or the killer might have taken time to mourn his loss, in which case the name would figure in none of the current records. If they could find no match they would have to contact the four pages of families one by one.

There was no effective way of splitting the work between them. Liz read from the lists of dead and institutionalized, and Donovan hunted up and down the theatre list for a match. They had an interesting half-hour sorting out the various members of the Smith clan but when they had it was clear that the dead ones hadn't been operated on and the hospitalized ones hadn't died.

There were other names that recurred. When they first turned up two Edwardses they thought they'd hit paydirt. But the Edwards on the theatre list was a middle-aged man with a hernia and the dead Edwards a teenage girl. The Swann in hospital was a baby and the dead one a woman. The sick Taylor and the dead one were both young men and looked promising until they realized that the first died of his injuries in Intensive Care. He was a motorcyclist brought in as an emergency midway through the morning's operating list.

'Possible?' asked Donovan.

'Not impossible,' allowed Liz. 'But we're back to wondering why, if he's been dead four years, someone should start avenging him now. We'll check it out but I bet it's someone else.' She moved on to the next name.

After a moment it struck her that Donovan was no longer with her. Physically he was still sitting on the far side of the desk, hunched on a chair that seemed too low for him, his long legs bent like a stick insect's, his plastered forearm resting across his knees. But a gap had opened between them. The forefinger of his good hand was no longer tracing down the hospital list in response to the names she read out; his body had grown still and his face had gone distant, out of focus. She stopped reading and waited. After a minute she said quietly, 'Sergeant? What is it?'

He started and his gaze jerked round to her. His eyes were flayed. 'Nothing. Sorry, I—I just went AWOL for a minute. Where did we get to?'

She put the papers down. 'Never mind that for a moment. Are you still blaming yourself for what happened to Saunders?'

'No. No, of course not.' But there was no conviction in the way he said it.

Liz sighed. 'Donovan, listen. We're not responsible for the things we can't prevent. The man who killed him is responsible for Emil Saunders' death. Maybe Saunders gave him a reason. But all you're guilty of is trying to fit a thirty-hour day into twenty-four hours. Yes, it would be nice if we could sit on people's doorsteps until they were ready to talk to us. Once in a blue moon it would make a difference. But most of the time we'd have to neglect other duties, other people's problems, in order to do it. Your decision not to wait for Saunders was a proper one. I'm sorry it worked out badly but that was the luck of the draw. You've nothing to reproach yourself for.'

She didn't understand his fierce look. Words rushed from him in brief, savage torrent. 'Have you any idea the number of times I've been told that?'

She blinked, surprised by his vehemence. 'DI Clarke, you mean?'

'Alan. Lucy. Colleagues, acquaintances, friends, family—dear God, so many I've trouble remembering them all!' He spun off the chair with an abrupt, fluid movement as if he might leave the hurt behind, and fetched up by the window looking down at the car park. His voice was bitter. 'You must have heard of Donovan's

Luck. Even at Headquarters they've heard of Donovan's Luck.'

She didn't know whether honesty would appease or disappoint him. 'No. Sorry.' She could have left it at that. But after a moment she added, 'What do you mean?'

He looked round with a twisted parody of a smile. 'It's a bit like Hobson's Choice—it's no luck at all. I get people hurt. Sometimes I get them killed. It's never my fault. Only people who work with me, and people who know me, and in the dim and distant past people I dared care about, drop like flies round me. It's like carrying the plague, you know? I don't get it myself— OK, a bit of a side-swipe from the car that killed Alan— but mostly I'm left standing in a sea of bodies. These days I use a loose-leaf address book: it's easier to update.'

She didn't know what to say. It was tempting to dismiss it as hysteria, but though he was clearly depressed she didn't see him as either hysterical or self-indulgent. So maybe he did have bad luck. No, that wasn't what he was saying—that he *was* bad luck. To people around him. People like her.

She dismissed that with a quick shrug, as if it were an insect that had settled on her, cleared her throat, and picked up the print-out again. 'Where were we—Taylor? No, we did him. What about Gregory—Miss Marjorie Gregory, Hampton Cottages? Did anyone feel strongly enough about an eighty-seven-year-old maiden lady living in sheltered accommodation to murder three people over a botched operation four years ago?'

Donovan left the window and slouched back to his chair. He looked awkward, avoiding her gaze as if regretting his outburst. His index finger, strong, narrow, and slightly crooked like a raptor's talon, scored down the page in search of Miss Gregory. Not finding her on the first sheet he flipped to the second, then to the third. Then the moving finger stopped and tapped once, and Donovan said, 'Hold on,' in a puzzled, pensive tone that made Liz look up.

'You've got Miss Gregory too?'

'No,' he said. 'Sorry. Er—go back a bit. What have you got on Swann again?'

She read it out. 'But it's a different Swann. The hernia op was a baby. The death was a middle-aged woman.'

'Yeah. But I think it's the same family.'

EIGHT

LIZ STUDIED the relevant entries. There were no obvious connections. Certainly the address was different.

'What makes you think so?' It was possible the family had moved in the last four years, more likely that there were two Swann families in Castlemere.

'I've met them,' said Donovan. 'Well, more than that actually. It was George Swann stepped in when I was having the crap beaten out of me down at the cemetery. His wife's grave's near Alan's, she's not been there much longer. Swann was planting some flowers. He had his kid beside him in one of them buggy things.'

Liz thought about it, dismissed it. 'Coincidence. He wouldn't have a five-year-old in a pushchair.'

Donovan shook his head. 'He called the kid Danny. The baby's down on the theatre list as Daniel Swann. At the time I didn't register it but there was something wrong with the child. It kind of looks through you. Maybe it can't walk.'

'And this Mary was his wife?'

'That I can't swear to. But she died a fortnight ago and this grave's a few days older than Alan's so yes, I guess that's Mary Swann.'

They sat back, looking at each other, unsure what it meant. 'How could he blame Saunders for the death of his wife?'

Donovan shrugged. 'Search me. How could he think he's free to act if he has a retarded five-year-old to look after?'

'It doesn't hang together, does it? Do you know what he does for a living?'

'He's an antiques dealer. Shop in Castle Place, you've probably seen it—that's the address given for Mary Swann. They must have sold their house.'

'Antiques,' mused Liz. 'Not really Mac the Knife territory, is it?'

'You think not? There's big money in antiques, and it's harder to prove who owns them than a car or a video. No serial numbers. There are villains enough in the antiques trade. I just wouldn't have said George Swann was one of them.'

'What's he like?'

'Oh—pretty average. Mid-forties maybe. Decent kind of individual. Gentle, you know?' He grinned suddenly. 'You appreciate gentleness when you've just had three feet of chain wrapped round your head.' His eyes changed then, grew sharp. 'So average, in fact, he could be every third man in Castlemere.'

Liz understood. 'And he had a gun?'

'Well, yes and no. It was a gun—a pistol, not a shotgun, First World War job I think—but it wasn't capable of being fired. I checked while he was driving me to the hospital. It was in a trunk of stuff he bought once, he said, he hung on to it for fear of being held up sometime. I told you antiques wasn't that genteel a trade.'

'I suppose, though,' Liz said slowly, 'a man who could come by one gun in the way of business might come by another. What kind of car does he have?'

Something like a shock-wave swamped Donovan's expression. His head rocked back and he groaned. When he surfaced his face was rigid and there was a breathless quality to his voice. 'Oh dear God... Detective, is it? I get paid for being a detective? I *knew* what that porter said meant something to me, I just couldn't get hold of it. I don't know what kind of a car it was. I was a bit groggy, OK? But the thing you couldn't miss if you'd half an eye in your head was, it was yellow.'

THE FIRST THING new staff at Castle General learned about Desmond Hawley was that the chief administrator was three different men. With the consultants he was punctilious, with junior doctors and nurses superior, with domestic staff so overweening as to leave scant change out of rude. So none of his fellow employees would have been surprised to know that, just as he treated Inspector Graham in a different manner to Sergeant Donovan, so he treated Chief Inspector Shapiro in a different manner to Inspector Graham.

His manner was not all that had changed. His perception of how this might turn out had moved on too. He no longer believed it was possible to avoid scandal. His priority now was to establish that what happened was the fault of individual members of staff, not of the hospital.

Ushering Shapiro to a chair in his office he launched a pre-emptive strike. 'I was about to call you, Chief Inspector. I've just heard about Dr Saunders. I think I know what this is all about.' He told the story of George Swann who believed his child was a victim of medical negligence.

Shapiro stopped him to make a phone call, then asked him to continue.

'I had no idea,' insisted Hawley, 'that the poor man had become demented. I knew he blamed us for his son's condition but that's not uncommon. People don't realize that surgery is not an exact science. Every year something that works fine for ninety-nine patients makes the hundredth worse. But people think we're only doing our job when it comes out right and must have been negligent when it comes out wrong.'

'Swann accused Dr Saunders of negligence?'

The administrator sniffed. 'He accused everyone of negligence. At first he was upset, which was understandable. Later he became obsessive. He waylaid members of staff and tried to bully confessions out of them. We received letters on his behalf from half the solicitors in Castlemere. Of course I put it in the hands of our lawyers and let them deal with him. I'm a busy man, Chief Inspector: I sympathized, I assured him that what happened to his baby was nobody's fault, but I really wasn't prepared to listen to his tirades month after month.

'I said if he thought he had a case against us he must pursue it. I didn't expect him to get anywhere and he didn't. But it took him four years to accept that. At least, I thought he'd accepted it. We got a letter from his solicitor—his last solicitor—a month ago saying he was taking no further action.'

It was a text-book description of a bureaucrat stonewalling. Shapiro could imagine the effect it had on the bereaved man. 'Did you ask the surgical team about the case?'

'Of course. They said the operation went smoothly. I interviewed them individually and put to them Swann's allegation that Dr Saunders was intoxicated. They all denied it, including Staff Nurse Carson whom Swann said he had the story from. What more was I to do? I'd no reason to call them liars. I still haven't. It still seems likeliest to me that Mr Swann was wrong, that he believed it but he was wrong. People are not at their most rational when their emotions are involved.'

Shapiro nodded slowly. He refrained from observing that people are not at their most truthful when their jobs are involved either. 'It's a pity you didn't tell us this when Kerry Page was murdered.'

Mr Hawley was apologetic. 'Chief Inspector, if it had occurred to me I would have done. There was no reason to think her death had anything to do with the hospital. I understood her husband was the prime suspect.'

'And when Mrs Board was shot outside the nurses' home?'

'I remembered, of course, that they'd worked together. But I still didn't make the connection. It was four years ago, and anyway it seemed Swann had finally bowed to the inevitable. I'd told Mrs Board he'd dropped it, phoned Dr Saunders to tell him, and he said he'd let Mrs Page know—apparently he saw her from time to time, they worked for the same organization as you know. Then I drew a line under it. Only when Dr Saunders too was killed was the connection with the Swann case apparent to me.'

Shapiro breathed heavily down his ancestral nose. The man was clever: he knew stupidity wasn't a criminal act. 'If you'd told Inspector Graham what you've told me, Emil Saunders would still be alive. I don't think you're legally culpable of his death. But between you and me, Mr Hawley, I reckon you're responsible for it. If you'd been a little less concerned with the hospital's reputation and a little more concerned about the welfare of its patients and staff, none of this need have happened. Your attitude drove George Swann to a kind of madness and you let him kill three people rather than admit it. Even if the law has no call on you, I'd like to think your own conscience had.' He sighed. 'But I'd be kidding myself, wouldn't I, Mr Hawley?'

As they stared at each other across the administrator's desk the phone rang. After a long pause Hawley picked it up. Then he passed it to Shapiro. 'Your office, Chief Inspector.'

LIZ SENT A MESSAGE to Shapiro to meet them at the shop. She still didn't know how it was going to work out but she believed they were on the right trail now.

As they hurried to her car she glanced at Donovan's arm. 'If this gets rough will you be able to cope? I could second a beefy constable.'

Donovan shook his head. 'Swann won't get rough. I told you, he's a gentle man.'

Liz gave him a sceptical look. 'Dr Saunders might not agree with you.'

Donovan rocked his good hand. 'What happened to Saunders was four years in the making. You can build up a lot of hate in four years. I don't think that basically he's a violent man—a man who'd react violently to any-one crossing him.'

'He might consider being arrested for murder as rather more than just being crossed,' murmured Liz.

'No. It's like you said: he doesn't care what happens to him. If we get to him in time he'll go to prison; if we don't he'll kill himself. It's all the same to him. He's done what he set out to do, he doesn't care what happens now.'

Liz drove the dark canyons of narrow streets hemmed in by high black buildings rather faster than she could have justified to Traffic Branch.

Castle Place was the oldest part of town, older even than the canal basin and the warehouses. The current buildings were Georgian—workaday rather than Grand Design Georgian but pleasing in their proportions, although unfortunate alterations, in the way of plate-glass shop-fronts, neon signs, and low-maintenance energy efficient double-glazing, had been added to many of them. The ruins on Castle Mount, not much more now than a jumble of stone piers towering against the sky, glowered down in mute disapproval.

Castle Antiques was one of the prettier buildings in the square. The ground floor had been painted Wedgwood blue with the frames of the twelve-pane windows picked out in white. The name and that of George Swann, Proprietor, arched in curly script over the elegant fan light of the doorcase. It all looked original. Of course, an antiques dealer would have the inside track when it came to restoration.

But the other thing Liz noticed about Castle Antiques was that while a great deal of work had been done to it, with both skill and taste employed in its renovation, very little had been done recently. The paint was showing signs of wear and a cracked drain-pipe had left a trail of mossy damp down one side of the frontage. With a little imagination, Liz thought, you could suppose it had been untouched for four years.

The heavy wooden door, cherry-red, was locked. A card in the window read *Closed*. There was no sign of movement in the shop or at the windows above in response to Liz's knock. She stared at the building in dismay. That door wouldn't yield to a good kick: it would take tools and time and they had neither. She could have broken a window but the narrow mullions would have kept a child out and there were locks on the fastenings.

'Round the back,' Donovan said curtly, and she turned to see him sprint off round the corner. Abandoning the unassailable front she followed.

A narrow entry gave access to the back yards. Logic said there was one but you had to know where to look, for it opened on to the side-street through what looked like someone's garage door. Diving through in Donovan's wake Liz found herself in the kind of townscape where the Artful Dodger would have felt at home: close, sunless, grimy, confusing. It did not escape her notice that Donovan seemed at home here too.

He'd counted the front doors on Castle Place and now he was counting the yard doors. When the numbers tallied he threw the door open almost without breaking pace. Liz, breathless, was on his heels as he crossed to the back of the house through a yard full of broken drawers and wardrobe doors: the bones of old furniture that had gone there to die.

The back door was up a flight of stone steps; it too was locked. But the kitchen window was modern and big enough to admit whatever light found its way into the yard. Donovan hurled half a Windsor chair through it and glass crashed into the stone sink within and on to the steps without.

But his wrist was a significant handicap and Liz couldn't see how he could climb over to the window one-handed, though she had no doubt that if he'd been alone he would have tried. A detective sergeant with a damaged wrist had his limitations but one with a broken neck would be a positive liability. She laid her hand on his arm. 'Step aside, Sergeant. This is a job for Wonder Woman.'

While Donovan stared, steadying herself on his shoulder she climbed first on to the rail, then across to the windowsill. Avoiding the glass as best she could she snaked through and disappeared inside. A moment later the key turned in the lock and she opened the door, sucking a cut finger. 'Impressed?'

He shook his head. 'You'd never catch the real Wonder Woman bleeding.'

They moved into the house, keeping together, unsure what they would find: a multiple murderer, the body of a multiple murderer, or an irate antiques dealer demanding compensation for his broken window.

The kitchen no longer performed its original function but, with the rest of the ground floor, served the shop. Two of the four rooms connected through an arch to make a showroom, behind were an office and the kitchen which was used for cleaning and repairs. They checked each room but found no one. Liz moved towards the stairs.

Without seeming to hurry Donovan got there first. 'My turn, ma'am.'

She was about to order him aside but thought better of it. Unfit as he was for any kind of physical encounter, he needed his self-esteem more than he needed her protection. She gave a faint smile. 'I'm not going to fight you for the privilege.'

He grinned. 'I'm only going first 'cause I know he hasn't got the shotgun.'

Half-way up the stairs, too late to change places, Liz murmured, 'At least, we know he hasn't got *that* shotgun.'

On the first landing they had a choice of three doors and another staircase. Behind the nearest door Liz found a dining room furnished with good but slightly shabby pieces in a variety of periods and styles: stock which had failed to sell. From the dry, slightly stale air Liz thought it hadn't been used much recently. Donovan found the new kitchen with unwashed pots in the sink.

The third door was a living room with the television, a
tea-tray on a low table, and in one corner a playpen
where a rabbit in evening dress hung by one ear from
the bars. Apart from the rabbit, which greeted them with
a knowing look, there was no one in any of the rooms.

Donovan indicated the stairs and Liz nodded. She
said softly, 'If he's here, that's where he has to be.'

There were two bedrooms and a bathroom. Donovan
checked the bathroom but it was empty so they tried
the bedroom doors.

The master bedroom was a large room at the front of
the house decorated in pastel chintzes and featuring a
walnut wardrobe, an oak one, and a chest of drawers
and dressing table in rich red mahogany. Brocade curtains made for larger windows hung from a vast pelmet
pleated to fit. The curtains were pulled across the window but showed the universal sign of having been
drawn by a man: they didn't quite meet in the middle.

Swann was sitting on the half-tester bed. He glanced
up at her entry with a slightly surprised but not wholly
displeased look and smiled. His wife had trained him
well: he'd taken his shoes off before putting his feet on
the bed.

'Boss.' Donovan was in the open door of the other
room, half in and half out. The stillness of his long body
and the timbre of his voice said he'd found something.
Liz backed out of the master bedroom and joined him.
When she touched his arm he stood aside to let her
through.

It was a child's room, decorated in primary colours,
with circus scenes on the walls and a hot-air balloon for
a lampshade. Rainbow-coloured curtains had been
drawn more carefully than the brocade ones next door.
A child's bed lay along the wall and a duvet covered

in cartoon characters was humped over a child-sized mound.

Liz stepped softly across the floor. She didn't want to startle a sleeping child but she needed to know if he was all right. As she approached the bed she said, quietly reassuring, 'Are you asleep, Danny? Don't be afraid—I'm a policewoman, I'm just here to see you're all right.'

There was no response from the bed. Liz wondered if the little boy was genuinely asleep or cowering in silent terror under the bedclothes at the sound of a stranger in his room. She reached out to ease the duvet away from his head, still talking in the same quiet, friendly voice. 'I like your room, Danny. Did you choose the pictures? I like this one of the clown. Do you like the circus, Danny? Does your dad take you sometimes?'

Her outstretched fingers reached the upper edge of the duvet. 'Will you come out for a minute while we have a quick chat?' she asked. 'Danny?' She lifted the top of the duvet.

The little white face that greeted her was set in such sweet repose, the eyes shut, the long lashes curving down to the rounded cheeks, the rosebud lips pursed in a thoughtful pout, that at first she thought all her reassuring noises had failed to rouse him. With a careful fingertip she brushed a lick of fair hair off his satiny brow.

Donovan heard the breath catch in her throat. A stride brought him to her side.

The satin skin was as cold as ice, as smoothly unresponsive as wax. Nothing she could do would startle Danny Swann from his sleep. He was dead. The little body was already stiffening.

After Emil Saunders she had thought nothing would shock her again. But she was shocked by this. The eyes she raised to Donovan's were deep with tragedy: this beautiful child lying dead in his bed in his perfect child's bedroom. Her voice cracked. 'Donovan, his *son!* He's killed his own son!'

Donovan's good hand fastened on her arm with enough pressure to steady her. She was glad of his strength. Gradually a little of it seemed to pass from his body into hers, warming the cold veins. By degrees the horror settled in her brain, finding its own level, no longer monopolizing her thinking. With hardly a tremble she said, 'He's in the other room.'

Donovan moved towards the door. 'You stay with the kid.'

But there was nothing she could do for Danny Swann. She went with Donovan into the main bedroom.

Swann looked up again with his amiable smile as if they were customers in his shop not police officers in his bedroom. He recognized Donovan, more by the plaster than the face, nodded a friendly greeting. Then he saw the hollowness in Liz's eyes and nodded again, understandingly. 'You've seen Danny.'

'Did you kill him?'

There was sorrow but nothing she recognized as guilt in Swann's voice and he answered without hesitation. 'Yes, I did.'

'How?'

There was a small brown bottle on the dressing table by the bed. Beside it lay a syringe charged with an all but colourless liquid. 'With that. Morphine. I got it from Dr Saunders. I told him it was for Danny. It did a good job, he's safe now. Danny's safe with his mother, and if you'd been five minutes later I'd be on my way to join them.' He glanced between Liz and Donovan and said, as if he already knew the answer, 'I don't suppose—?'

Liz shook her head once, sharply. 'Sergeant.'

Donovan put himself between Swann and the syringe. Swann, resigned, smiled at him. 'How's the wrist now?'

'Fine,' said Donovan. He didn't know what else to say.

Liz's voice was hard. 'You killed Dr Saunders as well? And Maggie Board? And Kerry Page?' At each name Swann nodded again. Liz's iron control cracked. 'In God's name, man, why? And why Danny? Why your son?'

Swann swung his legs to the floor and stood up. His face was curiously untroubled. 'I will tell you,' he promised. 'Everything. I want you to understand. I'm not a bad man. I'm an ordinary man. One thing, though, before we go. Can I say goodbye to Danny?'

Liz's eyes widened. She said nothing, but her eyes said: You killed him, and now you want to say goodbye?

Swann's tone was quietly reproachful. 'I loved my son, officer. Everything I did was for him. Only a minute, that's all. Stay with me if you like. I'm not going anywhere.'

In the bottom of the house sounded a hammering like hollow thunder: Shapiro seeking admittance. Liz moved towards the stairs. 'You have as long as it takes me to answer the door. My sergeant will stay with you. Then we're going to the police station and you're going to tell me why four people are dead.'

'Five,' said Swann.

'Five?' Liz's neck-hairs prickled up. 'There was a fifth?'

'My wife. When the inquest is held the coroner will find that she took her own life while the balance of her mind was disturbed. But Mary was as much a victim as Danny was. Two innocent victims; too much innocent blood.'

Shivering, Liz went to answer the door.

III

ONE

DONOVAN DIDN'T COME to the police station with them. 'If you can spare me for half an hour I'll drop in on Page, tell him we've got the guy and what it was all about. I don't want him hearing it on the radio. Anyway, I'd like to see if he's OK. I'm uneasy about him. This was bound to knock the stuffing out of him, I'm not saying the man isn't entitled to grieve but somehow it's more than that. He could end up needing a shrink, you know?'

Shapiro knew. A few days ago he'd been thinking the same about Donovan. 'That's all right, you go. We've only the gory details to get from Swann, we'll have this finished by tonight.'

Donovan's glance lingered. 'Then tomorrow—?'

Shapiro nodded wearily. 'Yes, Sergeant. Tomorrow we'll see if we can make CID history by pulling DI Clarke's killer out of a hat.'

'You know whose hat, don't you?' said Donovan in a forcible murmur.

Shapiro spoke like a man saying something he's already said several times and expects to have to say several times more. 'I know what you believe, lad. I know you're very likely right. But I still have no evidence against him, and until I have I'm not jeopardizing the case by going at him like a bull at a gate. If he did what you think I want to make sure of him.'

Donovan nodded, mollified if not wholly convinced.

'I'll go see Page.'

'You do that,' said Shapiro.

GEORGE SWANN, local businessman, devoted husband and father, and mass murderer, was as good as his word. At the station, still speaking mainly to Liz, he told them everything—what he had done, how he had done it, why.

'I was thirty-nine when Danny was born and Mary was thirty-six. We'd been a bit slow off the mark: we didn't marry till we were in our thirties and though we wanted children time was against us. We had other things to be grateful for. The business was doing well, Mary was made head of department. She was a teacher, did I tell you that?' George Swann looked up with pride in his eyes. Liz nodded wordlessly.

'She was a fine teacher,' Swann went on, 'everybody said so. I wish you could have known her, Inspector. I wish you could have known us both then. You'd have liked us. If someone had told you that one of us would commit suicide and the other kill four people, you'd have sent for a psychiatrist.

'Then one day, long after we'd given up, we were no longer a childless professional couple on the brink of middle age, we were expecting a baby. Do you have children, Inspector?' Liz shook her head. 'I don't mean to be rude, but until it happens you can't imagine how your life changes. Your job, your house, your nice car, all the things that mattered to you, suddenly they mean nothing beside this developing bump. Your life revolves around it long before it's born. I'm telling you this so that you'll understand how devastated we were by what happened.

'He was a beautiful baby. You've seen him.' He was

still addressing Liz, though Shapiro was in the interview room with them, as if he needed something from her: understanding or forgiveness. But he'd be a long time waiting. Liz resented the implication that, as a woman, she would be more tolerant of crimes motivated by love. 'He was still a beautiful child, even afterwards, but as a baby he was lovely enough to make you cry.' He sniffed apologetically. 'I'm sorry, I'm embarrassing you. I'll just tell the story.

'He had a little hernia. It was nothing much, our GP said it was a common problem with boys, a little op would fix it. He referred us to Castle General and they said it'd be a good idea to do it fairly soon: not because it was dangerous but so that we could forget about it. It was no big deal, it wouldn't cause him any more problems.' He gave a little laugh, half angry, half tragic. 'And it never has. They flushed my child's brain out but by God, that hernia's never given us a day's anxiety.'

The first intimation that something was wrong came when Mrs Board told them that Danny wasn't coming out of the anaesthetic as quickly as he should. A ventilator was helping him breathe. After two days they took him off the ventilator and he breathed for himself but still he showed no signs of waking.

'Mrs Board said it was an allergic reaction to the anaesthetic, something no one could have predicted. She couldn't say when, or even if, he'd come out of it now. So that was it: our brief foray into normal parenthood. Then we became statistics.

'He was in a coma for six days, then he started to stir and finally woke up. But it wasn't our Danny who came back. It wasn't anybody's child, just a little pink machine taking in food at one end and ejecting waste at the other—never looking at you, never smiling. He

never even cried. If he was hungry or wet or the sun
was in his eyes, he just lay there. Like a log. Sooner or
later someone fed him or changed him, or the sun
moved away. Danny could wait. Danny was good at
waiting.

'All this time he was in the hospital. They wired him
up to different instruments and compared graphs, and
stood over him nodding and clucking as if they knew
what they were doing. Finally they admitted it was mas-
sive, irreversible brain damage. He'd be a baby, wholly
dependent on someone—Mary and me or an institu-
tion—for the rest of his life. When there was nothing
more they could do we brought him home.'

As the shock wore off the Swanns wanted to know
more about what had gone wrong. At first there was no
time, and no spare emotional capacity, to go into it. But
when Danny was home and they'd found their feet—
'Mary gave up her job and we moved over the shop so
I'd never be more than a shout away'—they wanted
more information. Not because they wanted to blame
someone but because this was how their life was going
to be, how their son was going to be, and they needed
to understand how it had happened.

'I wasn't ready for the hostility we met. Mrs Board
acted as if I'd developed an unhealthy preoccupation.
She used jargon I couldn't understand and said it was
no one's fault and there was nothing to be gained from
keeping going over it. This was my son's life she was
talking about, and the way my wife and I had to live
now, and all she cared about was getting rid of me. I
didn't deserve that. If she owed me nothing more she
owed me an explanation. I went to see the chief administrator.'

'Hawley,' said Liz, the trace of a thaw in her voice.

She knew what trying to get information out of Hawley was like.

'Mr Hawley,' agreed Swann. 'I said I'd clearly got Mrs Board on a busy day and perhaps he'd get me the information I wanted.'

'But he didn't,' murmured Shapiro.

'He did not. He said there was no information to be had: it was just one of those things, like lightning—it always can strike, it seldom does. No one was to blame for Danny's condition. It was time we accepted that.

'It was the repeated insistence that nobody was to blame that made me wonder if perhaps somebody was. That maybe Danny was the victim of an accident rather than an Act of God.'

But Swann's solicitor advised against pursuing a claim. If something had gone wrong in the operating theatre the only witnesses were the surgical team who clearly weren't talking about it. The chances of finding independent corroboration were so small that the best advice she could give him was to forget it.

'And she was right. But it took me four years and every penny we had to find out. I tried to talk to Dr Saunders. He wouldn't see me, referred me back to Mr Hawley. He was working at the Feyd Clinic by then so I made an appointment under a false name and saw him there. It didn't do any good. When I asked what had happened he repeated the same line about an allergic reaction. It didn't happen often, he said, but it was always a risk with surgery. And he said—'

For the first time in the telling of his story George Swann's voice broke. Until now he had managed to preserve an almost eerie calm, a detachment from the tragedy that had enveloped his family, as if now he'd brought it to an end he was able to step back and view it dispassionately. But the anguish was there, under the surface, suppressed but not dealt with, and momentarily it burgeoned forth in the twisting of his lips and the soaring note of his voice. 'And that man said to me that I couldn't just order a new nose here, a different shape of ears there, without being aware that surgery always carries some risk and shouldn't be entered into frivolously.

'He said that to *me!* I let him take my son because the best medical opinion I could get was that he needed the operation, and he'd come back as a kind of doll— one of those dolls that opens its eyes if you prop it up a certain way. And he dared accuse me of frivolity!' He swallowed. After a moment he went on. 'I knew then that there *had* been negligence, and who was responsible. Only a man with something to hide could be that cruel. But I still had to prove it.'

He spoke to Staff Nurse Carson. Kerry had been deeply disturbed to find herself assisting a gas-happy anaesthetist but she didn't want to talk about it. The surgeon who had chosen to cover for him was still a senior staff-member in the hospital where she worked, even though she had transferred to another department, and she felt she had to protect herself. But she also felt Swann was owed an explanation, and at last he got it.

'They didn't realize at first. He wasn't reeling drunk, they thought he was just in good form. There was a real party atmosphere going. But midway through the operation Mrs Board realized Danny was turning blue. There was an obstruction in the oxygen: if Saunders had been doing his job he'd have seen it and fixed it and there'd have been no problem. But he was too full of the joys of spring to pay much heed to a minor op so

Danny'd been without oxygen for a couple of minutes before anyone noticed.

'Even then Saunders couldn't pull himself together. Mrs Board took over. She got the oxygen flowing, flushed Danny's lungs out, gave him some kind of a stimulant. The nurse said she couldn't have done any more or done it any quicker. Then they had to wait to see what damage had been done.

'Dr Saunders recovered before Danny did. He begged them not to report him. It couldn't do Danny any good, it could only ruin him. He swore it wouldn't happen again. The Staff Nurse wouldn't listen. But Mrs Board saw her afterwards and said that she wouldn't be making a complaint. She too had suspected Saunders was intoxicated but now she thought she'd misjudged him. If Miss Carson was confident of her facts she could file a complaint but Mrs Board would not feel able to support her.'

'*Why?*' hissed Liz. 'Why would she do that? Protect him—after what he'd done.' Then her tone changed. 'Oh—'

Swann nodded. 'Yes. She was in love. She was a middle-aged divorcee, and Saunders was just old enough to attract her and immature enough to play on that. Mrs Board had been alone long enough to take it for the real thing. She cared for him, couldn't bring herself to ruin him. But she told him if she saw him in theatre again she'd have him struck off.'

'Why didn't you go to the authorities?' asked Shapiro.

Swann looked at him as if he were mad. 'Do you think I didn't try? I tried Hawley. He set his lawyers on me. I tried to brief lawyers of my own: they asked for evidence. When I tried to produce Staff Nurse

Carson I found she'd been got at. Between talking to me and talking to my solicitor she changed her mind. She said she'd made a mistake, that in the heat of the moment she'd thought Saunders was negligent but she now realized it was the inevitable chaos of dealing with an emergency. She insisted that everyone involved in Danny's operation had done their best for him and what happened was an unavoidable accident. A month later she took up her new job at the Rosedale Nursing Home. I suppose you know it's owned by the same people as the Feyd Clinic where Dr Saunders worked.'

'You could have tried us,' Liz suggested softly.

'Oh, yes? You'd have listened, would you? I was the distraught parent of a brain-damaged child. I hadn't been present at the operation, and all those who were now agreed that everything possible had been done. You'd have done what Hawley did: given me coffee, a little sympathy, and a word of advice to the effect that accusing a doctor of negligence in the absence of concrete evidence could prove expensive.

'I have to say he was right. I hired private detectives. I consulted lawyers. It wasn't just the compensation that Danny was entitled to: I wanted a public acknowledgement that what happened to him was preventable and the attempt to cover it up was wrong. I kept it up for more than three years. I spent every penny we had, I let the business slide, and in the end I'd achieved nothing. Nothing. When the last lawyer expressed the view that we'd exhausted all the options and sent his bill, I didn't have the money to pay him. All we had left was the shop, the flat, and a son who was going to need looking after for the rest of his life.

'I suppose it didn't seem very much to live for. I hadn't given Mary the support she needed. I was too preoccupied with my crusade to see how faded she'd become, how run away to nothing. After she gave up her job she only had me and Danny, neither of us fit company for an intelligent woman. The prospect of losing the flat was too much. She couldn't face it. She wouldn't face it. The future held nothing for her: if we got through this crisis there'd have been another one. She didn't want a life that was only struggling today and dreading tomorrow. Suicide didn't just seem an easy way out, it was one. I miss her—oh God how I miss her—but I don't blame her.'

When he found her Swann wanted to follow, immediately, take Danny and hurry after her. 'But I had something to do first. They were owed something for all the misery. I'd tried to get legal redress but the system was loaded against ordinary people. I tried to play the game but they moved the goal-posts: now we were going to play by my rules, the main one being that every action has a reaction and you can't escape it by lying.'

So he killed them, the nurse first because her offence was least. 'I had to punish her. She shouldn't have lied. But I didn't want to frighten her. She only got three seconds' warning, then she was dead.'

Then the surgeon. 'I don't think Mrs Board realized Mrs Page's death had anything to do with her. When I aimed the gun at her she was surprised. She didn't remember me. There was no time to explain: I shot her and drove away in the confusion.'

He smiled at Liz then, so far as she could tell with genuine amusement. 'I went to the cemetery to tell Mary. To tell her there was only one more and then we'd be on our way. That was when I got involved in the incident with your sergeant. I couldn't think what to do for the best. I'd just come from shooting Mrs

Board, I still had the shotgun in the car—if that was found I'd never get Saunders and he was the one I wanted most. But I couldn't watch four thugs beat the living daylights out of someone when I had the power to stop them. I didn't dare produce the shotgun, though, I had to gamble on the Luger being enough to scare them off. Thank God it was. Then when he said he was a policeman—! My heart was in my mouth till I could get him to the hospital.'

Finally he described how he had dealt with Saunders. For the first time he showed signs of remorse. 'It all got out of hand, rather. I wanted to show him the enormity of what he'd done, to feel it for himself. Once would have been enough. But I enjoyed watching him suffer. I didn't think you could cram enough hurting into the few minutes I had to pay him for what he'd done. But I was wrong. I had a better cause than vengeance.'

WHEN SWANN'S statement was complete Shapiro delivered him to the holding cells, then took Liz outside for the fresh air they both needed. The police station, like most buildings in Castlemere, was an old structure adapted to its present use: from its genesis as a private house it had retained a small back garden and access to one of the canals. They walked along the towpath side by side, easy in their familiarity, Shapiro with his hands in his pockets, Liz with her head tipped back to drink cool air. The spectre of Emil Saunders, suffocating by inches, haunted her still.

After a while Shapiro said, 'You know the saddest aspect of all this? It's that five people are dead, and one's going to prison for the rest of his life, and actually there wasn't a genuinely bad person among them.'

Liz shot him a startled glance. 'You don't consider Swann a bad man?'

'Lord, no,' said Shapiro, breathing the words like a benediction. 'Wrong-headed, certainly. Arguably insane. But bad? If ever a man was driven literally to distraction by events over which he had no control, that man was George Swann. He tried to act properly. The system frustrated him, shut him out. He had either to accept the unfairness of it or fight back.' He shook his head, bemused. 'Who'd have looked at George Swann and guessed he'd fight?'

'Saunders, then.'

Shapiro shook his head. 'Saunders wasn't a bad man either. He was a weak man, a foolish one, but he never meant to create this situation. What he did was reprehensible but he's not the first to need Dutch courage to do a stressful job.'

'He let Swann bankrupt himself rather than admit his fault. He played on the affection of one colleague and the anxiety of another when both women wanted to tell the truth. He bribed Kerry Page to change her story. He got her the job at Rosedale, and he went on seeing her—he said as much to Hawley, what Julian Perrin saw confirms it—to keep her on his side.'

'You think she was blackmailing him?'

'Probably not. He had influence at the place where she worked, she couldn't threaten him without making problems for herself. Once the time for telling was past they had to keep one another sweet. But he couldn't lean on Maggie Board, so he pretended to love her.'

'He was afraid, Liz! It was too late to do anything for the baby so he tried to save himself. Irresponsible as he was, Emil Saunders never meant to hurt anyone.'

They had reached a bend in the canal. Ahead dark

buildings loomed over the ribbon of water until they swallowed it entirely and it plunged into the darkness of Mere Basin.

Remembering an earlier conversation, and changing the subject but only a little, Liz said, 'Whatever was Donovan going on about? That is a strange young man.'

Shapiro grimaced. 'Isn't he just? But he's a good copper, Liz. I know he gets up your nose but try to remember that. He's worth the trouble he causes. Get him on your side and you'll never have a stauncher ally. His heart's in the right place, he's all the guts you could ask for, and he has a better mind than you might think from talking to him. But strange—yes, I really couldn't argue on that. What was he saying?'

'I'm not sure. Something about things happening round him and it never being his fault.'

Shapiro nodded sombrely. 'Donovan's Luck.'

She looked at him in surprise. 'That's right, that's what he said. You're not telling me anybody else believes in it?'

'Alan Clarke didn't.'

'But Alan Clarke's—' She stopped, her eyes widening.

'Quite,' said Shapiro, walking on.

'It's true, then? People who work with him get hurt?'

He gave her a laconic smile. 'Want a transfer?'

'Of course not,' she said testily. 'But—'

She was about to ask where the myth began and how much of it was founded in fact. But they heard feet running on the towpath and turned to see a constable sprinting after them. As he came within ear-shot he stopped and panted, 'Message for you, sir. Will you go to Rosedale Avenue right away? Sergeant Donovan says he can prove it was murder and who did it.'

Liz was confused. 'Of course it was murder. We've got the murderer. We've got a confession.'

The constable made allowances for the fact that she was new, didn't yet appreciate the single-mindedness of DS Donovan's style. 'Sorry, ma'am, not the Swann case. DI Clarke. Sergeant Donovan reckons he can prove who murdered DI Clarke.'

TWO

JULIAN PERRIN answered Page's door. He looked pale and drawn, crumpled as if he'd spent too long in the same clothes. But his eyes warmed at the sight of Donovan and he practically dragged him inside. 'Ladysmith is relieved,' he whispered dramatically.

Donovan knew better than to ask where Lady Smith fitted into all this. He glanced round what he could see of the flat from the hall. 'David's here, is he?'

'Oh, he's here all right,' said Perrin. 'He shouldn't be. He should be in a psychiatric unit under the care of someone who knows more about depressive illness than I do. But he won't leave here. So I sit with him and the hours pass. Every time he goes to the bathroom I wonder if I missed something—I moved the razor, the aspirin, and the Harpic but there's nothing so ingenious as a would-be suicide. And every time I go to the bathroom I wonder if he'll still be here when I come out.'

Donovan whistled in his teeth. 'That bad?'

'Oh yes.' Everything in his tone and manner confirmed it.

'What can we do for him?'

'Stay with him,' Perrin said simply. 'We can't force him to go anywhere. But I can stay with him. I've told the hospital I won't be in for a while. They didn't like it but what the hell, I'm a nurse, if I can't help sick people who can? But listen, Sergeant, I have to get out for half an hour—some things I need, some things I have to do. Honestly, half an hour would do it. Can you stay with him till I get back?'

Donovan was anxious to get out of the house as well. He was here from duty not inclination. He was itching to return to what remained for him the important business of proving that Jack Carney killed Alan Clarke. It seemed now that closing the file on Kerry Page wouldn't be that easy. But Donovan wasn't a social worker: he might feel for the bereaved man but he could achieve more elsewhere.

'Sure,' he said tiredly. 'I have to talk to him anyway.'

'You're a *dear,*' averred Perrin, disconcertingly, as he fled for the landing.

Donovan found Page in the cluttered little living room. Not reading, not watching TV, just sitting. He didn't look up at the sound of the door.

He still hadn't shaved, washed, or changed his clothes. An aura of apathy surrounded him like cigarette smoke. The flat was neater—because Perrin was there, Donovan supposed, he'd be as uncomfortable amid squalor as a cat with butter on its paws—but it emphasized rather than disguised the little island of misery in the corner of the room.

Donovan knew something about misery. He knew the power of it, how it clung to the body of its victim like a vampire, cloaking his spirit in darkness, drinking his soul. Because of the long dark nights when Donovan had heard its wings beating over his head it frightened him in a way that less personal horrors did not. But he had to stay until Perrin returned so he might as well do what he'd come here for. Perhaps knowing the reason for what happened would help Page deal with it.

'Mr Page?' He didn't look round. Donovan hoisted a hip on the edge of the dresser in front of him and perched there, cradling his plaster, like a stork taking a breather en route to deliver a baby. 'I thought you'd want to know. We have him—the man who shot Kerry. It dates back to something that happened at the hospital, before you knew her.'

He gave a brief digest of what he knew—he'd left before hearing the full explanation but even if he'd known more Page could not have taken it in. Even keeping to the outline, using simple words and short sentences, Donovan felt that the effort of understanding was almost more than Page could manage. He made no response. Donovan couldn't be sure if anything he was saying was reaching him, filtering into Page's brain through the complex layers of rage, grief, misery, and despair.

The casual observer would not have listed rage among the emotions swamping David Page. But Donovan had been there. He knew that of the various states that could mimic calm, one was a turmoil so violent that given any rein at all it could tear a man apart. Donovan was uneasy in his company, not because he didn't understand David Page but because he understood him too well. They were vulnerable to the same demons: Donovan looked at Page and saw not only a man in distress but a reflection of his own frailty. His instincts told him to get away from Page before the infection consuming him identified another host.

But on a less primitive level he was concerned what happened to Page. The man was manifestly failing to cope and somebody had to try and help him. Donovan had neither training nor talent for such a role but at least until Perrin came back he was stuck with it. He ventured, 'If you need help getting things organized there are some people I can call.'

'I don't need any help.'

'Suppose I talk to your boss.'

Page's head rocked back in a peal of laughter except that no sound came. 'And tell him what? That I've lost control of myself so he should put me in charge of one of his aircraft? Tell me, Sergeant, would you be happy in an aeroplane I was flying?'

'Not *now*,' agreed Donovan. 'Of course you can't fly now. But this'll pass. I know it doesn't feel like it, it feels it's going to last for ever, but it won't. You'll be able to do anything you could do before, including your job. And it'll pass quicker,' he added sharply, 'if you stop wallowing in it.'

That provoked a reaction. Page's eyes kindled. 'You think I'm enjoying this? That maybe it was worth losing my wife for the sheer fun of having do-gooders stalk me with paper hankies and Freud? You have no idea how I feel. You think that losing your wife is like losing your job, or crashing your car, or having your dog run over—upsetting at the time but these things happen and life goes on.

'Only it isn't like that. It's like somebody reached into the body of you and ripped out an organ you can't live without. And the flesh is throbbing, and the wound is bleeding, and the nerves are screaming, and you know that any moment the pain'll overwhelm you and you'll go down. And then you'll die because it isn't possible to go on living after something that vital's been ripped out of you, however many people tell you to pull yourself together. So you wait for it to end. And after four days you're still waiting. Still dying and not yet dead. That's what it feels like. Like being butchered in slow motion. How dare you tell a man with his guts hanging out to pull himself together?'

'I do understand,' Donovan began.

Page wouldn't let him continue. 'No, you don't. You don't begin to understand. Your boss got killed: do you suppose that remotely qualifies you to judge real bereavement, real grief?'

Donovan had had enough of this. He'd supposed that if Page would talk about what had happened that would be the first step in coming to terms with it. Well, Page was talking all right. He was talking as if the cavity inside him had filled up not with blood but with words; as if a dam had cracked and all the words that had built up behind it were flooding out. But it wasn't Kerry he was talking about. He was talking about himself—his loss, his pain. In his agony was a powerful streak of self-pity. He couldn't see how he could manage alone.

'So who gave you a monopoly on suffering?' snarled Donovan, his patience exhausted. 'You lost your wife. I'm sorry. George Swann lost his wife, his son, his business, and his home, and he's going to be an old man before he walks free. That's my idea of losing everything. You're young, you've got everything ahead of you. You can get over this, if you want to.'

'Swann!' Page's voice soared till it cracked. 'You want me to feel sorry for the man who murdered my wife? Because four years ago a doctor made a mistake and Kerry was too scared to report him? OK, it was hard to have that happen to his baby. Life is hard sometimes. And then you die.'

Donovan had his mouth open to snap back when Page's words hit him in the belly, knocking the breath out of him. His eyes rounded, otherwise his expression froze.

After a pause so long the electric silence crackled he managed, '*What* did you say?'

Page stared at him irritably. 'What's the matter with you, aren't you even *listening?* I said it was tough on him to have that happen to his child. But it didn't give him the right to murder three people. He had no right to kill Kerry.'

'No—no, you didn't,' stumbled Donovan, white-faced, shaking his head. 'You said it was hard. You said, "Life's hard, and then you die."'

'So?' demanded Page, exasperated almost beyond bearing.

So he'd heard those words before. Those very words, that odd dour expression that he'd never met anywhere else. Lying in the dirt under the viaduct behind the gas-works, his vision a slice of tail-lights and shiny shoes, his body a pulsing mass of hurts and his mind numb with terror because he knew the car was coming back for him and he couldn't get himself out of the way. And the man standing over him had rolled him, lifting his shoulder with the toe of one shoe for a better look at his face. And seeing he was still alive, still at least marginally conscious, he'd said, 'Life's hard, Donovan. And then you die.'

That was the thing buried in his subconscious that Shapiro had stirred up, that he'd known was worth digging for. He knew the man had said something to him. Concussion, and a degree of terror he couldn't cope with, had blanked it out; but he'd known there was something distinctive about it, something he would recognize when he heard it again. He thought it was the voice. But it was that: that lugubrious little aphorism. That, and the fact that the man knew his name.

For the briefest of moments he considered the possibility that David Page was the man in the car. But it made no sense. Page wasn't a killer: all his destructive urges were aimed at himself. Still it had to be more than random chance. There had to be a connection. The killer heard that expression from Page or Page heard it from the killer. He breathed out in a soft explosion, 'Where the hell did you hear that?'

Page stared at him as if doubting his sanity. 'My wife's dead. Kerry's dead, and the people are dead all over this God-damned town, and you're worrying where I heard a God-damned Russian proverb?'

'Is that what it is? A Russian proverb? Page, for pity's sake, try and remember! It's important—I promise you it's important. You heard it recently? Where—who said it?'

'I don't know,' said Page, petulantly, offended by the shift of the conversation away from his troubles.

Donovan fought with a devil on his shoulder. He knew where Page had heard it—where he must have heard it, he had the man in his aeroplane only a week ago. The devil on his shoulder could see no harm in reminding Page of this. But Donovan wanted evidence that would stand up in court, and the connection was tenuous enough without the defence counsel being able to claim that the name of the accused was suggested to the witness by a police officer. The devil thought he was fussing. The value of the connection was not that it would stand up in court but that, deftly used, it would prise out a confession. Page would never have to testify to the genesis of the improbable epithet.

But what if he does, Donovan asked the devil.

Then lie, the devil said.

'I remember,' said Page, just in time to save Donovan from the prospect of perjury. 'Last week, the run I did to Cartmel. There was a pile-up in the third race and one of the fallers broke a leg. Coming back Mr Carney said a friend of his had big money on it. Then they both chuckled and the other one said, 'Life's hard, then you die.'''

'The other one?' Donovan's voice was so low as to be barely audible.

'Terry something. McMeekin. Terry McMeekin.'

The phone was in the hall. 'Stay here,' said Donovan. 'I'll be right back.'

HE MET HIS INSPECTOR and chief inspector on the stairs and took them up to Page's flat. Page was still slumped in his chair in the corner of the room, but the aura of despair that had hung over him had given way to the faintly electric crackle of incredulous annoyance. Where sympathy and concern had failed to reach him, the sheer tactlessness of Donovan's reaction had goaded Page to an altogether human and healthy regard for his own importance. He was sulking because Donovan wanted to talk about somebody else's troubles.

Liz greeted him quietly, received a sullen nod in return. The last time they met she'd been working up to charging him with the murder of his wife.

Shapiro had taken longer coming up the stairs and was out of breath. He still sought Page's permission before he sat down. Then he said, 'Sergeant Donovan thinks you can help us clear up another matter, Mr Page. He says you know how DI Clarke died.'

'Does he?' Page's whole attitude was unhelpful. 'It's news to me.'

Shapiro's head gave a little jerk and he frowned. 'You mean it isn't true?'

'I don't know what he's talking about. I've understood almost nothing he's said since he came up here.'

Liz was watching Donovan. Donovan was watching

Page and trying hard not to intervene. She said levelly, 'Sergeant? Can you explain?'

So Donovan told them what Page had said, and how it had hit him like a fist. He told them where Page had heard it, and where he had. His eyes burned with the intensity of how much he wanted this to work. He wasn't a naïve young constable, he knew that Page's contribution wasn't the pink ribbon bow that would tie the Carney case up neatly for the court. He knew a good brief would make it sound like nothing, the flimsiest of coincidences.

But for the moment persuading a jury wasn't his problem. He wanted to persuade Shapiro. If Shapiro believed in this he would have Carney, go after him and not give up until he brought him down. If this fragment of information, this oddly shaped little piece of jigsaw that had been lying unsuspected in David Page's back pocket all the time they'd been working out what happened to his wife, was accepted by Shapiro as independent corroboration of Carney's guilt, the rest would follow.

For a moment after Donovan had finished, even with the man's eyes burning his face, Shapiro refused to commit himself. He said to Page, 'This is right enough, is it? You heard Terry McMeekin say that?'

Page's manner was both bitter and negligent but his answer was unambiguous. 'Yes.'

'And Donovan, you're sure that's what you heard before you passed out? There's no wishful thinking at work here? Minds are funny things, sometimes they tell you what you want to hear. If there's any doubt in your mind about this, I want to know now.'

The accent was thicker than ever in Donovan's voice. 'I didn't imagine it. I can't prove it, but that's what I heard. What I was trying to remember.' He waited, his long body profoundly still, his concentration focused minutely on Shapiro. Liz thought he looked like a gun-fighter, watching for the fractional signal in the muscles of the other man's face that would be the only warning he'd get of what was coming.

Finally Shapiro let out a breath like a sigh. 'You don't have to prove it, lad, at least not to me. Convincing the DPP's another matter, but that's not today's problem. By the time we get there we'll have a case. For now, this is enough to work with.'

The blaze in Donovan's eyes flared up like fireworks.

As they were leaving, with a sudden pang of shame Liz excused herself and went back inside. Page was watching her: she winced under his acid gaze. 'We owe you an apology, Mr Page.'

His voice was cold, remote. 'Do you?'

Her eyebrows took on a wry slant. 'Well, Donovan does mostly. But you'll be a while waiting for it from him so I hope you'll accept it from me. Anyway, none of us has much to be proud about as far as you're concerned. You're entitled to feel let down. I'm sorry.'

'I don't know what you're talking about.' But there was a faint yielding in Page's manner that suggested that perhaps he did.

'That must have been very hurtful,' Liz said. 'It's no excuse that he didn't realize how offensive he was be-ing—he should have done. He'd no right to behave as if Kerry's death was less important than DI Clarke's, as if the main purpose of your suffering was to provide him with evidence in another case. It was crass and insensitive, and more than that it was wrong. Nothing that's happened was more dreadful than the murder of your wife.'

The bitterness was dying in Page's heart, leaving only ashes. Robbed of his anger he seemed childlike again, small and damaged. 'That's right,' he said softly, insistently. 'That's right.'

'The only excuse I can offer is the pressure we've been under—four murders in a week, one of them the man best qualified to deal with the other three. I don't suppose it alters anything but when we've had time to catch our breath we'll all be rather ashamed of how we've treated you. All I can say is it wasn't deliberate.'

'I know that,' Page said slowly, resignedly, as if giving something away. 'I know. It's all right.'

'Will you be all right? I can get someone to stay with you if you'd rather not be alone.'

'I think,' David Page said tiredly, 'being alone is what I'd like most. I think it's what I need. Go on, go catch your murderer. Really, I'll be fine.'

Liz smiled and nodded. 'Yes. I know you will.' Then she followed the men downstairs.

THREE

FOR CASTLEMERE CID the day ended more happily than
it had begun, with a celebration in the public bar of the
Ginger Pig. Wrapping up the Swann case, that so recently had seemed an impenetrable knot of contradic-
tions punctuated at intervals by sudden acts of ferocious
violence, had left them with an unexpectedly clear deck.
Tomorrow they would resume work with a vengeance,
switching thoughts and efforts from one grim pursuit to
another, hungrier than usual for a result because of the
sharply personal turn the case against Jack Carney had
taken. But tonight they were relaxing. Being policemen,
they seemed to know no ways of relaxing that were
either dry or quiet.

Shapiro and Liz had found a corner a safe distance
from their colleagues and watched with the good-
natured tolerance of people out of range of a game of
Lager Roulette. DC Scobie had shaken one can thoroughly before hiding it in an identity parade. Now he
and DC Morris were taking turns to open the cans close
under their noses. They were down to three and the
tension at surrounding tables was becoming unbearable.

There was a notable absentee from the festivities. Liz
peered through the press of bodies. 'Where's Donovan?'

'He'll be here.'

The loaded can went off, lager spraying DC Morris
and much of the room. DC Scobie almost fell off his
chair with the sheer hilarity of it. Doris the barmaid

gave Morris a resigned look and a towel. WPC Wilson gave him a piece of her mind.

About then the door opened, admitting a flurry of cold air and something else. By degrees the noise died away and the eyes of all present, even those who were not policemen, were drawn to the open door and the gaunt figure stood there like an omen.

It was Donovan. His face was a mask of barely constrained fury, his voice aquiver with rage. 'What the hell are you doing here, all of you? Do you think you've *finished?*'

Shapiro raised a hand and, mildly, his voice. 'They're having a breather, Sergeant, and so are we. Come and join us.'

For a second Donovan stayed where he was. Then he strode to where his superiors were sitting and leaned over the table, his voice dropping to a querulous murmur. 'There isn't time for this, sir. We can have them now, both of them: McMeekin because it was him under the viaduct and Carney because McMeekin doesn't even blow his nose unless he's told to. We're wasting time. When we've nailed Carney: that's when we celebrate.'

Shapiro's voice hardened slightly. 'Sit down, Sergeant, and stop talking into my face.' It was an order so reluctantly Donovan obeyed. 'We're in here for some R and R because everybody's been working hard, everybody's tired, and we're glad to have cleared up a really rather dreadful case. It doesn't mean we've forgotten about Alan, it doesn't mean we won't find out what happened to him. It just means we're not doing it tonight.'

'Find out what happened to him?' yelped Donovan. 'We know what happened to him! A stolen car driven by Carney's mechanic wiped him all over the road.

Then that cocky bastard McMeekin got out for a gloat. I know he was there, I heard him say my name. And that same weird proverb that Page heard him say to Carney. I even saw his God-damned shiny shoes! What more do you need? Together me and Page put Mc-Meekin at the scene. Then we have Carney too.'

Liz cast a nervous glance round the bar. The patrons had resumed their own conversations when Donovan sat down but there still wasn't enough noise to cover the argument. 'Keep your voice down, Sergeant, you're not in the police station now.'

He encompassed all his colleagues in a scathing sweep of a look. 'You could have fooled me.'

Shapiro didn't want to finish the day trading snide remarks with a detective sergeant. 'Donovan, listen to me. I know you think we've got this case wrapped up. Believe me, even with what Page will say, what we have so far will not convince a jury. Look at it from their point of view. You were unconscious six hours, you had a bad concussion. And you want them to send two men to prison for a long time on the strength of what you think you heard and saw between being hit by the car and passing out? McMeekin does have an alibi, you know, of sorts.'

'A doctor saw him half-dressed at Carney's house ten minutes after the event! He wasn't just up, he was just back!'

Shapiro shook his head. 'Maybe. Maybe we can even prove it to a jury's satisfaction. Tomorrow we'll start picking at the knots, see what we unravel. But tonight we're taking a break.'

'Tomorrow may be too late,' said Donovan through clenched teeth. 'Sir. Look, it was a botched job. They got interrupted: they didn't mean to leave me alive. OK, it's taken till now for me to get my head together enough to know I can nail him. But Carney's known it all along: he must have decided what he'll do if I say I saw McMeekin under the viaduct.'

'Then perhaps you shouldn't,' suggested Shapiro. 'At least not so loudly; at least not in public.'

Liz frowned. 'What can he do? He can hide McMeekin away for a while. But if he's keeping out of our way he's not doing his job. If Carney's any sense he'll stand his ground and invite us to prove something. I don't think we can.'

'We can so!' exclaimed Donovan. Liz blinked. 'Sorry, ma'am, I don't mean to shout, but— We can have him, if we do it now. You're right, he won't want to hide McMeekin: Terry's his right arm, he won't trust anyone else with the things he needs Terry for. I should have known it was him I saw: how many heavies dress like that? I underestimated him, I thought he wasn't ready for the big time yet. But Carney *is* big time: there's not that much difference between breaking legs for him and breaking necks.

'What I want to know is, who was driving? Was McMeekin there as an observer, looking after Carney's interests, or did he do the job himself? We can have McMeekin, we can have Carney. But if there's a third man, he's the one who took money to smash up a man he'd never met, and I want him too.

'OK, so what I remember won't convince a jury. But we weren't idle these last three months: Alan scraped together a lot of information before they got him. We know who we have to talk to. Once they see that we're going to do this, that we mean to make it stick, somebody's going to come down off the fence. Now we have something to work with it'll only take a bit of a shove to start the dominoes falling. You know that, sir.' The appeal to Shapiro won a slight nod, that was all. 'Anyway, it doesn't have to convince a jury. We can use it another way.'

Despite her misgivings about its author, Liz was getting interested in the theory. 'How?'

'The first thing we do is put an armed guard on Page.'

'What?!'

'Oh no you don't,' said Shapiro sharply. 'That young man's been through enough. You're not using him for bait.'

'I don't need to. We can protect him, make sure nobody gets near him. But by God it'll put the wind up Carney. He'll think we've got our case. He'll have to do something about it.'

'He'll come after Page. If it's that or going down he'll give it his best shot, and you know as well as I do that you can't *guarantee* anybody's safety. I'm not risking Page's life so you can panic a dangerous man into a desperate act. We'll get him, but we'll do it by the book. That way nobody gets hurt.'

'And maybe nobody gets caught either,' spat Donovan.

Liz neither raised her voice nor significantly dropped it, but there was no mistaking the warning in her tone. 'Sergeant, you're out of line again. Operational decisions are not your province. We've heard you out: if Mr Shapiro doesn't think the end justifies the risk, there's nothing more to be said. Sit down and have a drink.'

'I don't want a frigging drink!' he exploded. 'Listen to me. I don't want to risk Page's life. I don't have to. If Carney knows he's safe he has to come for me. He has to break the chain of evidence, yes? It takes both of us to put McMeekin at the scene: if I'm dead it doesn't matter what Page heard. So it doesn't matter which of us he shuts up. If he can't get to Page he'll come for me.'

'And what'll you do?' demanded Shapiro. 'Hit him with your plaster?'

To Donovan it was no laughing matter. His eyes flashed angrily and his lip curled. 'I kind of hoped I might get some back-up. Sir.'

For a long minute it seemed as though Shapiro was considering it. His eyes went distant and seemed to follow the flight of an invisible butterfly across the heads of his officers at the bar. Liz waited with interest, wondering what she would have said if it had been her decision.

Finally Shapiro's gaze found its way back to Donovan and, half apologetically, he shook his head. 'It's too risky.'

'It's a risk I'm willing to take!'

'It's not a risk you can take alone, though, is it?' Shapiro snapped. 'Whoever gets the job of covering you is at risk too. If Carney comes mob-handed somebody'll get hurt. However many people I can spare for you, however well armed and well prepared they are, if Carney thinks his safety depends on killing you there's going to be bloodshed.'

'And if we don't get him there'll be bloodshed too! At least we're paid to take the risk. If we let him stay in business a whole lot of ordinary people who have the right to our protection will suffer instead. That's not fair. They pay the piper, we play the tune.'

Then, his temper rising as their voices had risen in the heat of the argument, Shapiro said something unforgivable. 'It's easy for you to talk. We all know what'll happen if we set you up as the target. The poor sod next to you'll get smeared all over the pavement.'

Liz flinched. She saw the words hit Donovan in the face and the shock-wave ripple through his eyes. For a second he was literally breathless. Then he gasped, 'You bastard!'

Liz leaned quickly between them, laying a hand on each man's wrist—or Shapiro's wrist, Donovan's plaster. 'Sergeant! Sir. That's enough. If either of you has any more to say, let's go back to the office where at least we can be offensive in private.'

It was a vicious and petty jibe, uncharacteristic of him, and perhaps already regretting it Shapiro turned away. But Donovan had shot to his feet, shaking off Liz's hand. 'Is that it?' he demanded, his voice climbing. 'Is that why you won't do anything I ask? You blame me for Alan's death? My God, is that why Marion won't see me—did you tell *her* I got him killed?'

Shapiro shook his head irritably. 'Of course I didn't. Sergeant, we're tired—we're all tired—'

'You're damn *right* I'm tired.' Liz thought Donovan was actually shaking with passion. 'I'm tired of being the scapegoat every time something goes wrong. I'm tired of trying to do my job and getting damn-all in the way of back-up. I joined CID to catch criminals, not to exercise my elbow in the local pub. We could catch this man: now, today. But you're not going to, are you? It's easier to let him be and hope he'll do the same for you.

'Well, if you've lost interest in catching criminals you won't be needing detectives any more.' He threw something on to the table. It was his warrant card and it landed with a splash in a shallow pool of spilt beer. 'Write a report about that. You're good at writing re-

ports. Not too much of a risk element; not too much to
go wrong.'

Shapiro eyed him wordlessly for a long moment.
Then he picked up the card, wiped it carefully with his
handkerchief and held it out. 'You give me this thing
one more time, Donovan,' he said quietly, 'and I shall
keep it.'

'Keep it,' echoed Donovan, the accent thickening
round the words. 'You might as well, I've no more use
for it myself. If I can't do the job it empowers me to
do it's just so much excess baggage. Keep it. File it.
I'll manage without.'

Shapiro came to his feet angrily, throwing the card
down on the table. It landed in the beer again. 'I'm
warning you, Donovan, stay away from Carney. If you
won't work with me you have no further interest in the
case. Keep out of my way. If you obstruct my investigation I'll see you behind bars, by God!'

'Bars?' snorted Donovan derisively. 'Dear God, the
only people you ever see behind bars are barmaids! A
man could die of old age waiting for you to arrest him!'
With that parting shot, and with every eye in the place
on him, he turned on his heel and stalked out.

Somebody whistled. Somebody else said, 'He's done
it this time.'

Liz stared into her glass, mainly to avoid looking
anywhere else, and breathed lightly for a minute. Then
she said, 'That was edifying.'

Shapiro had sunk back in his chair. Discomfiture was
etched on his face and he shuffled his shoulders inside
his coat. 'I don't think I handled that very well, did I?'

Liz kept her eyes glued to the sliver of floating lemon
and said nothing more.

FOUR

SHE WAS A WORKING GIRL. Actually she was a woman of close to middle age and because of the work she did she looked older than that. Not at first glance. At first glance she looked like any other twenty-five-year-old waiting for her date, long legs stretched between a short leather skirt and high heels, masses of unruly black hair piled on her head, ear-rings that jangled audibly as she moved.

Close up, though, the deception was obvious. She wore more make-up than twenty-five-year-olds. Thick mascara gave her a surprised expression. Under the make-up, behind the mask, was a tiredness that had nothing to do with the lateness of the hour. She wore a tight leather waistcoat, no blouse, and a velvet jacket that fell from her bare shoulders with practised ease whenever she sat down. She was a working girl, but it was midweek and the work wasn't coming easily. By the time she walked into the Rose and Castle she was looking for a sit-down and a drink more than a customer.

And a sit-down and a drink were all she was likely to find in the Rose and Castle that evening. Half an hour before closing time the place was already emptying. There was a single man at the bar but he was drinking too seriously to be worth chatting up. A little muscle relaxant oils the wheels nicely but a real drunk is a pain in the neck to a working girl. They take too long doing what they can do, some things they can't do at all, and even if they don't fall asleep on the job they tend to think they've got a bed for the night.

But it had been a very quiet evening, Friday was still some way away, and perhaps he wasn't as drunk as he looked. She eased herself on to the stool beside him and ordered a lager and lime. The man didn't look at her. He had both forearms ranged along the bar in front of him and one long-fingered hand wrapped round a pint mug. The other wore a grubby plaster.

'Been in the wars, love?'

He didn't answer. He dropped his chin on his arms and went on staring at the half-empty mug as if he could see something more than chains of slowly rising bubbles in the straw-coloured liquid.

The woman shrugged, pulled her coat back over her cold shoulders. 'Pardon me, I'm sure.'

The barman brought her change and a little advice. 'Save yourself the trouble, ducky. He's a cop.'

The woman startled, her painted eyes widening dramatically. She hauled the coat tight around her as if to keep out more than the cold. Then she looked again. 'Are you sure?'

Donovan gave a silent laugh and nodded. 'He's sure. But he's wrong.' His voice was thick with accent and alcohol.

The woman didn't understand. 'Then you're not a cop?'

Donovan looked at his watch. He took time working it out. 'Not for the last three hours.'

She should have known better but she was intrigued. 'How come?'

'I got fired. No,' he said then, carefully, as if it was important to be accurate, 'I got myself fired. You keep throwing things at your chief inspector, sooner or later he's going to throw something back.'

The woman grinned. The dark lipstick on her wide mouth was like a slash across her face. 'What did you throw at him?'

For the first time he looked at her. His eyes were sunk in the hollows of his face. He looked more ill than drunk. His voice was languid, weary and half amused. 'About the worst thing you can throw at your governor: the truth. I told him he wasn't up to the job.'

The woman whistled softly into her drink. 'I can see how that'd make you popular.'

Donovan's lip curled. 'You get no prizes for popularity in this job. You can't do it if you're worried about collecting flak. You got to be ready to kick ass.'

'And you were, and he wasn't?'

'Oh yeah. Donovan's always ready to kick ass,' he slurred. 'No matter what the consequences. No matter who gets hurt. He can afford to: it's never him.' He drained his glass. 'But oh God, I get so tired always being the lucky one.'

She looked at him without much sympathy. 'Are you always this sorry for yourself?'

He gave a little snort of laughter. 'Yeah, I think maybe I am.' He bought refills for them both. 'You got a name?'

She did the easy, practised smile and let the coat slip once more from her shoulders. 'You can call me Tina, love.'

He acknowledged that with a lift of his mug, and when he put it down it was half empty again. He drank savagely, without enjoyment, as if it were medicine for a hurt he had.

She watched him for a minute longer, plainly wondering if it was worth the effort. Then she made her play. 'Listen, dear, many more of those and you'll be sleeping in your own cells tonight. Why don't you come with me instead? We'll have a bit of fun, then you can sleep it off. What do you say?'

Donovan laughed queerly, more at himself than her. 'I lost my job today. I lost my chance to nail the bastard who killed my friend. I was right, but I cocked it up just the same. Now I got nothing. I wouldn't be much company for you tonight.'

She put a long arm round his shoulders. 'That's all right, dear. I'll cheer you up, see if I don't.'

He shook his head doggedly. 'Tomorrow I have to think what to do. See if I've any friends left; see if my enemy'll settle for anything less than my head on a platter. The hell for it: tomorrow can wait.' His eyes groped for her. 'You got a car?'

She looked surprised. 'Sure. Why?'

'They'll be closing here. You want to go for a drive?'

There was no enthusiasm in her response. 'I don't know, dear, it's getting late.'

'I'll pay. For a driver.' He held up his damaged wrist. 'I'm a cripple, I can't drive myself. Come on—it's easier than turning tricks.'

For a moment she wavered, undecided. Then she nodded. 'Where do you want to go?'

He finished the beer with a grimace. 'Just drive. I need to think and I think better on the move. Wait a minute, I know a place. Yeah, OK, I'll tell you where to go.' He swayed as he got down from the stool and she steered him outside.

They walked for five minutes through the centre of town. A light rain was beginning to fall slick on the grimy pavements when they came to where her car was parked under a street light, as improbable a survivor in that run-down place as the dinosaurs at Crystal Palace.

It was a very ordinary car. Not pink; not upholstered in fake leopard-skin; not even a pair of furry dice hanging from the rear-view mirror. It was a car for shopping in, for visiting her mother, for the occasional luxury of a long drive alone in the countryside with nobody's whims to satisfy but her own. It was part of her private life, nothing to do with her job.

For a moment Donovan forgot himself and headed for the driver's door. The woman diverted him with a hand on his shoulder. 'Oh no you don't. The state you're in I wouldn't let you drive me on the dodgems.'

He chuckled darkly and walked round the bonnet, pausing as he did so to look back up the street the way they'd come.

The woman looked too. 'What is it? What can you see?'

'Nothing. Just thinking, it's a good place for an ambush.'

She leaned across the car to open the passenger door. 'You've been watching too much telly, dear.'

Donovan folded his long legs inside. 'No,' he said pontifically. 'Telly makes sense. Telly plays by the rules. It's real life that beats the hell out of me.'

He told her where to go. For a time they drove beside the canal. Then the black buildings looming over them began to shrink, to separate, to space out and admit the sky. Soon the town fell behind them and Castlemere Levels spread out ahead.

They hardly spoke. Donovan slumped in his seat as if half asleep, except that every time the car went round a corner he looked back. Sometimes there were headlights behind them, sometimes not.

It was a clear night with a gibbous moon climbing. The slow meanders of the river gleamed like a silver ribbon dropped in careless loops, meeting the road and wandering away again. There was a sheen of dew and gossamer on the water-meadows.

Lying back with his eyes half-hooded Donovan still saw the turn-off in time to warn his driver. The trees closed in as they bumped down the gritty track. The moon penetrated the branches overhead unevenly or not at all.

The track ended in a clearing in the woods shaped like a wine-glass, with the rim of the glass a shallow escarpment dropping down to the Levels. The river was quarter of a mile away and the meadows stretched as far as the eye could see.

The woman stopped the car, wound her window down, and exclaimed into the open night, 'I know where we are. Why—?'

Donovan shrugged. He opened his door and let one long leg dangle outside. 'Why not? It's a beauty spot, isn't it? Where else would a man take a woman?'

'You're a romantic, Donovan,' she said, not unkindly. 'If you'd ever been with hookers you'd know there are three places and none of them's a beauty spot. A cheap hotel, the back of a car, a dark alley. Strolling in the moonlight is strictly for lovers: working girls do it with an eye on the clock.'

The Pages had come here as lovers. Time had meant nothing to them. They had parked and walked down to the river by moonlight, and coupled in the long soft grass to the murmur of the water. Then they strolled back to the car and sat in companionable silence until George Swann stepped out of the darkness and blasted

Kerry Page to bloody fragments through the windscreen.

The woman shuddered. 'You really are a bit weird,
aren't you? Fancy wanting to come here.'

Donovan was undisturbed. 'It's quiet. It's pretty. And
the killer isn't coming back here, and even if he did he
wouldn't give us any trouble. He saved my neck once.'

Because the passenger door was open the interior
light was on. Apart from the moon and the cold sharp
pricks of stars it was the only light they could see.

Nothing happened. After a while, a shade petulantly,
she said, 'How long do you want to stay?'

He didn't open his eyes. 'You rushing home?'

She snorted. 'Hardly.'

'A bit longer then. OK?'

She shrugged. 'You're paying, I'm just the driver.'

'Yeah.' With his lazy grin and his eyes shut and one
long leg trailing into the car park he looked as switched
off, as relaxed, as she felt uneasy.

Finally she'd had enough. She opened her mouth to
say, 'That's it, I've had enough—I'll take you back to
town or you can damn well stay here,' though the words
had yet to form, when she became aware that he was
no longer drowsing with his eyes half-hooded but staring into the blackness of the wood ten metres away.
She touched his arm and he was rigid, the long muscles
tense. 'What is it?' she whispered, a thread of fear puck-
ering her voice. 'What can you see?'

The darkness moved and separated, and a piece of it
came towards them—black against black the shape remained amorphous but it moved like a man walking. It
said, 'He's seen me, love.'

The woman moaned. 'Oh, God. I thought you said

you'd caught him—the man who killed that girl. You said it was safe, God damn you!'

She was clutching his sleeve. She felt him shrug. He slurred, 'There's more than one fish in the sea. More than one shark in Castlemere. And baby—what's your name again?—nowhere's that safe. Once the sharks are after you, they find you someplace.'

She said, 'Then who—?' and her voice shook.

The man interjected quickly. 'Tell her, Donovan, and you're both history.' Donovan said nothing. 'All right. Who is she?'

The drunken grin was audible in his voice. 'She's a hooker. Her name's Gina.'

'Tina,' the woman corrected him indignantly, then wondered why. She addressed the other man, urgently, the words tripping over themselves in her hurry. 'Oh listen, mister, I don't know who you are and I don't want to. I didn't want to come here. He paid me to drive him, that's all. I don't want to know your business, I just want to go home. Let me go home. Please?'

'I've got some business with Mr Donovan,' said the man, explaining carefully. He did not seem to share her haste. 'I don't want to be interrupted.'

'No, sure, I understand,' babbled the woman. 'Look, I'll go. I don't want any trouble. I won't talk to anyone. Anyway, what could I tell them?'

'All right then,' said the man kindly. 'But you'll have to leave the car.'

'My car? But it's miles back to town! I can't walk that far.' Then it seemed to strike her she was putting her convenience ahead of her safety and her tone changed abruptly. 'No, sure, that's OK. Keep it. I'll walk. Jesus, mister, please let me go.'

The man nodded. 'That's OK, Tina. You go now. Go

through the woods and you'll hit the road in about quarter of a mile. Wait half an hour, then you can start thumbing. If I come along and see you before that, I'll carve you. You understand?'

She understood perfectly. It was the kind of talk, and he the kind of man, she had no difficulty understanding. It was too dark to see if he carried a weapon but she believed him implicitly. If she disobeyed him he would do as he said without compunction. She knew he would cut her throat with a smile on his face if it would serve his purpose. He was letting her go only because she couldn't harm him.

She almost fell out of the car in her hurry. 'I'm gone, mister. You do the business you've got to do, it's nothing to do with me.' Her heels were not made for gravel car parks and woody tracks, she was tripping at every step.

'Thanks a bunch, Gina,' Donovan said slowly.

'Tina!' she yelled back as she stumbled out of sight.

When she was gone the man said, conversationally, 'You've done your good deed for the day, Donovan.'

Donovan squinted up at him. There was just enough light from the open door to illuminate the lower part of his face. 'How's that, then?'

'You didn't tell her my name,' said Terry McMeekin. 'If you had, I'd have had to kill her too.'

FIVE

'COME ON, Terry, who're you trying to impress?' Donovan yawned. 'There's only you and me here and we both know your limitations. You're not bad at putting the frighteners on people but you haven't the stomach for murder. Not even women. Not even hookers.'

'You reckon?' McMeekin's voice was barred with irritation. 'Then why do I keep tripping over you? Why do I keep having to say where I was while you and your governor were playing chicken under the viaduct?'

'Because you were there,' insisted Donovan. 'I don't know who was driving—like I say, somebody tougher than you—but you were there. I heard you; I saw you from the waist down. Who the hell else dresses like that round here? You're going down, McMeekin. You aided and abetted the murder of a police officer and you're going to pay for that. The best thing you can do now is give us the driver. That's got to be worth three years to you.'

McMeekin chuckled. 'You're still talking like a policeman, Donovan. From what I hear you're in no position to be making promises.'

'I can get you a deal,' swore Donovan. 'Give me Carney, and the driver, and I'll get you a deal if it's the last thing I do before I sign on the dole.'

'You don't want much, do you? The man who pays my wages and this top hit-man he hired to do your governor. And for that I don't even walk?'

'Three years takes a lot of serving. Don't underestimate what I'm offering you.'

McMeekin seemed to be considering it. Then he reached through the open door of the car, fastened big hands in Donovan's clothes, and hauled him bodily outside. 'Come here.'

Even sober and with two hands Donovan would have been no match for McMeekin. He was as tall but only half as wide, and though he had more than a layman's knowledge of street-fighting he was trained to the use of minimum necessary force. He'd learned a few tricks the Police Complaints Commission didn't know, and didn't want to, but a man in McMeekin's trade must have forgotten more than Donovan knew. He could move faster than the big man, but with one hand in plaster and alcohol dulling his reactions it seemed unlikely to make the difference.

He didn't resist, only complaining mildly as McMeekin hauled him out of the car and slammed him up against it. 'What are you doing, Terry? You think I'm carrying? Shapiro kept my warrant card: you think he left me a gun?'

'I heard about your slanging match in the Ginger Pig. Jesus, Donovan, you were some loss to the Diplomatic Corps.'

'Yeah, well,' grunted Donovan, 'I suppose it wasn't too smart, shouting the odds in a public bar. You never know who's listening.' Slowly, in the glimmer of light from the car, his face changed with the recollection of what he'd been shouting about. He didn't remember every word but the main thrust of his argument, the reason he'd cornered Shapiro in the pub instead of waiting for him to return to his office, was that the infor-

mation they now had was enough to make the cat jump.
Well, it had jumped.

McMeekin nodded, his voice humorous. 'That's
right. You told half Castlemere that you and Page together could convict us of Clarke's murder. You wanted
to use the kid as bait but Mr Shapiro wouldn't wear it.
So you stormed out, went on a blinder, and drove up
here in the middle of the night with some tom. What
did you think was going to happen? Michael Aspel was
going to jump out from behind a bush with a big red
book?'

Donovan shrugged. 'So it was stupid. It's been a long
day: I was tired, I lost the rag. It wouldn't have stood
up in court anyway.'

McMeekin sniffed. 'That's not what you said in the
Ginger Pig. What I heard was, you had it sewn up. As
long as you and Page could both testify.' He waited but
Donovan said nothing. 'Guess what, Donovan? You
aren't going to testify.'

Donovan felt the alcohol like lead in his belly and
his veins. He'd have given anything for a clear head.
He'd had a reason to drink, but with hindsight it had
been a bad move. McMeekin was either warning him
off or threatening to kill him: he wished he could be
sure which. It mattered.

He got round it with a spurt of bravado that came out
as a sneer. 'So what now, Terry? You want me to wait
while you find out if it's convenient for your man to
come over and bust my head in?'

McMeekin sighed. 'I keep telling you, Donovan, but
you don't listen. There's no hit-man. There never was
a hit-man. Anything Mr Carney needs doing for him, I
do. I look after him. I tidy up for him. If he gets something on his shoes, I clean them. That's all you are,

Donovan, something he's trodden in. You'll wipe off.'
He sniffed. 'I thought I'd wiped you off once before. I
knew Clarke was finished: I thought you were too.
You're a lucky bastard, Donovan. At least, you used to
be.'

'I knew it was you I saw,' breathed Donovan. 'You
were alone in the car? It was you driving? You that hit
us?'

McMeekin nodded. He seemed pleased with himself.
'I don't need help dealing with the likes of you. Not
then, not now.'

Now he had his confession it almost seemed that
Donovan doubted it. 'How did you get rid of the car?'

'The scrap-yard I borrowed it from put it straight in
the crusher. It was a half-ton paperweight before you
reached the hospital.' The smugness in his voice was
intolerable.

Donovan ached with the desire to shred it. 'I bet that
wasn't your idea. Too clever for you by half, that. The
boss?'

The big man shrugged. 'I do what Mr Carney says.
Always. You know that. And Donovan, he says he
wants you dead.'

That was neither a warning nor a threat, it was a
statement of fact, delivered as unemotionally as a gro-
cery list. Donovan knew the only reason McMeekin was
talking like this—was talking to him at all—was that
he saw no problem about carrying out his orders. He'd
be armed and Donovan wasn't; he was sober and Donovan wasn't. He'd waited till Donovan had cut himself
off from his colleagues, until he came to a time and a
place where the chances of an interruption were tiny.
Donovan would fight, he'd have to fight, this was his
life they were talking about, but he wouldn't fight well,
he wouldn't fight for long, and when he went down it

would be over.

'How you going to make this look like an accident, Terry?'

McMeekin laughed out loud. 'You *were* going to be another victim of the Castlemere Crazy. That's why I brought this.' He produced a sawn-off shotgun from under his coat. Moonlight touched the abbreviated barrel with a blue gleam, the polished stock with a palely golden one. 'I've been on your tail most of the evening, I couldn't believe my luck when you came out here, where it all began. I thought that was so neat, hiding your death in the work of a mindless serial killer. Even if the guy was caught later and he denied it, who's going to believe a homicidal maniac? By then the situation would have been so confused they'd never have sorted it out. I was really pissed off when I found out you'd caught him already, that was why you were all in the Ginger Pig. Your security's crap, you know that?'

Donovan gave a lop-sided shrug. 'We had the guy. No one thought there was anything to keep quiet about.'

McMeekin nodded resignedly. 'So now it'll have to be those bikers you had a run-in with. They'll be along in a little while, you'll be found with the tracks of motorbikes all round you. And over you. Why? Maybe you reported them once for riding without the proper headgear. Another nasty skirmish in the long-running war between rebel youth and the forces of law. Sad, really. But Donovan's Luck was bound to run out one day.'

Donovan had heard all he wanted to. If he didn't make a move soon he was going to run out of time. McMeekin had allowed himself half an hour to do this, longer than was either safe or sensible but not very long at all when a man thought of it as the rest of his life. The arrival of the bikes would end any chance he had to out-manoeuvre McMeekin. What he didn't do soon would go undone.

He nodded at the weapon. 'Bikers don't use guns.'

'No,' agreed McMeekin. 'They use knives and chains and boots. And iron bars.' Without changing his grip on the shotgun, with sudden violence he struck out at Donovan's head.

There was neither time nor, with McMeekin in front of him and the car behind, space to evade the assault even though Donovan saw it coming. He tried to roll with it and absorb some of the force that way. It wasn't enough. The impact exploded fireworks behind his eyes and flung him to his hands and knees on the gritty ground. Nausea rolled over him in a tide. A rough edge where the barrel was sawn had opened a gash under his left eye: he felt the blood wash down his cheek as he knelt by the car, blind and hanging his head, trying to hold back the crowding darkness, the kaleidoscopic pain.

McMeekin bent beside him, peering into his face. He raised Donovan's head by a handful of hair the better to inspect his workmanship. Then he turned the gun unhurriedly in his gloved hands. 'And pick-axe handles.'

The stock of the gun, swung like a club, hit Donovan under the ribs, driving the air out of him, spilling him across the gravel in a sprawl of limbs; and when he tried to lift his face out of the grit it smashed across his back, beating him down. He tried to roll out of range but McMeekin followed, calmly, unhurriedly, and kicked him in the belly and in the face.

After that he could not have risen to save his life. He was breathing knives. His body pulsed in agony and his head reeled. Fear swamped him. What strength remained to him he used to draw his arms about his head and his knees up to his belly, protectively; and with what wits remained to him he thought, If this goes on much longer I'm going to die.

But McMeekin didn't hit him again. Instead he put the gun aside, lifted Donovan and propped him against a wheel of the car. His head rocked back until it collided softly with the metal panel. His eyes slid open, vacant and appalled.

'Oh, Donovan,' sighed the big man, squatting in front of him, his arms resting across his knees. 'You wouldn't believe it, would you? You had to have proof. This proof enough? *Now* will you believe the only mechanic Mr Carney needs is me?'

Donovan's gaze was vague, focusing only blurrily. Finally it found its way to McMeekin's face. Flecked with blood his lips moved in a whisper. 'So what are we waiting for?'

Another shadow detached itself from the fringing trees and stepped round the back of the car. 'For me, Sergeant Donovan. He's waiting for me.'

It was Jack Carney, and by appearing at the scene of a crime he was breaking the habit of a lifetime. It was a calculated risk. McMeekin had made sure there were no witnesses before he stepped out of the darkness, and McMeekin would make sure that nothing Donovan heard or saw could harm him. There remained the remote risk of a chance discovery. Jack Carney was not a man who liked taking even remote risks. That he wanted to be here for this said everything about his feelings for Donovan.

'Carney.' He managed a bloody grin. 'Brought your motorbike?'

Carney laughed, a high light peal that sounded like

genuine amusement. There wasn't enough light to judge his expression but in his voice were mingled malice and something almost like affection. 'Do you know something, Donovan? I'm sorry it's come to this. I'm going to miss you. Not much but a bit. Like an old dog that's constantly tripping you up and getting in your way: you finally get rid of it but you miss it, just a bit.'

'You could give me to the RSPCA,' suggested Donovan weakly. 'Somebody might give me a good home.'

Still chuckling, Carney shook his head. 'Sorry, boy. You've become dangerous. I can't have that. I could put up with you being a nuisance but not once you started to bite.'

'Is that why you killed Alan? He was getting close enough to hurt you?'

'Inspector Clarke? Yes, that's about it. He was a cleverer man than I gave him credit for—clever and determined. I knew he was rooting round, of course. I didn't think there was anything for him to find. But it seems my tracks weren't as carefully covered as they should have been.' His head moved as if he were flicking an acid glance at McMeekin. 'Well, that's all in the past. Neither of you can hurt me now.'

'Page—'

'Yes, I know,' nodded Carney. 'You really shouldn't discuss police business in pubs, you know. Page heard Terry say the same words you heard under the viaduct. It doesn't matter now. It wasn't much to start with: when you're dead it won't be anything at all. Oh, I expect I'll have Mr Shapiro or Mrs Graham round asking about it. What can I tell them? That Terry watches a lot of TV, he picks up some funny expressions, God knows where that one came from but this reckless driver must have seen the same film. So maybe you thought you recognized Terry's voice; but you were concussed, weren't you? Anyway, there's no way of knowing now. Without you there's no case.'

'Lucy,' slurred Donovan. His grip was slipping, he was afraid he was going to pass out. That would be the end. Carney was only holding McMeekin back because it amused him to talk with a man who'd tried to bring him down and was about to pay for his insolence with his life.

Carney frowned. He didn't understand. 'Lucy?'

'The bag-lady. The old woman who asked to see us behind the gasworks. What happened to her?'

Jack Carney was a busy man. A criminal enterprise requires as much organizing as any other; indeed there are more considerations to occupy the mind. No man with an expanding business can deal with every aspect of it, he has to delegate. He tries to keep his finger on the pulse of major events but often the minor details elude him. That was what had happened here. With devastating honesty he admitted, 'I don't remember.'

It knocked the wind out of Donovan like another blow. 'You killed an old lady, and you don't remember?'

Carney's head turned. 'Did we kill her, Terry? You dealt with it. What did you do with her?'

McMeekin's voice was bleak. 'She went on a trip…Birmingham, I think. Third class. Actually, in a shipment of grain.' He grinned. 'They'll find her when people start complaining about the lumpy bits in the bread.'

Donovan's head tilted back until the starlight was in his eyes. 'Oh, Jesus,' he moaned. 'She was an old tramp—how could she be any danger to you?'

'She couldn't,' agreed Carney calmly. 'Not after Terry'd fixed her up with an Away Day to Birmingham. He really didn't have much option. She saw him disposing of Mr Potter's dog—you know, the one he liked almost as much as his children? Well, you can't cut somebody's kid's throat and dump it in the foundations of his latest building project, can you? Not till you've exhausted the other possibilities.'

'Potter got the message,' said Donovan. 'He never said another word to us. You didn't need to kill Lucy.'

'I'm sorry, Sergeant,' Carney said, though not as if he meant it, 'but that was down to you. Everyone in Castlemere knows Lucy lived on what you gave her for street-gossip. We could have frightened her off but it wouldn't have lasted: next time she was cold and hungry she'd have called you. You're the reason Lucy's dead.'

'You made her call me. You knew I'd come where she told me. You knew I'd bring DI Clarke if she asked to see him.'

'Me?' said Carney, the negligent little half-smile broadening. 'I was miles away, tucked up in bed with a nasty attack of palpitations. Ask my doctor.'

Donovan gave a languid drunken grin. 'Hey, Carney, this is me you're talking to. I know how long your reach is.'

Like many men who think themselves a cut above the average, Jack Carney was susceptible to flattery. He took it as a compliment and preened visibly. 'Well, all right—just between the three of us. What I can't do in person Terry does for me. You know that. You underestimated Terry, Sergeant. You thought he couldn't handle the heavy stuff, that I needed outside help for that. Terry was really quite offended, weren't you, Terry?'

'I was, Mr Carney,' McMeekin agreed obediently.

'But Terry's a big boy now. He can deal with the likes of Lucy. He can deal with the likes of you. I don't need to be here tonight. Do you know why I am?'

'Nothing on the telly?'

It wasn't a great joke but anyway it was wasted on Carney. All the humour had died out of his voice. He sounded at last like what he was: a vicious little thug with a cold hatred in his heart for anyone who opposed him. 'Because I want to watch you die, Donovan. You've done your level best to destroy me. You tried to snare me in your laws. You spied on me. You tried to make it impossible for me to conduct my business. You tried to make me a laughing stock, in my own town, among my own associates. And you failed. Now you're going to die, and I'm going to watch so I'll never be tempted to worry about little things like policemen again. There's nothing special about policemen. You bleed like men; you die like men.'

'We breed like flies. There'll always be another, every way you turn.' In spite of the nausea, fear was pushing the words out faster than he would have wished. They were true, but they weren't much consolation.

'Don't flatter yourself, Donovan. No one's going to make a crusade of avenging you. Terry?'

Carney stepped back. The last thing he wanted was blood on his overcoat. McMeekin was wearing a plastic mac. He reached for the gun and, after a moment's consideration, picked it up slowly by the barrels. 'Sorry, Donovan,' he said.

And Donovan groaned, 'Beam me up, Scottie.'

Powerful lights sprang out all round the car park, catching the little tableau—the man on the ground, the man poised to beat the life out of him, the third man watching—like actors on a stage. A woman's voice rang out. 'Armed police officers. Stay where you are.'

For an instant McMeekin seemed to think of using the gun. If he'd picked it up by the stock perhaps he would have done. But he couldn't turn it quicker than a marksman could drop him, and by the time he'd thought that he knew there was no point anyway. He couldn't get away. He was surrounded, he couldn't reach the woods, if he went over the escarpment there was no cover between here and the river.

Slowly he let out the deep breath he'd snatched for action. Still holding the gun by the barrels he offered it to Donovan. 'Some you win, some you lose.'

Without moving from the ground Donovan took it. It was heavier than he expected. The weight of it seemed to carry the stubby barrels slowly, inexorably towards Jack Carney, settling on his broad belly. The little man jolted with the unfamiliar emotion fear.

There was light enough in the car park now for Donovan to see his face, to see his eyes. By concentrating hard he could keep the black mist far enough back in the corners of his head to see the shock there turn to panic and then to a recognition that it was over. That the cleverest brief on his payroll couldn't get him out of this. That he'd been played like a fish, like the wily old trout he was, but he'd finally met a bait that was too damned tempting and snapped at it. Now he'd condemned himself out of his own mouth with most of Castlemere CID listening. They had him. It was over.

When he saw in Carney's eyes the sick understanding of how he had been trapped, Donovan nodded his heavy head ponderously, raised the heavy barrels till Carney was staring down them. He drawled, 'Life's hard, Jack. Then you die.'

Still he waited. For all the people in and around it, the car park was silent. No one spoke, no one moved. They wouldn't let him get away with murdering Jack Carney but he didn't think they'd shoot him first to stop him. He watched Carney's face along the barrels.

He waited until he saw in Carney's eyes the stark terror of certain and imminent death. Then he broke the gun open and thumbed the shells out.

SIX

CARS TOOK CARNEY and his mechanic away. An ambulance came for Donovan. Still sitting on the ground by the wheel of the car, resting his head on the paintwork, so weak and dizzy it was plain he could not have stood up to save his life, he tried to persuade Shapiro it was an unnecessary precaution. 'I'm all right. I'll creak for a couple of days, then I'll be fine. I don't need to go to hospital again.'

'Yes, you do,' Shapiro said with conviction. Donovan still had the gun. Shapiro took it gently from him.

'If I have any more X-rays I'll glow in the dark!'

'Sergeant, do as you're told,' the Chief Inspector said wearily. 'Just for once. For me. Just to show that you can.'

Donovan opened his mouth, then shut it again. His eyes shut too.

Hampered by the tight skirt Liz knelt beside him. 'Excuse me.' She put her hands inside his shirt.

Without opening his eyes he grinned lazily. 'Back home in Glencurran this'd mean we had to get married.'

The wire had been taped to his skin under his belt where only a strip-search would have found it. A man looking for a gun could have patted him up and down all day and never known it was there. Liz gave the slender thing to Shapiro who couched it in hands that were not quite steady, looking at it as if it were something alien, something outside his experience.

As if she were his mother Liz buttoned Donovan's

shirt again. As she did so his good hand came up and held her wrist for a moment. He looked her in the eye and said, 'Thanks, boss.'

Liz stared at him. In the glare of lights his face was a death's head, the skin bone-white except where it had been blackened. He'd been beaten within not too many inches of his life. Every breath cost him pain. She looked at the hand he was holding and there was blood on her fingers from inside his shirt. She said faintly, 'Whatever for?'

'For the back-up. I couldn't have managed alone. And for keeping your nerve. A lot of people would have stepped in to finish it before the big man showed. Don't worry about that.' He'd noticed his blood on her fingers. 'There's plenty where that came from. I'd have given a damn sight more of it to get Carney where we have him now.'

For a moment Liz was unsure how to respond. If he'd been on his feet she might have slapped him down, reminding him tacitly if not explicitly of their respective ranks and the fact that she had higher imperatives in running an operation than obliging her sergeant. Somehow she couldn't say that to an injured man, and by the time she'd worked out why she was glad. It was an honest expression of appreciation from someone who'd literally risked everything to do his job and he deserved better than to have his head bitten off for a breach of protocol.

'Wait till tomorrow,' she advised, 'see if you're still grateful then.'

'We got the bastards,' said Donovan. The edges of his words were growing woolly but there was no mistaking the satisfaction, happiness even, in his voice.

'We got the man who killed Alan and the man who sent him. I don't care how I feel tomorrow.'

'I'm glad it worked out,' she said. 'It was a clever idea of yours. Risky, but clever. I'm glad it worked out how you wanted.'

Donovan's hand slipped off the cuff of her velvet jacket, the bony knuckles brushing down the leather of her skirt. 'I couldn't have done it without Sheena.'

'Tina, damn it,' she exploded softly, half of her wanting to laugh and half, inexplicably, to cry.

He didn't answer. His eyes slid closed again but a trace of the grin remained on his broken lips. Shapiro nodded to the paramedics and they took over.

When the ambulance had gone he turned to Liz and smiled sombrely. 'I hope you know how honoured you are.'

'Honoured?' She didn't understand.

'Donovan. He calls me sir because he has to and he calls you ma'am because you told him to, but *boss* is what he used to call Alan.'

They began the slow walk up the track to the main road, where four young men on motorcycles were trying in vain to convince the check-point that they were only out for a moonlight ride round the Levels. Shapiro's car was with the other police vehicles.

They'd followed the primrose BMW out here—at a safe distance, once it began moving this way there was no question but that it was on Donovan's trail. Only after Inspector Graham radioed in that McMeekin had reached the car park did Shapiro move his vehicles up to close the road and lead his men down into the trees.

He needed them near enough to halt the action at a moment's notice, near enough to prevent either of the targets disappearing into the dark wood, far enough away that an unlucky step wouldn't betray them. He set up his cordon about sixty metres out from the car park. Three officers were armed with guns, the others with torches.

His only contact with Liz was by radio. She was covering Donovan from as close as she could escape detection and any movement towards her would certainly have been seen. As the person with the best overview of what was happening she was effectively running the operation.

'Why did he wait so long?' wondered Shapiro as they walked. 'He damn nearly let them kill him. Why?'

'To make sure,' explained Liz. There was a shake in her voice of which she seemed unaware. 'He was sick of being told he needed more evidence. He wanted taped confessions from both of them. He wanted them to admit to DI Clarke's murder. Then he wanted them to admit to killing the bag-lady. In case there was a cock-up and the first charge wouldn't stick.'

Shapiro turned to look at her. 'And what's your excuse?'

She didn't know what he meant. 'Sorry?'

'You were in control. You could have blown the whistle at any time. You let that animal beat the living daylights out of him. Why?'

It was a question she'd known she would have to answer some time. She had not expected it to come so soon, or from him. 'Because of the stakes. Because it was the only sure way to put behind bars criminals who'd killed one police officer and tried to kill another.'

'That's why we gave Donovan's idea a shot,' agreed Shapiro. 'That's why we engineered the argument in the pub, why Donovan spent the evening drinking and then came up here with no back-up to speak of. Because

Carney had to believe he was out on his own, an easy target.'

'What do you mean, no back-up?' Liz waved the curly black wig indignantly.

Shapiro allowed her a smile. 'Apart from Tina the tom with her Saturday night special in her handbag. But if McMeekin had thought to search you, or thought it wiser to kill you too, I don't know if you could have stopped him. It was a hell of a gamble. I could have lost you both. As it is the lad's taken more damage than I ever imagined. God knows how long he'll be out·of action, or even if he'll make a full recovery. A beating like that can stay with a man for life.'

'It *was* a gamble,' agreed Liz. Her tone was determined: she was aware she was defending her credibility. 'But whatever was going to happen wasn't going to happen till Carney arrived. He didn't want Donovan dead in a nice, quick, discreet accident—not this time. He wanted him to know why he was dying: that there were some people he couldn't push around even with the weight of the law behind him. And he wanted to watch.

'If Carney hadn't turned up we'd have had to take McMeekin on his own. But there was every chance that Carney'd be there. That's why it was worth waiting, even with Donovan getting hammered. He thought so or he'd have called me in sooner. He wanted it wrapped up so it couldn't come untied. That was worth a couple of cracked ribs to him.'

'Donovan is a sergeant,' Shapiro reminded her. 'You're an inspector. That gives you both the right and the duty to override any decisions of his which, because of emotional involvement or plain bad judgement, don't stand up. That's what I require of my inspectors. Power *and* responsibility.'

'That's what you got, sir,' Liz said quietly. 'It was my judgement that the risks we took, including the risk of injury to Sergeant Donovan, were justified by the likely outcome. That judgement was vindicated by events. I'm sorry if you feel I was wrong to let it go on so long. I accept that there's room for other views on the matter, that it would also have been a valid judgement to stop it before the officer got hurt. But if I'd done that we wouldn't have got Carney. I'll defend my decision at a disciplinary hearing if you feel that's appropriate.'

Shapiro sighed and shook his head. 'I'm not suggesting that. I'm not even saying you're wrong. I just wanted to be sure that you'd thought it through. That you hadn't let the thing run out of control.'

'It wasn't out of control,' insisted Liz. 'It could have ended badly. If it had I'd still have defended my judgement.'

'And if Donovan had shot Carney?'

'There was never any question of that.'

'Liz, I saw him! You saw him—we all bloody saw him. He decided against. But he thought about it.'

'Of course he thought about it. After what he's been through he'd have been superhuman not to. But he didn't do it, and he didn't try to. We're responsible to society for our actions: our thoughts are our own.'

'If he'd done it his defence would have been that he was too punch-drunk to think straight. Any jury in the land would accept that. I'm not sure what they'd think of an inspector who watched her officer beaten witless because she wanted her case to have a belt as well as braces.'

'Legal errors occur. People do walk on technicalities. If for some reason we can't put them away for killing DI Clarke we can have them for killing Lucy. If they went free they'd do a lot worse than beat up the odd policeman before we could get them again.'

Shapiro sighed. 'I'm not challenging that. I'm just concerned that you don't make that kind of decision—that kind of pay-off between damage and results—too easily.'

'Easily?' Incredulity caught in her throat. 'Sir, I've sweated blood! I didn't want to leave him with Mc-Meekin. While I was hidden in the wood waiting for you to get in position, every moment I wanted to stop it. I had the gun, I had the element of surprise, I could have done it. Donovan would never have forgiven me but I could have lived with that. Every time McMeekin hit him I thought, That's it, he's going to kill him—even if I stop it now, maybe he's crippled already.

'But Donovan was conscious, I could hear him, he was still making sense and he hadn't called me in. You think I enjoyed watching that—obscenity? We agreed I'd stay out until we had what we wanted unless he absolutely needed me in there sooner. It was my judgement that that moment had not quite come.' She shook her head and her voice broke, angry and distressed. 'You don't need to throw this at me, Frank. I'm going to have enough trouble sleeping after what I let them do to him. If I got it wrong, if he's badly hurt, you'll have my resignation in the morning. You can have it now if you want. I don't know what I'm doing in a job that asks you to make that kind of decision, those kinds of choices.'

Shapiro took her into the fold of his arm, felt the rigidity that would any moment turn to shaking. 'The

best you can, like all of us. We do our best, we hope
it's enough, mostly it is and sometimes it isn't. But it's
never easy. I'm sorry, I shouldn't have said that. I think
I'm a bit punch-drunk too. Come on, we're about finished—let's get out of here.'

They went back to town, Shapiro driving. Because it
was just the two of them, and their friendship went back
a long way, Liz felt able to ask him what could have
been an impertinent question. 'If it had been your call,
Frank. If you'd been the man on the spot. If you'd been
standing where I was, in the wood, watching, with a
gun in your hand—would you have stopped it? If
McMeekin had laid into your sergeant with both ends
of a shotgun, knowing what interfering would cost,
would you have blown the whistle?'

Shapiro didn't even hesitate. 'Oh, yes,' he said simply. 'Whatever the consequences I couldn't have
watched an officer I was responsible for take a beating
like that without trying to stop it.'

'Then you think I was wrong.'

'Not necessarily. I don't know which of us is right.
Maybe there's no right and wrong about it. If Donovan's OK it'll have been worth it; if he isn't it'll be
harder to judge. All I can tell you is what I'd have done.
But then, I always knew you were tougher than me. You
had to be, to come this far. Maybe the new generation
of coppers are all tougher than me. Maybe I'm getting
old.'

'There's something else,' Liz ventured after a pause.
'Something I took into account which you mightn't
have considered. Perhaps I shouldn't have but I did.
Donovan. He needed a success. If he was going to be
any use in the future, to himself or anyone else, he
needed to break the jinx.'

Shapiro thought about it. 'At the cost of blood?'

'Especially if it cost him blood. You know about Donovan's Luck: other people collect his flak, pay for his mistakes? But not this time. This time it was his plan, his neck, his risk; and he pulled it off, and the only one who got hurt was him. I think, by the time somebody's strapped up his ribs and stitched up his face, he's going to feel pretty good about that.'

She heard a soft snort which for a moment she failed to identify. Then she realized Shapiro was chuckling. She stared at him until he felt her eyes and explained. 'You two. Have you any idea how alike you are? Oh, you talk nicer than Donovan, you're better company, but beneath that nice middle-class veneer you're as much of a street-fighter as he is.'

Liz blinked, astonished. 'A street-fighter? Me?'

'Undoubtedly. A beautifully brought-up street-fighter, a street-fighter with a grammar-school accent, but the velvet glove doesn't alter the essential nature of the iron fist. You'll go a long way. I've always worried too much about the minutiae, about justifying every detail—occasionally it's paid off but more often it's bogged me down. I can't see you making the same mistake. You have the courage of your convictions. You're like Donovan in that too.'

Liz was troubled. She wasn't sure that Shapiro was paying her a compliment. She'd known him too long to think he admired ruthlessness, even when it was effective. She said in a low voice, 'I don't know if that's the sort of copper I want to be. I'm not ambitious, Frank. Not enough to want promotion more than respect.'

He glanced fondly at her. 'Liz, whatever you choose to do—if you want to be the first female chief constable or the best detective inspector in the country—wherever

you want to go from here you will always have my
respect. Even if we don't agree on everything. Look.
Police work, particularly CID, isn't an exact science.
You do your best and hope it'll work out, but often
enough the results are disappointing. It's hard to keep
on trying, but you have to. That's where street-fighters
come into their own. It's better to try too hard than not
hard enough.

'That's Donovan's strength: that he'll put himself on
the line for something that matters without wanting a
cast-iron guarantee that he'll come out of it all right.
You have to watch your back in this job, but if you're
always watching your back you lose sight of where
you're going. Donovan doesn't mind making himself
unpopular. He doesn't mind being in a minority of one.
It doesn't make him the easiest man to work with but
it means he sometimes gets results that almost nobody
else could get. You do that too. Eyes on the prize: isn't
that what the Americans say?' He sounded pleased and
surprised that he knew that.

They drove another mile in silence. Then Shapiro
said, 'I want to make a call on our way in, if that's all
right?'

It was a purely rhetorical question. Liz nodded automatically. 'Of course, sir. Where are we going?'

'It's time I talked to Marion Clarke. For both their
sakes—hers and Donovan's. I shouldn't have let *this* go
on so long: her blaming the lad for Alan's death and
both of them hurting because of it. It's time I put a stop
to it.'

Liz studied what she could see of his profile by the
gleam of the instruments. 'At two o'clock in the morning?'

Shapiro nodded warily. 'I know. I should have done

it sooner. I've been busy. She'll be in bed, I'll have to get her up. But I think—I think—she'll be glad I did. I think she might want to go down to the hospital, see if he's all right.'

Liz didn't know Alan Clarke's widow, didn't know how she was likely to react. And she was learning something new about Shapiro all the time. When he'd parked the car she said, 'Shall I come in with you?'

'No need,' he said, 'and anyway better not. She won't be wondering who's on her doorstep, she'll know it's me. And we might get cross with one another before we're done so we'd better be left alone for ten minutes. Then you can drive us both to Castle General.'

But as he was climbing out of the car, a man past middle age weary with all that had happened in the last eight days, he came slowly to a halt and turned back to her. 'There is something you can do.'

'Name it.' She was tired too but she meant it.

'Think if there's any way you could stay here—take Alan's job on a permanent basis. Brian's an art teacher, isn't he? Could he get work in Castlemere? There are some good schools. If not, would one of you consider commuting? I don't want to put you on the spot, Liz, I'm not expecting you to choose between your marriage and your career. I haven't said anything to Head-quarters, if the idea doesn't appeal to you all you'll be turning down is an informal approach, there'll be noth-ing on your record. But if there was a way I'd like to have you here.'

Momentarily she was dumbfounded, amazed and not amazed.

She'd been here a week. Together they'd solved two cases involving six deaths—seven counting Mary Swann. In one way she'd hardly had time to think where she was, what she was doing, where it might lead, where she wanted it to lead. In another, all the years she hadn't been working with Frank Shapiro seemed to have dissolved to nothing.

She had a good job where she was. She had prospects. She wasn't sure if DI at Castlemere amounted to progress. But already she knew she wanted it. She wanted to work in the real world again, not just with computer files and other police. She wanted the immediacy, the direct evidence of making a difference that came with hands-on detecting. She wanted to work with Shapiro. She could even get used to the idea of working with Donovan.

'Frank, I don't know. I can't say, not off the top of my head like this. Can I think about it? See what room I have for manoeuvre?'

For a moment Shapiro's tired, amiable smile was framed in the car's open door. 'Of course. Take all the time you need. Talk to Brian. Talk to Headquarters. Then do what's best for you.' Then he straightened and turned, and she watched his back in Harris tweed trudge up Marion Clarke's garden path.